TULLEY THREW OPEN THE DOOR AND CAME TO A HALT

Cass stood on the doorstep, a film of mist glistening on his hair and the shoulders of his parka. He reached out and touched her face— he'd come back.

He stepped across the threshold and caught her to him. Tulley hugged him and curled her fingers into his hair, her throat tight with happiness.

Their lips played upon each other in quick, hungry samplings. Cass scattered small kisses at the corners of her mouth and caught her lower lip softly between his teeth. She touched her tongue to his lips—it was the end of play. Their mouths joined in a deep, bottomless kiss.

Forgotten was her reason for sending him away. She knew only that she wanted to ignore everything that lay between them and lose herself in this man. . . .

ABOUT THE AUTHOR

Like the heroine in *Scenes from a Balcony*, Jenny
Loring is no stranger to the newspaper world. A
former reporter and columnist, Jenny decided to use
a small-town paper as background for her third
Superromance. Her many fans will be thrilled to
find that this California author's latest work is filled
with humor, endearing characters and an abundance
of romance.

Books by Jenny Loring

HARLEQUIN SUPERROMANCE
  74—A STRANGER'S KISS
129—THE RIGHT WOMAN
202—SCENES FROM A BALCONY

These books may be available at your local bookseller.

Don't miss any of our special offers. Write to us at the
following address for information on our newest releases.

Harlequin Reader Service
901 Fuhrmann Blvd., P.O. Box 1397, Buffalo, NY 14240
Canadian address: P.O. Box 2800, Postal Station A,
5170 Yonge St., Willowdale, Ont. M2N 6J3

Jenny Loring

SCENES FROM A BALCONY

Harlequin Books

TORONTO • NEW YORK • LONDON
AMSTERDAM • PARIS • SYDNEY • HAMBURG
STOCKHOLM • ATHENS • TOKYO • MILAN

Published March 1986

First printing January 1986

ISBN 0-373-70202-7

Copyright © 1986 by Jenny Loring. All rights reserved.
Philippine copyright 1986. Australian copyright 1986.
Except for use in any review, the reproduction or utilization of
this work in whole or in part in any form by any electronic,
mechanical or other means, now known or hereafter invented,
including xerography, photocopying and recording, or in any
information storage or retrieval system, is forbidden without
the permission of the publisher, Harlequin Enterprises Limited,
225 Duncan Mill Road, Don Mills, Ontario, Canada M3B 3K9.

All the characters in this book have no existence outside the
imagination of the author and have no relation whatsoever to
anyone bearing the same name or names. They are not even
distantly inspired by any individual known or unknown to the
author, and all the incidents are pure invention.

The Superromance design trademark consisting of the words
HARLEQUIN SUPERROMANCE and the portrayal of a Harlequin,
and the Superromance trademark consisting of the words
HARLEQUIN SUPERROMANCE are trademarks of Harlequin
Enterprises Limited. The Superromance design trademark
and the portrayal of a Harlequin are registered in the
United States Patent Office.

Printed in Canada

To my friend, Nell Leake,
and all the newspaper people
we have known and loved;
and to Georgia Bockoven,
friend and writer,
who knows how to listen.

My thanks to

John Bockoven, Alan Fishleder, Larry Amundsen,
Wesley Reiff and Dr. Harry Walker
for their generous research assistance.

CHAPTER ONE

THE RETURN on the registered letter, postmarked Hilby, North Carolina, and delivered to the newsroom of the large metropolitan daily, read "Samuel Clemens Matthews, Attorney-at-Law." In the stiff, cautious wording common to lawyers, it advised Elizabeth Tulley Calhoun that her uncle, one Lamarr Calhoun, was dead, and that she, as the only apparent heir, was entitled to assets including a few municipal bonds, a small savings account, a modest amount of cash, some real estate, including the house he'd lived in, and *The Hilby Herald*, a daily newspaper in the county seat of Hilby, N.C.

The whole proposition was so bizarre that Tulley's immediate reaction was to wonder which of her antic colleagues in the newspaper world had bothered to rig up an elaborate hoax that involved out-of-state mailing and a fake letterhead, or for that matter, knew of her family connection with the town of Hilby. Raising her eyes in speculation, she scanned the newsroom, a trifle annoyed that someone should imagine her so gullible. The thought that the joke was on the prankster stirred a rustle of wry amusement in her.

Whoever it was obviously didn't know that she'd been no more than peripherally aware that she had an uncle until after her father's death five years earlier, when her mother asked her to notify his brother, Lamarr Calhoun. Tulley could not forget the voice of wintry detachment that came to her that day over the phone.

"Prentiss Calhoun, my brother? You're mistaken, young woman. I have no brother."

Detached, yes, but the voice had also echoed bitterness harbored over imagined injustices twenty years past. It would be bizarre, indeed, even to find herself among those notified that her uncle had died—much less mentioned in his will.

Will...?

Her hazel eyes, slightly uptilted at the outer corners, lighted in a delayed double take as a single word from the letter flashed back to her. *My God!* she thought, the word—the key word—hadn't registered in her mind.

Feverishly she scanned the letter a second time, sure the word had been there when her eyes skimmed over the message a moment ago.

Intestate! There it was, in the second paragraph. Intestate! Her uncle had left no will. Suddenly the whole thing made sense.

"Inasmuch as Lamarr Calhoun died intestate, and you are the child of the deceased's late brother, Prentiss Calhoun, and as such, presently appear to be the deceased's only surviving relative...etc." There it was in unimpeachable lawyer language, there in immaculate IBM Selectric pica type, dutifully signed, "Yours very truly, Samuel Clemens Matthews, Attorney-at-Law." It must be true!

A ripple of excitement raced through Tulley. She blinked, and in response to an involuntary shiver that flicked across her shoulders and up the back of her neck, gave a dazed shake of her head that sent her shoulder-length ash-blond hair swirling in a veil across her face.

At the next computer terminal Stan Rice turned away from his screen to eye her curiously. "Hey, Tulley! That letter you just signed for... It must be an exclusive from the White House."

Tulley peered rakishly out from behind the curtain of hair for a moment before she straightened her shoulders and reached up with both hands, gathering her pale hair into two silken skeins, pulling it back from her face to give the young man a bemused smile.

"Better than that!" she assured him in a voice of stunned half belief. As she spoke, the full impact of the letter's message finally hit her. "You're not going to believe this, Stanley!" There was a quaver of awe in her voice. "I've just fallen heir to a newspaper... *I think.*"

TWO DAYS LATER Elizabeth Tulley Calhoun, wearing her one designer garment—a stunning three-year-old amethyst tweed suit that made her look every inch the cool female executive—sat on the other side of an ancient oak desk from Samuel Matthews in his Hilby, N.C., law office. She restrained her impatience to get down to the substantive matters she was there to hear. The stout, bald-pated gentleman in the somewhat rumpled gray worsted suit was not to be hurried. Taking his time about it, he observed amenities with that particular unhurried gallantry seldom found outside the South.

"I most certainly hope we haven't put you to too much inconvenience, Miss Calhoun, askin' you to come down here on such short notice," he said in a voice that came from the bottom of a sorghum barrel, the words falling softly with a noticeable lack of ending gs. "Eudith—that's Miss Eudith Clover, my secretary—she's been tryin' to run you down ever since they called me to say Lamarr died. I knew for sure he hadn't left a will, so I reckoned it was only a matter of time before it'd be up to us to find you. It took a while. I'm right sorry we couldn't give you more notice."

In his midsixties, Matthews had a comfortable down-home manner that reminded Tulley of her father. She'd had apprehensions about meeting the attorney who represented the embittered voice that was her only memory of her uncle Lamarr, but in the presence of the low-key, courtly gentleman she relaxed. There was something reassuring about the serene heavy-jowled face that made the brief phone encounter with her late uncle seem irrelevant.

Interrupting himself with frequent digressions and pauses, the lawyer settled down to his business with her in his own good time. He'd been Lamarr Calhoun's attorney, he told her, but it was not in that capacity he'd summoned her here. Because her uncle had left no will and because she, his inadvertent heir, was from out-of-state, making her ineligible by North Carolina law to be the estate's administrator herself, it had fallen to Matthews, as public administrator for Hilby County, to manage his late client's estate.

Captivated by the butter-soft syllables that rolled from the lawyer's tongue, Tulley refrained from telling him she already knew it was the responsibility of the public administrator to see that property in probate—such as her uncle Lamarr's—was properly managed until distributed to the heirs. Such things she'd learned early in her newspaper career. Nevertheless, she listened with rapt attention to his explanation—not so much to the words as to their sound. They evoked memories of her father who, to the end of his life, had carried a gentle hint of pure North Carolina honeysuckle in his speech that twenty years on northern soil never quite erased.

After a time the lawyer paused and removed his wire-rimmed glasses to breathe a puff of mist on each lens. When he resumed talking, there was a different note in his voice that caught Tulley's attention. She had a feeling he was coming to the point he'd been leading up to all along.

"It's easy enough for a public administrator to find the right person to run the usual business-type business. All it takes in that case is to keep an eye on him and make sure he doesn't go wrong. But I don't know about running a newspaper," he confessed when the spectacles were back on his nose. "How'm I to know if someone I hire is doing it right? The whole operation could go down the tube before I knew what was happening." He rubbed a palm across the bare curve of his head in a worried gesture and hurried on. "That's why, young woman, I been in such a sweat to get you down here. You know papers, and since you stand to inherit this'n anyway..."

"You mean I'm to take over the paper now?"

The lawyer smiled indulgently. "Whoa! That's not what I mean at all," he drawled. "It's not yours till the court turns it over to you, which'll be some months. Meanwhile, it's up to me as public administrator to find some likely journalist to run it. The salary'll come out of the estate you'll eventually inherit. I figured you might like to have a go at it."

Such a possibility had never crossed Tulley's mind. It stopped her short to consider the pros and the cons.

Matthews reminded her craftily, "It'd save you some money. You wouldn't be obliged to shell out that salary to someone else."

A product of the Columbia University School of Journalism with two years' experience on a small-town daily in upstate New York and another three as a reporter on one of New York City's most prestigious dailies, Tulley respected herself as a journalist but feared being stampeded into a position. Good sense reminded her that her area of expertise had nothing to do with actually *running* a newspaper. It was as if a competent member of the chorus were to be suddenly thrust into the impresario role.

"I don't know if I could. My experience has been in the news end of the paper," she confessed reluctantly. "I don't know the first thing about running one."

"Miss Calhoun…ma'am…I yield to no man in my admiration of modesty in a young woman, but Eudith Clover's checked out your credentials. You're twenty-nine years old, and you've been learning the business for the best part of ten years. If you can't run this newspaper, I'd like to know who in creation can? Somebody's got to take over the operation," he finished querulously.

"I'm sorry. You'll just have to get someone else to run it for now," she said. "One of the publishers' associations can recommend a qualified person. It'd be better for me to go back to my job in New York and take some night courses in newspaper management so I'll know what I'm doing when the paper is really mine."

"May I remind you that the estate'll be obliged to pay anyone I hire considerably more to run the *Herald* than you're likely to be making up there in New York on your job," the lawyer said shrewdly. "You sure you want to let that kind of money go to someone else?"

"I realize that, of course. And I'll admit it tempts me to stay, but...no. It's crazy even to think about it."

The lawyer gazed at her reproachfully over his glasses for so long that she grew uncomfortable under his eyes. He heaved a sigh at last. "Miss Calhoun, I'm disappointed," he said sadly. "I calculated you to be a woman of spirit."

"It's not spirit I lack. It's experience," she began reasonably. She looked across at the round pleasant face of the lawyer whom she already thought of as her friend—a friend whose beseeching look made it clear she was letting him down.

"Look, Mr. Matthews, I know a fair amount about writing, editing and reporting," she said seriously, "but you must understand I don't know much about anything else that goes on in a newspaper plant."

"You know all you need to know to start out with," the lawyer told her. "You've got a good man—name's Charlie Kettleman—in charge of the business and production end. He'll teach you more on the job than you'll learn in any class. It's the paper itself—the end product—where your abilities are sorely needed."

"Who's been running the editorial end of it since my uncle died?"

"Fellow by the name of Shelby Haynes. Shelby pretty much printed what Lamarr told him to, and now he's just going through the motions. If you want a paper left to inherit, I suggest you get in there and turn things around.''

Tulley let out a small, whistling breath of dismay and grinned uncertainly. ''You don't give me much choice but to take a leave of absence from my job and give it a try.''

''Good for you. Now that that's settled, you won't take offense if an old country lawyer who used to know your daddy calls you Elizabeth?''

She glanced at him in surprise and answered with a grin. ''I'd feel honored, Mr. Matthews, but I'm not sure I'd remember to answer to it. Most people call me Tulley.''

''Tulley?'' He rolled it around in his mind. ''Well, Tulley it is, then, and inasmuch as you're going to be seeing a good deal of me for a while, you better dispense with formality and call me Sam. Now, Tulley, when can you start?''

''It depends on how long it takes to tie up all the loose ends in New York. There's my job and my apartment, and a day at home in Connecticut with my mother...''

Matthews cut her off with a wave of his hand. ''Go along and take care of what you're obliged to, but hurry back.''

''Don't worry, I will. To be perfectly honest with you, I can hardly wait.''

During the hour that followed, Matthews covered matters of the estate with a dispatch that she wouldn't have thought possible, considering his leisurely starting pace. The session was interrupted at last by a light knock on the door and the appearance of the white-haired, rosy-faced Miss Eudith Clover, saying a client was waiting on a matter of some urgency.

"I'm afraid I've taken too much of your time," Tulley said.

"No such thing. We're not through, but we'll have to wind it up in the morning. This client's problem won't wait. You weren't thinking about flying back to New York tonight?"

"No, I planned to stay over, but I came straight from the airport. If Miss Clover wouldn't mind calling a cab for me, and you could recommend a hotel—"

But Sam Matthews didn't wait to hear her out. "Mrs. Matthews has aired the guest room for you. She wouldn't hear of you staying anywhere else." Before Tulley could demur, he added, "You've got about a half-hour to look around before I'm done here and can drive you home."

"I'm dying to take a look at the paper. Would I have time to go over and introduce myself?"

She was puzzled to see a look of doubt cross the genial face.

After what seemed a moment of indecision, he said, "Maybe you'd better hold off until you get back from New York. Shelby Haynes is a might touchy. Knowing you're here to take over could be just the thing to set him off on one of his drinking sprees."

"I see."

Matthews shook his head and grimaced ruefully. "No, you don't. Not entirely. There's a lot you don't know about *The Hilby Herald*—some of it not good. Before you go over there, you'd best have all the background I can give you. Meanwhile, don't worry about it. Put it out of your mind."

Tulley felt a stirring of uneasiness. "Don't tell me I'm inheriting a paper that's about to go under?"

"Nothing that bad, I'd hope," said the lawyer. "Just that it needs some handling. Sorry I mentioned it. I just didn't want you to go away thinking I'd promised you a rose garden, as the saying goes."

Name of the game! thought Tulley. There were always problems on a newspaper. She might as well get used to being the one responsible for solving them.

"I'll be through here in about half an hour. Why don't you mosey down the street and take a look at our fine new annex to the Hilby County Courthouse while you're waiting," Matthews said. "It's not open yet, but it's about finished, and we're right proud of it. I'll call the custodian to let you in."

As Tulley started off, he called after her, "Step out on the third floor gallery on the far side while you're at it. You can get a right good view of the town from up there."

Tulley looked back and waved her thanks then walked on, smiling faintly, the click of her high heels muffled by a carpet of unswept leaves on the sidewalk. It was autumn: the air was heady with the smell of tobacco curing in barns and the aromas of ripe fruit hanging heavy on the boughs. She breathed deeply, savoring the satisfying fragrance of harvest that drifted in from the countryside encircling the town. The smells were of fall, and yet, somehow, to Tulley it felt like spring. In a sense it was. A new beginning. She was going to like Hilby, North Carolina, she thought. A feeling of contentment swelled within her. She felt on solid ground in a way she hadn't since the newspaper chain bought out the first paper she'd worked on. It had been three restless years since that small-town daily in upstate New York where she'd come to feel she belonged was turned into a money-making rag with neither conscience nor standards...and she had discovered Jerry's little clay feet.

She'd loved the newspaper. She'd loved Jerry, too, perhaps. No. Not loved, she amended. Idolized.

Jerry Helms was the first real newspaperman she'd ever worked with. The first she'd ever known. She was young, right out of journalism school, and bedazzled by his facile mind, his skill with words, his instinctive feel for a story. She had forgiven his unreasonable moodiness, imagining it fit the image of a man too wrapped up in important affairs of the press to have patience for lesser concerns. Even his willful good looks had seemed a part of the golden myth—until the paper was sold, and Jerry was promoted to managing editor by the new owners, thanks to a gratuitous proposal he made to implement policies that would gradually rob the community of its free press.

To learn that Jerry Helms could be bought had been a stunning blow, but she'd wasted no time nursing a broken heart.

She'd quit. It was easy enough to get over a man who'd earned nothing but her contempt. But the newspaper still hurt. It had been a good paper. It had served its community well.

Seeing for the first time how powerless she was to shape policy on a paper that belonged to someone else, she'd looked for and found a job on a large, impersonal metropolitan daily where she'd never know the people who read what she wrote. There she felt responsible only for the integrity of her own work and not for the overall policies of the paper.

It was during that time of frustration when her paper had changed hands and she still felt spiritually bruised by her father's death that her mother told her of *The Hilby Herald*—a paper founded by her great-grandfather and left by her grandfather to his two sons in joint ownership.

Tulley had always wondered what happened between the brothers to impel her dad to sell out to Lamarr, go north to Connecticut with its cool New England intellectualism and to settle in her mother's hometown of Holly, where three generations of the Tulley family had been born and raised. He'd started a printing shop there and operated it until he died.

Her mother, who even today didn't fully understand the passions of the South, had explained vaguely, "It wasn't any one thing. Lamarr was...difficult. They just didn't get along."

But if it was no more than that, why wouldn't her father talk about it, even to his own daughter when she'd decided upon a newspaper career? Whatever caused the breach between the brothers must have cut deeply. So deeply, she thought, that he'd closeted it away in some silent corner of his mind for the rest of his life.

It was something Tulley understood. In a way, she'd been there herself. Hidden away somewhere in her subconscious, she realized now as her feet stirred up the fallen leaves on the sidewalk, there had always been *The Hilby Herald*. Never imagining it could ever be hers, she'd shut it out of her mind just as her father had. She would have given almost anything to get her hands on a small-town daily and run it the way a paper should be run. Still, when she found out there was a family newspaper, she'd never allowed herself the frustrating luxury of daydreaming that she might one day own it. It had seemed utterly and forever out of her reach. Even now, with the *Herald* almost hers, she thought ahead to her future ownership with an almost superstitious caution.

Approaching the Hilby County Courthouse, she came to a stop and looked up at the venerable red brick colonial building resting at the top of a small rise of ground. It was an imposing Jeffersonian structure that was faced with white pillars and had a curved walkway leading up to it. Judging from the flurry of activity around the entrance, court had just let out for the day. She watched the people emerge and proceed down the broad steps to the walk. So she wouldn't impede traffic, Tulley moved to an open breezeway between two rows of lesser pillars.

She followed the breezeway to the side entrance of the annex. The addition was a remarkable blending of colonial and contemporary design that managed to appear as a natural appendage to the original, rather than an unfortunate afterthought.

"You the lady Mr. Sam called about, ma'am?" asked the white-haired custodian waiting at the door. "Like I told him, you got the building to yourself. It's near done, but there ain't nothing in it yet. No curtains, no rugs, no nothing. Nobody gets to see it until the ribbon-cutting ceremony after they get the furnishings in, but Mr. Sam says you are from away so I reckon it's all right to let you in."

"I wouldn't . . . want to get you into any trouble," Tulley said, hesitating.

"I reckon I'd be in more trouble with Mr. Sam if I *don't* let you in," he said with a chuckle. "Look wherever you like, ma'am. I unlocked all the doors for you, and I'll be right here. Just let me know when you're ready to go, so I can lock up again.'' With a wave of his hand he retreated into a room down the hall from the entrance. Through the open door she could see the screen of a small television tuned to *The Grand Ole Opry.*

Tulley wandered aimlessly through the building, the sound of her heels on the travertine floors echoing through the bare, high-ceilinged halls and chambers.

In spite of the smell of new wood and fresh paint that teased her nostrils, the annex had an inherent heirloom quality about it that pleased her. It seemed a fitting adjunct to the splendid courthouse that was some seventy-five years older and appeared quite ready to last as long. Her steps, echoing through the empty building, tempted her to try a yodel. Lacking that skill, she laughed aloud for the sheer pleasure of hearing the sound of her laughter billow out and roll back upon her. With the dying echo she ran up the last flight of stairs and stepped through the door onto the third floor balcony—the gallery Matthews had directed her to see.

Tulley looked out across a spread of gently rolling ground covered with trees and rooftops that made up the town of Hilby, North Carolina, eleven thousand five hundred sixty-two souls. Before her lay a patchwork of reds and yellows and oranges, with evergreens and late-turners lending accent spots of green. An errant breeze dropped a scarlet leaf on her hair. With a last lingering look at the scene below, she turned to start back to the lawyer's office and laid a hand on the gallery door only to find it locked.

It couldn't be! The custodian had assured her he'd left all the doors open for her. *Inside doors,* of course!

She rattled the handle in futile protest. It should have occurred to her that any outside door would be set to lock.

She paced the balcony restlessly, looking below for a stray pedestrian who might telegraph her predicament to the caretaker three floors down on the opposite side of the annex. It didn't take long to see that this portion of the courthouse grounds attracted no foot traffic. —

Minutes plodded by. To pass the time she perched on the railing and identified varieties of birds winging in and out of the trees. A cardinal made an appearance on a nearby limb. Charmed by the brilliance of its coloring, she watched it until it flew away.

"Tough act to follow," she murmured to an arriving wren, and turned her attention to the army of squirrels harvesting their winter supplies of acorns under the oak trees below.

"Hey, one of you guys, go tell someone I'm here," she muttered from the depths of her frustration.

When a half-hour had passed, Tulley's impatience erupted. She was long overdue at the lawyer's office. Sam Matthews must have got so preoccupied with his client's problems that he'd forgotten about her and gone home.

Another fifteen minutes ticked away before Tulley decided to take matters in her own hands. She looked over the railing. It was a long way down, but the pillars that supported the balcony were round and smooth and fairly accessible. In her tomboy days she'd been adept at sliding down poles. These pillars couldn't be that much different.

Tulley hesitated, but seeing no visible alternative, she crossed the long strap of her leather handbag over her head to the opposite shoulder so that the bag hung more securely out of her way and placed her hands on the railing. She realized then that she was not dressed for sliding down a pole. Though her slim skirt was slit deeply up one side to allow for a long, healthy stride, it was not made for shinnying. She looked around before slipping the skirt up over her thighs until it bunched in folds at her waist, leaving the greater portion of her long, trim-ankled, panty-hosed legs free for action and fully exposed. Her final act was to slip out of her high-heeled pumps and push them into the outside pocket of her handbag. The pocket accommodated one shoe handily but left the other only half tucked in.

When she was over the railing and had her stockinged feet firmly planted on the cornice, she paused, and clinging precariously to the rail, studied the logistics of the descent. She was about to begin the downslide when from directly beneath her she heard a door open and close and the muted sound of footsteps on the brick walkway. A second later a man, dressed in jeans topped by a tan windbreaker, a blue work shirt and a construction worker's yellow hard hat, appeared from under the overhang of the balcony.

She made an involuntary move to escape upward, unseen. The sudden movement sent the poorly anchored shoe plummeting out of her handbag. It hit the hat's hard surface with a resounding whack and bounced off onto the lawn. The workman uttered a salty expletive and turned to see what had hit him.

Frozen to the spot, Tulley held her breath as the man bent over to pick up the shoe, displaying a back and shoulders that might have belonged to a linebacker for the New York Jets. Instantly she unfroze and assessed her predicament. Though it had been reasonably easy to reach the spot where she now clung, to pull herself back up on the balcony would take some doing.

The man turned her shoe curiously in his hands, and Tulley debated her alternatives. Having come this far, she was of half a mind to slide the rest of the way. The thought of the fellow's surprise when a strange woman would catapult down the pillar to land at his feet was so irresistible that she was about to go through with it, but just then the man straightened and looked up, and the opportunity was lost.

Staring up at her as if hypnotized, he raised a hand to pull off the yellow helmet, absently exploring his thick thatch of reddish brown curly hair with his fore-fingers until they found the spot where her shoe had hit. Looking at him from over her shoulder, some instinct told Tulley that if she started down now she'd never make it to the ground. The man was standing there waiting to step up and pluck her off the column the moment she got within reach—waiting to be thanked for saving her life! He'd come too late to be useful but just in time to catch her, indecently exposed, clinging to the cornice of a public building.

She turned quickly and addressed herself to the awkward, not to say difficult, task of climbing back onto the balcony, all the while furiously aware of the audience below. Upon reaching her goal she pulled her skirt down and stroked it back into place before she let herself look down into the upturned face of the workman staring at her as if transfixed. She glowered at him haughtily. He held up her shoe.

"Yours?"

Still short of breath from her gymnastics, Tulley said raggedly, "You know it is."

"You didn't have to throw a shoe to get my attention," said the man plaintively. "All you had to do was call out if you wanted me to watch you perform."

"You know darned well I'm not up here to draw an audience," Tulley snapped. "I'm locked out. And I didn't throw the shoe. I couldn't slide down the pillar in my shoes, so I tucked them in my purse. I'm sorry one fell out and hit you. You're darned lucky you had on the hat," she finished nastily.

He stood almost directly below her now, still gazing up at her in a stunned sort of way.

Not that it mattered. All she wanted of the man was to fetch the caretaker—an errand he seemed disinclined to do until he'd had his fun.

"Those pillars are made of solid wood, ma'am," he said with barely concealed amusement. "If you made it all the way down without killing yourself, which is highly unlikely, you'd get splinters in your—"

"Would you mind?" Tulley said from between clenched teeth. What was she *doing*, she wondered wildly, defending her pole-sliding prowess at full voice to a smart-ass stranger.

Still, for the moment she was more or less at the mercy of her tormentor. She reined in her temper and said with chilly composure, "I wouldn't want to keep you from your work. If you will please go around the building and send the custodian up here to unlock this door, you can be on your way."

With no further words, hardly waiting to hear her out, the workman ducked under the overhang of the balcony and disappeared. She heard the click of a key in a lock, the opening and closing of a door and then nothing. Suppose the fellow had walked out on her. Suppose he'd decided to get back at her for her lofty treatment and left her to get down as best she could.

"Damnation!" she muttered in dismay. She had to climb down that blasted pillar, after all, and the clown had walked off with her shoe.

CHAPTER TWO

Before that thought had more than taken shape in her mind, Tulley's ears caught the faint sound of footsteps coming rapidly up the inside stairs. A moment later the door was flung open, and the man stepped out onto the balcony. She sucked in her breath in surprise.

It was almost as if her first glimpse of him had been in a convex mirror. The broad shoulders lacked the linebacker proportions she'd seen when she'd looked down on him moments ago. And from this new perspective the face she'd imagined to be without distinction seemed almost another face. Why, he was almost handsome! she thought grudgingly, but only for a moment. The features were too irregular; the lean, strong planes of the face too boldly drawn. The bridge of his nose veered slightly to one side, hinting at a badly set break. He was not handsome; if anything, perhaps he was a bit on the homely side. But if homely he was, she had to admit homely looked good on him. As for the long, splendidly built male body, she conceded it was superb.

She wondered uneasily what lay beneath the still surfaces of the clear blue eyes that measured her with candid appraisal from where he stood in the doorway. After a moment he crossed the balcony toward her. As she watched him all other thoughts gave way to a growing astonishment at his height. When she had looked down from above, he hadn't appeared particularly tall; square shouldered, close to the ground—not tall. Now as he came to a halt no more than an arm's length away, Tulley—five feet nine and a half inches in her bare feet, six foot in heels—underwent an Alice in Wonderland illusion of having suddenly shrunk.

Rarely did she have to tilt her head upward to look another person squarely in the face. But there he stood, one of her gray kid pumps with its three-inch heel clutched in his hands, and she had to look up. Way up!

"May I have my shoe?" she asked evenly, and not waiting for an answer, reached out and relieved him of the pump. Slipping both shoes on her feet she rose to her full height.

"Lawzy me, Miss Rapunzel, you sho' do have a way of cutting a man down to size," the fellow said with impudent humor. "Just the same, I want to know what the thunder a lady from Yankeeland is doing on the third floor gallery of a building that's closed to the public until two weeks from next Monday."

"I'm visiting Mr. Matthews, the public administrator, and his wife, and he suggested I take a look at the annex," she said distantly. "A matter of civic pride, I presume. He called the caretaker to let me in." Then in answer to a distinct sound of mistrust she caught in the man's voice, she went on the offensive. "The caretaker assured me there wasn't another soul in the building. So you tell *me* what *you* are doing here."

His grin turned wicked. "Aren't you forgetting one small but important detail?"

"That you're here at the moment because of me?" she answered, a hint of sarcasm in her voice. "At the risk of sounding unappreciative, I still want to know by what right you slip in and out of a building that by your own admission is off limits to the public."

With her words, all the big-city "street smarts" that had become second nature to her as a young female reporter on a newspaper in Manhattan, where "smarts" were a necessary tool for survival, sprung suddenly to full alert. Except for a custodian who had forgotten her and was too far away to call to, anyhow, she was alone in the huge, empty annex with an unsettling stranger whom she had no particular reason to trust.

As was typical of her, she covered her qualms with bravado. "For all I know you could be a jailbreaker from the local slammer. I was told I was alone in the building. I happen to know I wasn't. I heard you come out from below just before you picked up my shoe."

"Hardly surprising," the man said noncommittally. "I have a key. The building happens to be my job."

It seemed a reasonable explanation. Nonetheless, Tulley noted uneasily that the big, well-built body in workman's clothes effectively blocked any escape through the door. She was also acutely aware that during their entire exchange the clear blue eyes had been sizing her up. The fact that she saw in them a look of cool admiration did little to still her qualms.

Instinctively she inched away from him toward the balcony railing and was disconcerted when he moved forward, too, as if to regain the ground lost. Wondering skittishly if he intended to accost her, she felt like a fool when he bypassed her completely and moved to the railing. He leaned over and examined the cornice and molding of one of the pillars that supported the balcony. After a minute he straightened. His eyes scanned her again, pausing on her slender, well-turned legs.

The cavalier treatment was too much for Tulley. Turning on her heel, she walked through the open door into the building, keeping her steps unhurried to make sure her abrupt departure could not be mistaken for a rout.

On the second floor landing the workman caught up to her. "You might have made it at that," he said in a conversational tone, as if there had been nothing aberrant in his behavior. "The cornice is wide enough, so you must have had a pretty good foothold. From where you were when I saw you, you might have been able to hang on to the railing and lower your legs to where you could wrap them around the column."

The man blithely continued his descent at her side. Tulley did her best to ignore his presence, but halfway down the last flight of stairs, as if pulled by an invisible cord, her head turned to find him regarding her almost dreamily from beneath a thick fringe of long, dark lashes. She glanced quickly away, caught by some ineffable quality that made him seem . . . what? Attractive, certainly. Arresting . . . intriguing? Yes, but something more.

By the time they had reached the ground floor, Tulley knew she had overreacted. It was obvious the man had never had the slightest intention of laying a hand on her. A spark of helpless anger flashed through her. Not at the man, nor even at the uncaught hoodlum who had flung her to the concrete platform in a deserted subway station late one evening two years ago and made off with her handbag; she felt anger at herself because she'd let the incident make her painfully wary of every strange man she'd been caught alone with ever since.

If there was one thing her years as a reporter had taught her, it was to size people up quickly and accurately. But she obviously wasn't as good at it as she liked to think she was. For all his brashness this man had a look of decency and intelligence and humor about him that should have been reassurance enough.

Turning to make amends for her touchiness, she was surprised to find him eyeing her cheerfully, either unaware or unconcerned that he'd been wronged.

"If you don't mind my saying it, ma'am, I sure would like to have seen you slide down that pillar all the way," he said in a voice of lazy speculation.

No matter how she took the remark it could hardly be overlooked. "Well, I do mind!" she said, knowing she only half meant it. "I'm a woman. Ergo, you don't think I could do it. You think it would be great sport to see me stuck just over the cornice, bawling for help."

"You wrong me, lady." Though his tone pretended injury, there was no disguising the amusement in his eyes. "I concede you could very well do it. If you ever decide to, I'd like a grandstand seat. I can't imagine a prettier sight."

"I have friends who would consider that a pretty sexist..." But she couldn't go on. Not while his warm, teasing gaze embraced her. For a single lost heartbeat she was breathless. Then her heart righted itself and thumped wildly on.

The amusement in his face gentled. "If a little well-intentioned daydreaming that involves a beautiful and spirited lady is sexist, I stand guilty as accused," he said seriously, his blue eyes never leaving her face. After a moment he asked with an ill-feigned innocence that the wryness in his voice gave away, "Would you be any less offended if I told you this particular fantasy was as much aesthetic as carnal?"

Strange talk from a blue-shirted workman with a hard hat under his arm, thought Tulley, and for the life of her she could do nothing but meet his shameless grin with a reluctant smile.

"What's more, since I wouldn't risk one of those long, shapely legs or that lovely neck to gratify either fantasy, I'm right glad I came along," he finished with a rueful smile.

"How very gallant of you," she said, laughing now. She picked up the familiar colloquialism and handed it back to him in a teasing imitation of the Southern inflection he gave to whatever he said. "I'm right glad you came along, too. I'll have to admit I was none too happy about making my exit by way of that pillar. I felt like a fool. If I sounded prickly, it was because my dignity was under siege."

He surprised her with an approving laugh.

"Welcome to town, Rapunzel. Any woman who can shinny down a pole when the occasion demands is my kind of gal." The grin that lit his whole face sent a ripple of pleasure along Tulley's spine. Blue eyes met hazel and held, until Tulley realized she hadn't let out the breath she'd taken moments before. With a soft sigh she let it escape. By sheer will she turned her eyes away and down the broad corridor to the plate glass door that opened outside.

"I suppose I'd better report to the custodian before he comes looking for me," she said. "Thank you, and if I don't see you again, goodbye."

"Wait...."

But Tulley lifted her hand in a gesture of parting and moved out of his strangely pervasive sphere. Her last glimpse as she turned away was of his clear blue eyes. She imagined they followed her as she walked down the hall; she pictured him standing there, his hard hat tucked under one arm. Then, because she couldn't stop herself, she looked back when she reached the custodian's room. She was strangely disappointed to see that the workman was nowhere in sight.

SAM MATTHEWS LOOKED UP from clearing his desk for the day when Tulley walked in a few minutes later, armed with an apology for keeping him waiting and an explanation that fell short of the whole truth.

"I thought for a while I might have to slide down one of the pillars to get out. Luckily this workman came along and let me back in," she finished, not quite meeting his eyes.

"I get the feeling you would have done it if you had to," the lawyer said with an admiring chuckle. "My client took longer than I expected. Your timing's good. He just left."

With a parting word to Miss Eudith, who was tucking her typewriter under its hood for the night, Matthews directed Tulley outside to an old-model sedan parked at the curb. Its dun-colored paint was polished to the shimmer of nail gloss, and the 1962 Studebaker Lark looked as if it might have just come off an assembly line. The attorney turned the ignition key and observed grumpily that there hadn't been a good car made since.

As they pulled away from the curb, he said, "The town's having a big benefit party tonight for the new county hospital we're fixing to build. Caroline—Mrs. Matthews—is in charge of the festivities, so of course we're obliged to appear. Most of the folks you'll need to know once you start in at the paper are likely to be there. We'd be proud to have you come with us and meet a few of them in advance, Tulley."

"Thank you. I love a good party, and I'm delighted to have the chance to meet some of the townspeople," Tulley said. After a moment's hesitation she added, "Would it be terribly out of line if I asked you, at least for tonight, not to tell the locals about my connection with the paper?"

Matthews turned a critical eye upon her. "Folks'll have to know sooner or later, Tulley."

"I know, but I'd like this chance to talk to a few of them first. You've no idea how spooked people get when they know they're talking to someone connected with the press. It makes them afraid to let you know where they're coming from. It would be refreshing for a change to be judged just as another person rather than as a representative of the press."

The lawyer gave what Tulley took to be an understanding grunt, but she sensed he was not comfortable with the proposal.

"Well, let's see what Caroline has to say about it," he said after a moment's thought. Tulley did not press the issue.

CAROLINE MATTHEWS PROVED to be a woman of charm and tact whose soft round face and manner still held traces of the Southern belle she'd been when Sam married her. The two were a matched set, Tulley thought, like a pair of salt-and-pepper shaker figurines.

Mrs. Matthews welcomed Tulley to their home with genteel effusiveness in the best tradition of celebrated Southern hospitality. Then, to Tulley's surprise, after the initial pleasantries were over she homed in on the very subject her husband had thrown into limbo but a short time before.

"Sam, honey, I been thinking. At the benefit tonight how'd it be just to introduce Tulley around as our houseguest from New York, without mentioning her connection with Lamarr? Wouldn't that give the town a chance to... well... *accept* her on her own merits before—"

"I thought about that, Caroline, but it seems to me...uh, well...not quite forthright, somehow. And besides, somebody's bound to ask questions when they hear the name Calhoun," Matthews demurred.

Something in the two voices made Tulley wonder if being the niece of Lamarr Calhoun might be regarded a dubious asset in the town of Hilby. Certainly her own mother had called her uncle difficult.

Caroline Matthews continued briskly, "On the other hand, maybe not. Who in the world ever hears introductions at one of these big, noisy parties, anyhow? I have a hunch nobody'll even notice. 'Twon't hurt to try."

After having shown Tulley to the family guest room and making her apologies, Mrs. Matthews drove off shortly in her well-polished four-door sedan to tend to last-minute arrangements for the party, leaving Tulley to come later with her husband.

THE HILBY CENTER for the Performing Arts, a large, rectangular brick building where the benefit was being held, had once been a tobacco warehouse. At a sizable cost to the people of the county, with matching foundation funds, the long-abandoned warehouse had been renovated and converted into a public building of many purposes. Its name was considered by some to be grandiose, inasmuch as the activities it was used for—except for an annual chamber music concert and productions of the local theater group—leaned more toward basketball and benefits than the performing arts.

As Sam Matthews's venerable Lark pulled into the center's parking lot that evening, a roar of restrained power brought Tulley's head around curiously to watch a lean black foreign sports car zoom into the next parking slot. In the sudden silence after the powerful engine was shut off, the lawyer got out of the Studebaker and made his way ponderously around his own car to open the door for Tulley, pausing to flick a smudge of dirt off the front fender. Before Sam reached the passenger side, the driver of the sports car had stepped across the narrow space between the two vehicles and opened Tulley's door.

"Allow me," the man said, leaning forward with a suggestion of a bow as he extended his arm. He was wearing a watch Tulley recognized as solid gold and state-of-the-art. He peered in and offered his hand. His eyes, the color of dark rum, had a latently seductive ogle. His black hair was liberally laced with silver and expertly styled for a casual look.

Speaking of handsome, Tulley thought. A swashbuckling mustache partially hid a well-tanned, almost too-perfect face on which faint dark pouches beneath the eyes hinted at overwork or overindulgence.

He was dressed in a conventional navy blue blazer and gray flannels, but the cream-colored shirt was silk. Tulley recognized the designer's mark on his tie and could guess at its extravagant cost. The overall effect was...expensive. As expensive as the sports car he drove, Tulley thought as the full round face of Sam Matthews loomed up over his shoulder. The lawyer looked out of breath and not a little out of sorts.

"I couldn't resist opening the door for this stunning young lady, Sam. I was sure you wouldn't mind," the man said without taking his gaze away from Tulley. "Aren't you going to introduce me to your lovely guest?" He stepped aside to let Sam join them.

"Until now I haven't been in a position to do so, Leo," said the lawyer grumpily. "Miss Calhoun, may I present Mr. Drummond." The introduction, while succinct, was courteous.

"Calhoun? You aren't by any chance—"

Matthews eased his portly body between Tulley and the other man. "I understand you're fixing to appeal that condominium and shopping center you want to build. You think you can get the city council to reverse the planning commission's decision?"

"A piece of cake," replied Drummond. "The planning commission got the wrong idea about it. I put a lot of run-down areas back on the map in Florida, and I can do the same thing for the town of Hilby if they'll give me a variance to get around your antiquated zoning laws. The planning commission would have gone along with me in the first place if they hadn't listened to one man. Luckily, the council has the power to overrule them."

Something poisonous in Drummond's voice caught Tulley's attention more than his words. At the same time she observed a momentary look of cool skepticism on the lawyer's face.

Drummond broke the uneasy silence that followed by excusing himself to pull away and expansively greet another man and a woman.

"City council member," Matthews explained sotto voce to Tulley as they walked toward the big brick building.

Inside the converted warehouse, tables centered with bouquets of chrysanthemums and covered with cloths in autumn colors were semicircled around an open dance floor. A dozen or so couples were swinging to a five-piece combo playing Hoagy Carmichael's "Stardust."

"Maybe I should have warned you about the dancing," Matthews said. "You won't get much disco tonight. Most of the folks with the kind of money we need to build a hospital come from the Big Band generation."

Caught in a moment of nostalgia, Tulley smiled. "That's fine with me. I come from a family where the living room didn't have wall-to-wall carpet because my parents had to have a bare floor for dancing. Before I was five, my dad had taught me to fox trot by having me ride around on his shoes to Big Band tunes from the stereo."

"Well, I'm not the world's greatest dancer—" her host began and was interrupted by Leo Drummond, who had stepped up from behind to lay a proprietory hand on Tulley's shoulder.

"But I am," he said complacently with a pearly flash of teeth. Giving her no chance to demur, he slipped his hand down Tulley's arm to take hold of her elbow and steer her out onto the floor.

It was on her tongue to protest, but before she could rally against the arrogant seizure, she was swept into the rhythm of the music. She was at once captivated by the man's facile footwork and quite forgot the comeuppance on the tip of her tongue. Leo Drummond might be a tad overbearing, but when it came to dancing, he was almost as good as he said he was.

The man knew every variation of the fox trot and added further variations of his own. He dipped, turned, reversed and sidestepped in a swift succession of intricate patterns worthy of a professional. It took all of Tulley's considerable skill to keep up with him. By the time they were halfway around the floor, she put aside her instinctive distrust of her partner and gave in to the half-forgotten pleasure of a sweetly sentimental kind of music and dancing that had been relegated to the past by most of her generation.

Except for a moment of small talk between numbers they danced a fast fox trot and a rumba without speaking. As they stepped into the first slow measure of "Smoke Gets in Your Eyes," Drummond brought up the matter that Sam Matthews had headed off a short time before.

"So you are Miss Calhoun. Am I wrong in suspecting you are a relative of Lamarr's and that you are here to see Sam Matthews about the will?"

"That's right, but I'd rather hoped not too many people would catch the connection," she said. "That's why I asked the Matthewses not to make a point of it when I was introduced."

"Not everyone in town hated Lamarr," said Drummond. "Now I—"

"It has nothing to do with my uncle," Tulley broke in hastily. "It's my connection with the press that makes people freeze."

"Does this mean you'll be taking over *The Hilby Herald*?"

"In a couple of weeks."

"Then you'll be staying in Hilby. We must get better acquainted. How about dinner tomorrow evening?"

"Sorry. I'm leaving in the morning. I have a few things to tend to in New York before I settle in at the *Herald*."

"Unlike the natives, I had a very good understanding with your late uncle. We'll talk about it over dinner when you get back. And don't worry. Until you're ready to say so, I won't let on you are Lamarr's niece."

As the clarinet poured forth the last notes of the number in a poignant wail, Tulley's gaze threaded across the shoulders of other dancers in search of Sam Matthews. He stood back from the dance floor, partially hidden by the back and shoulders of another man to whom he was talking. Drummond didn't release her completely when the set ended but applied subtle body pressure to steer her toward the bar.

"Let's have a drink. The bar's this way."

"You go on," she said, pulling away from him in a manner that could leave no doubt she meant what she said. "Mr. Matthews will be looking for me."

She headed in the lawyer's direction with no further intervention from Drummond, though he laid a hand upon her elbow and escorted her to where her host waited.

As they approached, Tulley had a vague feeling she'd seen the man Matthews was talking to before.

When he turned unexpectedly, Tulley found herself face-to-face with the workman from the annex, dressed now in a well-cut dark blue suit. For a moment she felt herself drowning in the clear blue sea of his eyes. Her pulse leaped erratically and skittered on in triple time.

"Upon my soul, if it isn't Rapunzel!" the man exclaimed.

"Rapunzel? What's Rapunzel?" Drummond murmured to Tulley in a derisive aside that was obviously heard by a complacently grinning Sam Matthews.

"For your information, Leo, Rapunzel was the damsel locked in a tower who let her hair down for the prince to climb up on," Matthews informed him. "An old fairy tale parents read to kids, which it just so happens I read to my granddaughter the other night."

"I don't get the connection," Drummond said, clearly disgruntled.

"My dear, meet your rescuer, Cass McCready," said Matthews. "He's the contractor who built the annex. Cass, this is our charming guest, Miss Tulley—"

"Excuse me, Sam, honey. I need you. We've got a small emergency in the kitchen that won't wait." It was Caroline Matthews at her husband's elbow. Murmuring a hasty apology, the lawyer left the last half of the introduction dangling and hurried off with his wife, his ear bent fondly to receive her troubles.

Across the room the combo's clarinetist moaned out the first sweet strains of an old Johnny Mercer tune, and Leo Drummond made his move.

"I have this dance with the lady, McCready," Drummond said with clearly intended rudeness.

"That's not the first thing you were ever wrong about, Drummond," McCready said as he looped an arm around Tulley's waist and hustled her away.

CHAPTER THREE

FIRST DRUMMOND, now McCready! It was time to put a stop to this cavalier treatment!

Tulley set her feet in a stubborn stop at the edge of the dance floor. Then, to her surprise, instead of the cool reprimand she expected to deliver, she found herself asking curiously, "How do you know 'Rapunzel'?"

"Beats me. It just popped into my head when I saw you up there on that balcony today." He blinked as though he was trying to focus on something dimly remembered out of the past. "My grandfather must have read it to me, like Sam."

She didn't resist when he grasped her hand. Planting a palm firmly between her shoulders, he set off across the dance floor with more energy than finesse, in a rhythm strangely at odds with the music. Clutching her tightly, he steered her at a hazardous speed that had nothing to do with the tempo, in and around other dancers, barely avoiding collisions on all sides. Tulley could do no more than concentrate on keeping her feet from running afoul of his.

When the number came to an end, she glanced up to find Cass McCready looking remarkably pleased with himself.

"Not bad for a guy with two left feet." It was more of a statement than a question. "I got through that waltz without stepping on you."

With great difficulty Tulley swallowed an errant giggle and refrained from pointing out that the combo had been playing a fox trot, which explained his erratic rhythm. He'd been moving his feet in a three/four beat to music written in four/four time.

"Could we skip the next one?" she asked as the music began again. "I could really use something to drink."

"Was I that bad?" McCready asked with an abashed grin as they left the dance floor and made for the bar.

Smiling sweetly, Tulley said, "Not bad at all...if you were a ball player making a broken-field run, and I happened to be the ball."

He threw back his head and laughed with genuine amusement. Point for McCready, she thought. It was easy to forgive the fact that he was one of the worst dancers she'd ever gone around a floor with, as long as he had a sense of humor to go with it.

Having supplied themselves with wine from the bar and food from a bountiful buffet, McCready singled out a small corner away from the traffic flow.

Seated across from Tulley, he gave her a sheepish grin. "I may as well confess it's been a while since I was on a dance floor."

Tulley stared at him innocently. "You mean it wasn't your first time?"

"Listen! I learned to dance at Miss Cora Wimbley's cotillion class when I was twelve years old," McCready declared, affecting injury.

Tulley dipped her chin to look up at him skeptically from under lowered brows.

"All right, all right. Maybe that's using the term too loosely," he conceded. "Let's say my parents enrolled me, and I attended. Intermittently. When I couldn't escape. I figured there were a lot better ways to hug a girl than on a public dance floor."

"When was the last time you danced?"

"I just told you. When I was twelve years old."

"You're kidding! Well, Cass McCready, whatever brought you out of retirement tonight?"

"You, Miss Tulley. It was the only way I could see— short of decking the guy—to get you out of the clutches of Drummond."

"Call me Tulley, Cass. Miss Tulley sounds so formal," she suggested eagerly.

"Tulley? You have a first name, don't you?"

"Elizabeth, but all my friends call me Tulley, and I'd like for us to be friends."

Unexpectedly the man pushed his plate aside and reached across the table to take her hand in his. There was a new warmth in his eyes. Under their spell her breathing suddenly became shallow; her heart thundered in her breast.

"Is that all, Tulley?" the man asked quietly.

A thrill of pleasure darted up her spine. *What a remarkable face,* she thought. A face that promised many things, strength, purpose, intelligence and at the same time revealed a sense of humor. The restless passion in the eyes was tempered with an underlying tenderness.

He could be right. Maybe there could be something more than friendship ahead between them. It had been a long time—too long—since she had read something in a man's eyes that sent a delicious tremor coursing through her body.

"So, Cass McCready," she said softly, without intent and out of gentle bemusement, not knowing where the words forming on her lips would lead, "who are you? What do you do besides build big, noble buildings? Other than Leo Drummond and dancing, what don't you like? More important, what *do* you like?"

"You," he said, moving his chair nearer until their knees touched under the overhanging cloth. Her body tingled, but she did not draw away. Folding her arms along the edge of the table, she leaned toward him in the dim candlelight of the shadowy corner, until she imagined, rather than actually felt, his fresh, clean breath on her face.

He was both a McCready and a Hilby, the two surviving families of the town's original settlers in colonial times, he told her without fanfare or embellishment.

"It's only fair to warn you. Don't bad-mouth Cass McCready in Hilby County. Like as not you're talking to one of my shirttail kin," he said with a smile.

Tulley nodded thoughtfully. "I suppose in a county full of relatives you can just about write your own ticket, can't you."

Cass answered with a laugh. "I wish!" he said wryly. "After all those generations so many family feuds have built up and carried over that I'm lucky to have six relatives who are on speaking terms."

Unexpectedly his voice turned serious. "I'll have to say this for them, though, come what may, the kinfolks put aside feuds and celebrate any small triumph with a kind of fatuous pride. And they bleed with you

in defeat. Some might say our kind of family is a bur-
densome thing to have. You hate like anything to let
them down.''

In that shadowy corner of the converted tobacco
warehouse that was built by the McCready family two
generations before the business went sour, they talked
the evening away. Later Tulley could remember the
details only vaguely: favorite books, movies, sports;
pleasures and prejudices. Sealing wax and cabbages
for the most part, she thought afterward. But for all
the trivia, she found answers to Cass McCready—as
much from what she saw in his eyes and heard in his
voice as from what he actually told her. She noted the
quick flicker of humor in his gaze, the glint of steel,
the flare of passion. Her pulse quickened to the em-
bracing tenderness she heard in the sometimes teasing
voice, and to the zest in his laughter and the underlying thread of honesty that ran through whatever he
said. Still...she sensed something ominous in the
flashes of irony, in the occasional hint of inexplicable
bitterness—subtly hidden, but unmistakably there—
and that troubled her.

Gradually she became aware that a long time had
passed since they'd sat down at the table, and she
raised her eyes to peer half blindly across the dimly
lighted room. On the far side stood Sam and Caroline
Matthews, anxiously scanning the crowded dance
floor. With a guilty start she got to her feet. Still
seated, Cass reached out and caught her hand to de-
tain her.

''Wait. Don't go.''

''I've got to go. The Matthewses are over there
looking for me. There's nothing to keep you from

coming with me, is there?" she invited, not wanting to leave him, wanting him to come with her.

Still holding her hand, McCready got to his feet. He stood for a moment looking down at her, his mind clearly not on the Matthewses.

"Tulley. Miss Tulley," he said almost dreamily. "Mind if I call you Elizabeth? Somehow I don't feel comfortable calling you by your last name."

Tulley looked back at him in surprise. "Oh, that's not my last name. It's the family name of my mother. Her given name is Elizabeth, too, but she never really liked any of its many variations. To avoid confusion, they called me Tulley almost from the first."

"Then you're not really Miss Tulley?"

"No. I'm Miss Calhoun."

He let her hand drop. Tulley moved off, making her way among the tables and across the crowded room toward the Matthewses. A glance over her shoulder on the way told her McCready lagged behind, and she stopped to wait for him. She was disturbed by the expressionless mask that seemed to have dropped over his face. Her smile brought no answering one, and his eyes had grown suddenly cold.

"I shouldn't have holed up in that corner with you without letting the Matthewses know where I was," she said, hurrying on, disappointed to find him taking her departure so childishly. It was an unattractive trait she hadn't seen before in an otherwise perfectly attractive man. She felt somehow let down.

"Caroline just turned over her duties to the clean-up crew," Sam said after Tulley had apologized for her disappearance. "We're going to have a bite to eat before we go home. Maybe you two would like to dance, since you've already eaten. When we get done, maybe Tulley can meet a few people.''

"I was just going home, Sam. I'll turn Miss Calhoun over to you," McCready said tightly, at pains to avoid Tulley's eyes. "Now if you'll excuse me.... Good night, Miss Caroline. Good night, Sam."

Caroline Matthews stared after the departing back in astonishment. "Good gracious! What in the world has come over Cass McCready?"

"I wish I knew," murmured Tulley, stunned. She lifted her shoulders in a mute gesture of defeat and turned to Sam Matthews with questioning eyes. She was puzzled by the look of compassion on the lawyer's face.

"Don't be too hard on Cass, ladies," he said quietly. "He's going through a real hard time right now."

AT EIGHT-FIFTY the following morning Cass McCready was at the door to Sam Matthews's office. Finding it locked, he gave the latch a final frustrated rattle and walked back down the steps to his car, where he tucked his long body in behind the wheel and settled down to wait for someone to let him in. His eyes half-hooded, he looked out into the busy Court Street traffic absently, his mind filled with the single name that had stirred his wrath long before last night, when it had taken on a new relevance that was equally disturbing...but in a totally different way.

Calhoun. The South was full of Calhouns. Maybe he was jumping to a conclusion. It didn't necessarily mean she was related to Lamarr.

Slumped idly behind the wheel, he pictured her again as she'd been on the annex balcony when she'd slipped her feet into her high-heeled shoes and brought herself up to look him somewhat defiantly in the eyes. The smoky gold hair had fallen away from her face to expose a broad, intelligent brow and the creamy oval of her face, which tapered down to a delicately cleft chin. The perfect bow of her mouth curved into the natural pout of a full lower lip—a mouth that asked to be kissed. By an act of sheer will he managed not to succumb to the enticement. He'd heeded the spark of fire in the hazel eyes and known instinctively that he'd waited too long for a woman like this to risk blowing the potential on a stolen kiss.

The thought of that completely feminine, beguiling woman, dressed in Fifth Avenue clothes and shinnying down an annex pillar brought a faint smile to his face. She had climbed back over the railing from cornice to balcony with as much haste as caution permitted, exposing her firm, round buttocks and long, well-shaped legs sheathed in panty hose. The memory was irresistible, but he couldn't savor it fully. He wished Sam Matthews would get a move on. Why the hell couldn't he get to his office by nine o'clock like other folks?

Sam's secretary, Eudith Clover, came into sight shortly. Her white hair was looped into a tight crown at the top of her head, and she wore a lavender knit dress, purple sweater and orthopedic shoes. As the dumpy little figure plodded up the sidewalk toward Matthews's office, Cass got out of his car and stepped forward to greet her. The genial courtesy reflected in his eyes belied the impatience that seethed inside him.

"Here, let me do that, Miss Eudith," he said, hurrying up the steps to take the key she jiggled crossly in a lock that refused to yield. She looked around at him in surprise.

"Why, Cassius, that's right nice of you," she said. "I been telling Mr. Sam for the past six months he's got to do something about this door."

Under Cass's hand the door gave. He held it open for her. As he followed her in, she glanced back at him inquiringly.

"You coming in? Well, if you're fixing to see Mr. Sam, you may as well know you're likely to sit awhile. No telling when he'll get in," she said, then immediately corrected herself. "No, here he comes now, but he's got someone with him."

About to close the door behind himself, Cass glanced back to see Sam Matthews pilot his ancient sedan up to the curb in front of his office. At the same time he caught a glimpse of a straight back and an uptilted chin and a cloud of smoky blond hair. Cass felt a sudden constriction in his chest. The "someone" was the woman who'd been at the top of his mind since he first saw her; the woman he'd been all fired up to start a campaign on last night until she had told him her name was Elizabeth Tulley *Calhoun*.

Miss Eudith moved toward her desk beyond the raised platform of the reception counter. "Looks like he's going to be tied up awhile, Cassius. Why don't you come back around eleven? I'll put you down in the book."

With his back to the counter, Cass watched the two get out of the car and approach the office. They moved slowly, the woman listening attentively to what Sam Matthews was saying.

Her head—set like a rose on its slender stem—was inclined toward the short, round lawyer. On the top step Matthews brought Tulley to a halt. Her lovely head tipped back and Cass could hear the cascade of her sudden, delicious laugh. The face and the laughing mouth were hidden from his view by the fall of her hair. He felt singularly cheated and closed the door quietly.

"Cassius! Pay attention! I said for you to come back at eleven, y'hear?" Miss Eudith's schoolmarmish voice brought Cass out of his reverie, his moment of pleasure lost in the restless uncertainty of the business at hand.

"What I have to talk to Sam about concerns the lady out there on the steps with him," he said. "It won't take long. No reason she shouldn't hear it, too." A moment later the front door opened to admit Sam Matthews and the young woman.

"Well, Cass, good morning," the lawyer said in surprise as he extended his hand in greeting. "I wasn't expecting to find you here."

"No reason you should, Sam. You got a minute?"

Matthews turned to look at Tulley uncertainly. "Well...this young lady's got a plane to catch, and we've still got some—" He broke off and eyed Cass quizzically. "You met Miss Tulley last night, I believe."

Cass's jawline tautened ominously. "I met Miss Elizabeth Tulley Calhoun last night. Good morning, ma'am," he said with measured politeness. "Miss Calhoun is why I'm here. I have a question to ask, and it won't take long. She may as well hear it, too."

Still Matthews hesitated. Then with a resigned shrug as if bowing to an unpleasantness he couldn't avoid, he ushered the two back to his private office where he saw Tulley to a side chair and settled into his own swivel chair behind the big oak desk. Cass declined a seat. He went straight to the point.

"I want to know if Miss Calhoun is related to the late Lamarr," he said flatly. He saw Tulley's eyes widen in surprise. Sam Matthews took over, allowing no time for her to speak.

"I figured that's what you were here for. I guess you're entitled to know. She's Lamarr's niece all right, but you can't hold that against her, Cass. We don't get to pick who we're related to. Miss Tulley didn't even know Lamarr."

"Then what's she doing here?"

"She was his only living kin, and Lamarr died intestate—he neglected to leave a will."

Cass felt his stomach turn over. "She's the new owner of *The Hilby Herald*," he said in flat acceptance. He'd known it from the moment she said her name was Calhoun.

"I'm telling you she's the only heir to Lamarr's estate. She won't own any of it until after the estate's probated," Matthews corrected. "Now look here, Cass, just because Lamarr was a difficult man—"

"Difficult, hell! Lamarr Calhoun was a son of a b..." Cass bit off the word.

With growing indignation Tulley had listened to the men discuss her as if she wasn't in the room, then speak offensively of the relative whose worldly goods she was about to inherit. Who did this McCready think he was, calling her late uncle a son of a bitch? Whatever kind of a man Lamarr Calhoun had been, she couldn't stand still for that.

"Beg your pardon, Miss Calhoun," McCready was muttering, but the eyes he turned on Tulley were hardly friendly, even as he apologized.

"Well, you should!" she said in answer to his less than vigorous request for forgiveness. "That's a very unpleasant way to speak of a man who's no longer here to defend himself."

"You misunderstand, Miss Calhoun. A Southerner is exhorted at his mother's knee against using the kind of language I had in mind in the presence of a lady. That's what my apology was for," McCready said evenly. He paused. When he went on, his voice was like flint. "As for the rest, the man's death did nothing to alter my feelings about him. It would be bald hypocrisy if I begged your pardon for saying what I sincerely meant."

The controlled resentment she heard in his voice and the virulence in his words came as a shock. She liked the man. She'd been looking forward to getting to know him better when she got back from New York. In a funny, affectionately teasing way he'd made it clear the feeling was shared. There'd been something between them last night. Nothing more than a . . . potential, perhaps, but she couldn't just write it off.

With an uneasy side glance at Sam Matthews, wishing she could be alone with Cass for the uncomfortably personal confrontation about to take place, she forged on with a typically direct approach. "It seems we are no longer on a first-name basis, Mr. McCready. What makes us strangers today?"

"That was before I knew—"

"That I was my uncle's niece," Tulley broke in, driven by a sudden urgency to divorce herself from whatever quarrel he'd had with this relative she'd never known, a sudden need to make clear to Cass McCready that his quarrel was not with her.

"I don't know anything about the problem between you and my uncle," she said quietly. "All I know is that when you thought I was Elizabeth Tulley you were…cordial, and then I told you my last name, and the ice age descended."

McCready turned hot, accusing eyes on the lawyer.

"Dammit, Sam, you introduced her to me as 'Miss Tulley.'"

Not waiting for Sam Matthews to explain the interruption that had left the name unfinished the night before, Tulley said, "But my name *is* Calhoun. You can dislike me for my irritating habits or my character flaws, Mr. McCready, but you can't turn me off because of my name."

The faint cleft in her chin had deepened stubbornly. The wide hazel eyes challenged Cass. He groaned inwardly. Even if he wanted to, he couldn't turn her off. That was the rub.

Ramming his hands deep into his pockets, he gazed back at her unhappily, rocking on the balls of his feet—a man in a quandary. He came to a stop and brought a hand up to rake his fingers through his heavy thatch of hair with an air of uncertainty.

"The name came as a shock," he admitted, breaking the long pause. "Maybe I haven't been seeing it clearly. The only other Calhoun I ever had dealings with was out to destroy me. It warped my perspective, I'm afraid. I'm sorry."

"Destroy you?" Tulley repeated in stunned disbelief. "My uncle?"

"He libeled me in his newspaper and slandered me on the streets," Cass said, his voice rising with bitterness. "He set out to destroy the community's confidence in me as a building contractor. By casting doubts on my personal integrity, he's damaged not only myself but the honor of my family."

"But why? Nobody would set out to ruin another person for no reason at all."

McCready said levelly, "I hope you're not implying there was any truth in what he wrote...."

"I don't know enough about it to imply anything," Tulley broke in before he could get up a full head of steam. "I'm merely trying to find out what impelled my uncle to go after you in such a seemingly... unreasonable attack."

"The damage is done. What does it matter *why*?" McCready said, but he saw by her eyes that it mattered to her and by the set of her chin that she had no intention of letting it drop.

"It goes back to a grudge against my father—Lamarr had his heart set on marrying my mother—and then back to my grandfather. None of it had anything to do with me, but I seem to have inherited it," he said acidly.

"Are you saying he used his newspaper as a weapon in a purely personal grudge?" Tulley queried, her tone reflecting her bewildered disapproval. "I don't quite see how...."

His long workman's fingers tightened convulsively, but he fought to keep his anger and frustration out of his voice. "He recently wrote an editorial entitled 'Where There's So Much Smoke, Watch Out for Fire,' citing 'rumors' that some of the materials used in the annex building were below the quality specified in the contract. He took pains to point out that by using substandard materials, a contractor could milk thousands of dollars out of a project for himself without the public ever knowing."

"You think the editorial was aimed at you?" Tulley asked, shocked.

"Tell her, Sam," said McCready.

Matthews nodded. "Everyone who read that editorial knew he was pointing to Cass."

"He concluded by advising the commissioners to keep what he said in mind when hiring a contractor to build the new county hospital," Cass finished bitterly.

He made no move to distance himself from her as he talked, but a barrier like a wall of ice had suddenly sprung up between them. Seeing the bleakness that stripped his rugged face of its warmth and humor, Tulley felt unaccountably guilty and turned questioning eyes to Sam Matthews for reinforcement. Finding none, she turned back to Cass.

"What about these 'rumors'? An editor doesn't just manufacture something like that out of whole cloth," she ventured, praying the embattled man wouldn't again take what she said as an accusation.

For a moment she thought he was about to challenge her. Instead he said caustically, "There weren't any rumors until he ran that editorial in the paper. Now the whole county's abuzz with them. According to the *Herald*, an ad hoc committee has been formed to lobby the commissioners against awarding the hospital contract to me."

"You know any of the people on this committee?"

"I don't even know who they are. Lamarr said they weren't ready to announce themselves."

As a newspaperwoman, Tulley considered such subterfuge virtually indefensible. "You're entitled to know who you're contending with," she said indignantly.

"I demanded a retraction. Your uncle suggested an unacceptable compromise that I refused. Two days before he died he printed another blast of innuendo and inferences that clearly referred to me and again warned the commissioners that the 'flood of rumors' surrounding the courthouse annex must be listened to when the hospital bids are considered.''

"Oh, Cass, I'm sorry. I can't tell you how..." Tulley began in a stricken voice. "But please...you do see...it's not my... You mustn't... This has nothing to do with me."

Sam Matthews, who had been a silent witness to the exchange, cleared his throat and intervened. "I reckon that's not quite the case, Tulley," he began, but already a change had taken place in Cass McCready's clouded face.

"Oh, my God! That's right! Of course," Cass said softly. "The *Herald* belongs to you. All you'd have to do would be to pick up the phone and tell Shelby Haynes to print a retraction tomorrow."

Tulley had the sudden feeling one sometime gets on the edge of sleep of falling through endless space. She caught her breath and in an instant recovered.

"W-wait a minute," she stuttered. "I...really, Cass, the paper won't be mine for a long time yet. I'm not at all sure I can do what you ask. I've had no dealings with Shelby Haynes."

"It looks to me like when you inherit the paper, you inherit a responsibility to set right what the paper's done wrong. You could begin by calling Shelby," McCready said tightly.

Matthews came to Tulley's rescue. "Be reasonable, Cass. Tulley's right. It'll be six months to a year before she's the actual owner of the paper."

"You mean Shelby Haynes is going to run it in the meantime?" he asked, his voice shocked.

"Only until Tulley winds up her affairs in New York. I've asked her to take over when she gets back in a couple of weeks. You can talk about it then."

Cass groaned. "My God, Sam, I can't wait two weeks for a retraction. You know that! By that time the whole county will be locked into the belief that Cass McCready lined his pockets with their tax dollars. At that late date, no two-paragraph retraction will change their minds."

"I see your point, Cass, and I must say I sympathize. But I don't see anything Tulley can do about it."

"And I can't see why she can't do it before she leaves," Cass said stubbornly.

"Isn't the fact that I've never set eyes on Mr. Haynes and have yet to see the inside of the *Herald* building or a copy of the paper reason enough, McCready? Because, if it isn't, you've got a pretty sketchy idea of what a free press is all about. Surely you can't expect me to order a retraction for material I haven't read and know nothing about in a newspaper I've never laid eyes on."

The tension between them now was almost palpable. Tulley watched the man uneasily as she spoke, half expecting to see him go up in flames. The tightening of the cords of his neck, the slight upthrust of his jaw looked suspiciously like smoke signals. She had a terrible sinking feeling that the first man she'd been really attracted to since Jerry Helms was going to remove himself permanently from her life.

While a younger Cass whose ready temper had carried him to the brink of trouble more than once might have done just that, this older Cass saw the folly of such an act. Secure in the rightness of his cause, he gazed in speechless frustration at the woman the mere sight of whom a short time earlier had sent his juices rising in sensual response. He seethed. He'd been wronged, and he was entitled to a retraction, *now*.

And yet she had a right to her stand, too, he was forced to admit reluctantly as his self-righteous anger cooled. If she did what he asked, it would mean she must take him entirely on trust—a man she'd known less than twenty-four hours. They were at an impasse. It was time to withdraw and regroup.

Somehow he managed a conciliatory smile that brought a look of surprise to the woman's face. He noticed that the slight tilt at the outside corners of her hazel eyes gave her face its captivating, almost exotic air. Incredibly distracting! She met his smile with a relieved answering smile that deepened the cleft in her chin. It unlocked his speech.

"You're going back to New York today?" he asked.

"This morning, actually. A shuttle leaves for Raleigh at eleven forty-five. I believe Mr. Matthews has another matter or two to discuss with me, but I'd like to make it. It means a three-hour layover in Raleigh if I don't," she said with a concerned glance at her watch.

"Then I'll not keep you longer." He raised a hand to his forehead in a casual salute of farewell, and before Tulley or Matthews could say more, he was out the door and away.

As McCready moved away, Tulley watched the splendid shoulders, the big handsome head with its crop of unruly hair, and suffered her own frustrations. For all she knew, his exit words were to serve notice that he'd written her off. She was almost sorry she hadn't agreed to print the retraction he wanted. He was probably entitled to it. How could anyone be so straightforward, so open, so convincing in his account of how the *Herald* had injured him and not be telling the truth?

He was also the most attractive man she'd met in a long time, she reminded herself cynically in a sudden return to reason. What did she know about this so-called libel? Only what he'd told her himself. And what, after all, did she know about Cass McCready except that their chemistry had been working overtime from the moment he stepped onto the balcony the day before?

CHAPTER FOUR

THE SOUND OF SAM MATTHEWS clearing his throat brought Tulley out of her reverie with a sigh.

"Was my uncle really against Cass McCready just because Cass's mother married his father instead of Lamarr?"

"Lamarr could be mean as a pit bull when he got his back up," Matthews said, "but I doubt if the marriage has much to do with this business with Cass. There's more to it than simple malice. I've been doing a little digging, and if there's an ad hoc committee to investigate Cass, it was made up of Lamarr and maybe Shelby Haynes, or someone like that. As far as I can find out, nobody ever heard any of those 'rumors' until the *Herald* said they were floating around. Ornery as Lamarr could be, he wouldn't have gone to all that trouble for mere vengeance. My guess is Lamarr saw some personal gain in it, or he wouldn't have bothered."

Tulley stared at him sickly, quite unable to speak. At last she said dully, "What a rotten thing to do! You're satisfied Cass hasn't done anything wrong?"

"Positive, Tulley. I've known Cass and Cass's family on both sides as long as I've known anybody. They're fine, honorable people."

"The first thing on the agenda then is to find out what's been going on," said Tulley. "Cass'll just have to be patient until I get back and can look into it."

Matthews gave her a dubious smile. "You offer patience when what the man wants is a retraction?"

"Sam, you know I can't print a retraction just because he asked me to," argued Tulley. "It won't do him or the paper much good to speak out if we don't have some facts to back up what we say."

"You're right," Sam said thoughtfully. "If the hospital contract was all that was at stake, Cass might not be in such a stew, but he's got Amelia to consider. God knows what it would do to her."

"Amelia?" queried Tulley shakily. Why hadn't one of them told her there was a wife?

"His mother. It's taken most of the past three years for her to recover her health after the accident that killed Cass's father and nearly killed her. A drunk driver crashed into their car while they were vacationing in Arizona."

"Oh, Sam! I'm sorry."

"When Amelia finally pulled out of it, Cass urged her to accept an invitation from old friends who have retired to a villa on Majorca. She's been there several months."

"Then she doesn't know about all this?"

"He's managed to keep it from her, but she's talking of coming home soon," said the lawyer. "Naturally, Cass wants the matter cleared up before she gets here."

Tulley heard the lawyer out moodily. "We wouldn't be in this mess if my dad had bought out my uncle Lamarr instead of the other way around."

"You never knew Lamarr," Matthews said matter-of-factly. Tulley's eyes widened.

"But you were his—"

"Lawyer," he finished for her. "My dear Miss Tulley, if I was called on to admire all my clients, there'd be times when I'd have too few of them on the books to pay the rent. At the risk of speaking ill of the dead, I feel obliged to advise you not to blame your daddy for what happened."

"Oh, I don't *blame* Dad," Tulley hastened to say.

"He was a fine man . . . your father. A fine editor," Matthews said. "His idea of a newspaper was one that printed news with as little bias as was humanly possible, confined opinions to the editorial page and gave decent consideration to the people concerned."

It was a newspaper philosophy so near Tulley's own, and she was deeply moved by a new insight into the father she'd sometimes felt she'd hardly known. Her eyes were suddenly heavy with held-back tears.

The soft cadences of Sam Matthews's words rolled in around her. "Lamarr was just the opposite. To him the paper was an instrument of power—to use to get what he wanted out of the town. He was a year or two older than Prentiss, so what he said was the rule. They were too far apart to go on. Lamarr wouldn't sell out to Prentiss, so the best your father could do was sell to Lamarr and get out."

"I never knew. Thank you for telling me," Tulley said quietly with a soft glow of pride for this father she'd never really understood. She had to wait for the lump in her throat to dissolve before she could go on. "What I still don't understand is why my uncle held a grudge against my father for twenty years. After all, he got the paper, which was what he wanted."

"Being Lamarr, he figured that since Prentiss forced the sale it was the buyer's privilege to set the price," Matthews said. "It took an arbitrator to settle it. An independent appraiser placed a fair value on the property, which Lamarr was obliged to pay, and he never got over it! Grumbled to the last day of his life that his brother had cheated him."

Tulley sighed. "Ironic, isn't it? Wouldn't you think with all the bitterness my uncle had stored up in him he would have left a will? Why would he take a chance on the paper going to the one person he wouldn't have wanted to have it? Me. His brother's daughter."

"I reckon Lamarr never figured dying applied to him," the lawyer said dryly. "He may have mentioned making a will a time or two, but I didn't see any call to crowd him about it."

The face across from her was bland and innocent, the hooded eyes expressionless. *Why, the sweet old rascal,* Tulley thought.

Silence lay between them for a moment. Tulley sighed. "Maybe I ought to print the blasted retraction. It looks like I'll end up doing it eventually, anyhow."

Sam Matthews drew a deep, troubled sigh. "As public administrator and attorney for the estate, I can only advise you against it, Tulley, in spite of my sympathies for Cass. Somebody's out to get Cass, it appears, and they're not going to let it drop with a retraction unless you can give the public a good reason for printing one. Right now you haven't got a reason."

"Do you really think he'll lose the hospital contract if something isn't done pretty soon?"

"It's a possibility, but he'll survive. I wish I was as sure of the *Herald*'s survival if you order that retraction and it comes to the town's attention that you let Cass talk you into printing it without any facts to back it up."

"It would look bad, of course, but—"

"If you expect to be taken seriously as a newspaper publisher around here, you can't afford to go off half-cocked. Thanks to Lamarr, the *Herald* hasn't got all that much credibility in the county to begin with."

"That bad, hmm?"

"If you print that retraction with nothing to support it, you'll be 'that carpetbaggin' niece of Lamarr's who's no better than him.'"

"What about Cass? If the paper has wronged him—"

"Cass'll survive, even if he doesn't think so. He's a moving force in this town. The volunteer fire department, for instance, wasn't much better than a bucket brigade before Cass turned it into one of the best there is. We've got Cass to thank for that shuttle you're taking to Raleigh, which you won't find in most towns the size of Hilby. A local air corps flyer, name of Buddy Hill, wanted to start a service when he came back from Vietnam with a bad leg. It was Cass who got backing so he could do it. Cass comes from a fine old family and was one of the greatest quarterbacks the state of North Carolina has ever seen. Those things count around here. Folks *want* to believe in Cass."

"What you're saying is that it will harm the paper more now if I give in to Cass than it would harm him if I delay?"

"That's right. There's already serious talk that a Raleigh publisher is fixing to start a new daily in Hilby. Unless you can get the people behind you, it could put you out of business."

"But what about Cass's mother?"

Matthews's brow furrowed. "That's irrelevant. It hurts me to say it, Tulley, but until you've got some proof, I can only urge you to let the matter ride." He eyed her owlishly over the top of his glasses for a long moment. "Amelia McCready's been sick a lot, but inside she's a strong woman. Sure, it'll hurt her to come home to this mess, but you can't help it, and Amelia—like Cass—will survive," he said gently. "What we better hope for is to get it cleared up before she gets home."

Drawing a long breath, he took up a stack of papers from his desk and began to shuffle through them. "Now, enough of that. Let's get down to business. You've got a plane to catch."

"YOU ABOUT THROUGH, Mr. Sam? Cass McCready's been sitting out here in the waiting room for the past twenty minutes. Says he's here to take Miss Calhoun to her plane." It was Miss Eudith at the door, a questioning look on her face.

An unexpected warmth washed through Tulley. *He's back!* In the next instant her pleasure turned into dismay as she realized it meant only that Cass was seizing one last opportunity to resume the argument she'd hoped was closed for all time.

"Something wrong?" Matthews asked in response to the uneasiness written on her face.

"You bet there is! That man out there is here to con me into doing what you and my common sense warn me I should not."

"I was fixing to take you to the plane myself, Tulley," said Matthews. "I can just as well say we've still got some things to discuss and want to go over them on the way."

Unnerved though she was, Tulley couldn't suppress a grin. "You are a devious man, Mr. Sam. Thank goodness you're on my side!"

"You'd rather not go with Cass?"

Tulley vacillated. If she refused the ride with Cass, it would postpone a showdown until she got back from New York and had time to do some homework on the accusations. She might even come up with something that would clear McCready before she had to face him again. On the other hand, suddenly the time until she would see him again seemed to stretch off into eternity, and she realized that being with him energized her and made her feel exhilarated.

"Well, do you go with Cass or don't you?" the lawyer prompted.

Tulley's whole line of thinking went into reverse. Was she out of her mind? Cass McCready was trying to manipulate her, nothing else.

Her chin squared stubbornly, deepening its shallow cleft. "I'll go with him. If I missed such a golden opportunity, I'd hate myself. It's about time Mr. McCready understands he can't maneuver me into printing that retraction until I know it's the right thing to do, and why."

The attorney nodded his approval. "Hurry back, Tulley. Hilby County has been waiting a long time for a decent newspaper. I reckon you're just the person who can give us what we need.''

AFTER CASS TRANSFERRED Tulley's carryall from the trunk of Sam Matthews's car to his own, the couple rode through the town of Hilby without a word. When the car was on the straight two-lane highway that led to the small local airport, Cass turned his head to give his passenger a slight questioning smile. Once again she was struck by the pure blue of his eyes. A thrill of pleasure rippled through her and with it an instant of surety that there could be no chicanery hidden in their depths. But, she reminded herself, they told her no more than he wanted her to know.

His first words confirmed her expectations. "I'd hoped that after talking to Sam you'd want to have a few words with Shelby Haynes before you left town," McCready ventured.

"Why would you think that?" asked Tulley noncommittally.

"Sam knows I'm honest. He knows damn well I didn't—"

Tulley stopped him. "You're right. That's exactly what he said. He has an unequivocal faith in your integrity, to say nothing of a whole roster of other sterling qualities," she assured him a bit too heartily, knowing what was to come. "He could hardly have given you a more glowing vote of confidence if you were his son."

McCready drew a deep breath. He let it out and after a moment said seriously, "Thanks. I'm glad you told me. I hoped the stuff in the paper hadn't made him change his mind."

Tulley had a terrible feeling of sadness and a new sense of guilt as she recognized one unmentioned thing her uncle's writings had done to this strong, self-assured man. They had deprived him of the security of taking for granted the respect of lifelong friends such as Sam Matthews. Before she could bring herself to tell him the rest of what Sam had said, he pulled the car off the road and brought it to a stop on the shoulder. He shut off the engine and turned away from the wheel to reach for her hands.

"Look, Tulley, you know Sam Matthews wouldn't have said that if he didn't believe it's true. Isn't that assurance enough for you? You can call Sam from the airport and authorize Shelby Haynes to print that retraction tomorrow."

"No, Cass . . . I can't."

"Of course you can." Letting her hands go, he curved his long, strong fingers around her oval face. The rough calluses of his palms pricked her cheeks, and she felt an instant flurry in her breast, like the beat of a hummingbird's wing, and a tingling across the back of her neck. The heels of his hands pressed upon her chin, holding it steady. Under the spell of eyes that willed her to stay and were so near she could look deeply into the mystery of the blue-irised pupils, it never occurred to Tulley to pull away. She watched his eyes draw closer, forgetting to breathe as her own eyes went out of focus and his became a blur of blue. His full, hungering mouth came down and covered hers.

Her lips softened and parted in spontaneous invitation. A velvety sound rolled up from deep in his throat, and he completed the union in a long, questing kiss. He let her face go, and his callused fingers slipped under her hair at the back of her neck and moved to caress her shoulders and probe gently for the knobs of vertebrae and wings of shoulder blades under her soft wool suit. His arms tightened to draw her to him, but the gearbox between the bucket seats prevented a close embrace. They teetered in awkward imbalance until she pulled away. The kiss was lost. With a grunt of frustration he let her go.

Settled back in her seat, dreamily resisting a return to reality, Tulley was taken aback when Cass squared himself behind the wheel and reached for the ignition switch.

"There's no rush, Cass," she said with a glance at her watch. "The plane doesn't leave till a quarter to twelve."

"By the time you've made that phone call to Sam you won't have all that much time to spare," he said blandly.

Tulley sat bolt upright. "Hey, wait a minute. I'm not making any call. I thought that was understood."

"My God, Tulley! What does it take to convince you? You just said Sam Matthews was with me," McCready burst out in dismay, but when he spoke again she had to strain to hear above the idling engine. The anger in his voice had given way to a sound of hurt that tore at her heart. "You don't believe me, do you? Not even after what Sam said."

"That's not true, Cass. As a matter of fact, I do believe you, but not for any of the right reasons." She wanted desperately for him to see that she was trying to deal with the sticky situation fairly. "I believe you because I like the way you look and the way your mind works and the way you make me laugh...and because I like being with you. I believe you because...well, because I *want* to believe you." She was rewarded by a tentative, half-disbelieving smile that started in McCready's eyes and spread to the corners of his mouth.

"You mean that, Tulley?"

"Of course I mean it. It's not an easy thing for a woman to confess. The fact that I've trusted you enough to tell you should give you some idea what a believer I am."

The smile faded. The bleakness returned to his eyes.

"You're also telling me that it doesn't make a damn bit of difference whether you believe me or not. You have no intention of printing that retraction. Right?" he said tonelessly.

"I'm afraid so. Not until I come back from New York," she told him, her heart quailing as she read a kind of last-ditch disappointment in his eyes. "I'm truly sorry, Cass. My own personal reasons for believing you are just not valid for the people who read the paper. If I'm to run a newspaper in Hilby County, I've got to earn those people's confidence and respect. It would be a betrayal of my profession to order this retraction as my first act as editor of *The Hilby Herald*, without so much as looking into the charges, much less having proof they're false."

"Yeah...well, that's a highly admirable way for you to feel about it, but it doesn't do much to repair my reputation."

"But you do see, don't you, Cass, why I can't—"

"Of course I *see*, and from your standpoint . . . yes, I suppose it's the way you have to play it. But I also see you're going to ruin me when you could so easily. . . Look, you're not even responsible for the *Herald* yet."

"The minute I start issuing orders I'm responsible."

"You might at least listen to Sam Matthews's advice."

"I did listen to him. I'm afraid his reasons for believing you aren't a lot more concrete than mine," Tulley said with a ghost of a smile. She hesitated, wanting to spare him, yet needing more than ever to defend herself. "He says the *Herald* is done for in Hilby if I print that retraction without any facts to back it up. He advised me to do some investigative journalism when I get back from New York but to do nothing until then."

McCready looked stunned. "Sam Matthews said that?"

"Sam Matthews said that," Tulley assured him gently. "Sam also said that the town has more faith in you than it has in *The Hilby Herald*. He thinks it will hurt the people more if I print it than it will hurt you if I don't."

Cass turned away from her and stared moodily ahead, his jaw set in a hard line. "That's easy enough for Sam to say. He's not the one the paper has maligned."

"Please, Cass. . . . It's nothing personal, you know. Let's don't let it make a difference."

The man's hands flexed and unflexed on the steering wheel. Of course it made a difference! How could it not make a difference?

He reached for the stick shift to put the car in Drive and pulled out on the road with a silent goodbye to Tulley Calhoun. Whatever was blossoming between them had just suffered an early frost. If her uncle hadn't put everything Cass was in jeopardy—his name, his reputation as a contractor, the respect of his fellow men . . . But those things came first. There was more than one way to deal with defamation of character. He must not let the lady's charms distract him from the course he'd decided to take.

His foot heavy on the throttle, he let the car eat up the road as if the devil himself were after him. After the second mile he eased up on the gas pedal and heaved a deep sigh. She believed him because she liked him, she had said, and it had the solid ring of truth. So why was he lying to himself?

His own truth was that he liked Tulley Calhoun. He liked her spirit and intelligence and humor and candor...yes, and honor and decency sprang to his mind: she had a way of tackling issues head-on. And—though it was like swallowing a lemon to admit it—her uncompromising ethical sense. He probably wouldn't meet up with her equal again soon.

Tulley stared at his profile and the passing, irrelevant thought entered her head that a nose as prominent and askew as Cass McCready's would look out of place on a lesser man. On him it looked good. It was in appropriate scale to a sizable mouth and strong bones. Together they gave his face a clean-lined ruggedness. She loved the deep laughter lines that fanned out from the corners of his eyes and the way his eyelids squinched into narrow slits when he laughed, until all you could see was a sliver of pure blue.

Come to think of it, she hadn't seen him laugh since last night. Uneasiness stirred in her. The resolute thrust of his jaw, the straight, unyielding line of the mouth that had held hers in mutual yielding so short a time before, seemed suddenly formidable. There was nothing in his expression that suggested he had accepted defeat. It was sheer folly to imagine he'd given up his campaign for retraction! Nor did the silent treatment he was giving her mean Cass McCready sulked. Sulking was not his style.

McCready's style was action. The ominous silence meant he was planning a new attack. What kind of devious scheme was taking shape in his fertile brain to persuade her to change her mind? she wondered uneasily. Why didn't he *say* something, anything that would give her a clue to what was going on in his head?

They traveled in silence the rest of the way to the one-building airport whose hangar housed a few small planes that daily shuttled people to Raleigh. Cass pulled his car into a parking place near the corrugated side of the building and turned off the engine, his eyes focusing on the twin-engine plane that taxied away from the hangar to pick up a handful of passengers outside the waiting room door.

"There's your plane," he said, breaking the silence between them. Before she could speak, he glanced away from the airstrip to focus the full marauding intensity of his clear blue eyes upon her. She was not expecting it. Her mind blanked for an instant, as eyes are blinded from light beamed suddenly into them out of the dark.

"All right, Rapunzel, have it your way." The smile he favored her with was sardonic, unyielding. In spite of his words, there was no sound of surrender in his voice. "Better get going. The passengers are loading." He got out of the car and came around to open the door for her and lift out her traveling bag. Then he took her arm and urged her along at a fast walk.

Tulley felt a sudden shortness of breath. Everything was moving too fast. There was something she had to say to McCready—if he'd just give her time to find a way to say it: something that would tell him she understood; tell him how much she hated not being able to do what he'd asked her to. They were still some distance from the plane when she came to a halt and turned to face the man and was at a loss for words.

"Th-thanks," she said falteringly, wondering why she picked that to say. The word had nothing to do with what she'd wanted to tell him.

"Don't mention it. It was my pleasure," replied McCready. He added in the same conversational tone of voice, "By the way, before you leave, you may as well know I'm going to sue you."

"You're *what*?"

"Oh, not you, Tulley Calhoun, but *The Hilby Herald* and Shelby Haynes and the estate of Lamarr Calhoun. For defamation of character, libel and slander. The suit will be filed in the morning."

Tulley stared at him in stunned disbelief. The blue in his eyes was steel once more: he meant exactly what he said. Sam Matthews's warning about the shaky condition of the *Herald*'s credibility flashed to her mind, and she felt the muscles in her throat go tight.

"That's crazy, Cass," she managed to say weakly. "You say the retraction won't do any good unless it's printed tomorrow. Your case won't get into court for months."

"True, but in the meantime the people of Hilby County are going to know Cass McCready's on the warpath. No one's going to declare me guilty of the *Herald*'s charges by default."

"Not tomorrow. Please, Cass." She was about to cry out her concern that such a suit could wreck the paper, but remembered what had led them to this juncture and thought better of it. "At least wait until I get back."

"I believe the phrase is 'I'll see you in court,'" McCready said in a voice that held no trace of rancor. He thrust into her hand a roll of newspapers he had been carrying. "Here. Read what your great paper has to say about me on the way to New York City, Tulley. It's about time you know the kind of battle you're in for."

A man in mechanic's coveralls was standing by the portable steps up to the plane, and he motioned Tulley to board. Thunderstruck, she stood staring numbly at Cass until he took her arm and pushed her along. When they reached the stairs, he handed her bag up to a steward's waiting hand.

Tulley stepped up but before she could mount all the way, McCready pulled her back down to him. Wrapping her in his arms, he gave her a long, proprietary kiss.

"We're not going to let a little old impersonal thing like a lawsuit make a difference, are we, Tulley, honey?" he asked over the roar of the plane in a wicked parody of her own words. Her senses reeled. His arms relaxed and he let her go. She climbed the steps and took her seat inside. Through the dust-speckled window she watched McCready walk across the tarmac with a jaunty stride and not look back. As the plane started its taxi down the runway, she saw his long body fold into his car. Before the plane was airborne, he was gone.

Tulley sat through the short flight to Raleigh in a kind of daze. Once settled on the jet to New York, she stared at the roll of newspapers Cass had thrust in her hand, seeing again his strong face masked with anger and despair.

Then, as she began to unroll the papers to take her first look at the *Herald*, she thought of something that added a bright new gem to the crown she was beginning to see on Cass McCready's head. He hadn't used one argument she'd feared and had no answer for: his mother. How easy it would have been for him to plead with her to spare the tragic woman this new suffering. It was an emotional ploy that would have left her steeped in guilt. For that omission she thanked Cass from the bottom of her heart.

CHAPTER FIVE

TULLEY'S STATE OF MIND ten days later as she hunched down in her seat on the Raleigh shuttle was a match for the pitch of the twin-engine plane that butted its way through the wind-driven rain of an October storm. In spite of an instinctive mistrust of lesser aerial conveyances not propelled by jet, she dismissed the small craft's buck and sway with a fatalistic shrug. At least the fellow up there in the cockpit knew what he was doing. She only wished she had as much confidence in her own ability to publish a newspaper as she had in the captain's to pilot the plane.

She'd been stunned by the pattern of insensitivity she'd found in the copies of *The Hilby Herald* she'd read on the plane to New York. She'd opened them in curiosity, but after the first three, curiosity had turned to annoyance, which in turn gave way to outrage as she came upon instance after instance of outright malice; some was spelled out boldly in type and some whispered slyly from between the lines.

Other voices and other words she'd heard while she was in Hilby began to reassert themselves, and the loudest and clearest was Cass's dispassionate announcement that he intended to sue. As she read on, she was swamped by a growing alarm that Cass McCready stood a strong chance of winning if the case ever got into court. *The Hilby Herald* was hardly the simple, uncomplicated small-town daily she'd envisioned presiding over. She'd wished suddenly she hadn't been in such a hurry to let Sam Matthews's gentle persuasion override her own instinctive doubts.

More than once during her first days in New York, she'd reached for the phone to call Matthews and tell him she'd changed her mind. Let him find someone else to take over the *Herald* until the estate was probated and the paper belonged to her.

But each time her finger was poised to punch out the number of the Matthews law office, something stayed her hand. At last it came to her what the dear old homespun lawyer had known all along: that for all her inexperience, Tulley Calhoun, and Tulley alone, could restore the ailing paper to good health. Her late uncle had made the name of Calhoun synonymous with sleazy journalism in Hilby County. Until the people understood that a different sort of Calhoun was at the helm and that this one intended to give them the newspaper they deserved, the paper's standing in the community would remain unchanged.

It was her obligation to get the family paper back on course before it was lost for all time. She owed it to her father and her grandfather and to all the publishing Calhouns since the first Hilby County weekly was launched nearly a century ago. She owed it to all those generations of Calhouns who'd served the county with distinction until Lamarr inherited the press and betrayed the trust.

Staring out the rain-streaked window of the plane into the gathering dusk, Tulley unexpectedly gave in to a heady indulgence she'd deliberately denied herself too long. For the past ten days she'd sheltered in her heart the warm moments she'd spent with Cass, while her mind raged at the exasperating man who was bent on turning himself into the *Herald*'s nemesis.

Now, in the plane's last moments in suspension as it throttled down to earth, she dropped her guard and let her thoughts return to the scattering of delicious interludes she'd shared with Cass.

"We're not going to let a little old impersonal thing like a lawsuit make a difference, are we, Tulley, honey?"

Until now she'd had only to remember those last taunting words he'd flung at her as he walked away ten days before to wipe out the picture of the warm, rakish, wonderfully ingratiating Cass. The Cass who stirred in her sweet, sensual yearnings that echoed through her body still. She let herself harken back to those few short heartbeats spent in his arms and wondered ruefully when she would see him again.

She wasn't likely to—except in court—if she didn't find some quick, reliable explanations for her uncle's charges; explanations that would justify a public retraction and restore Cass's honor in the community's eye. But other matters came first. She had to learn her way around the *Herald*, not to mention the town. She had to throw herself on the mercy of the sterling Charlie Kettleman and establish a good rapport with all her staff. And there was the unpromising Shelby Haynes to be dealt with first of all.

Everything had to be done first! Silently she groaned. There was too much to do and too little time to do it in; in the meantime Cass McCready would take himself off to his lair in bitterness and gnaw on the bone of his lawsuit against her. Wouldn't you know! she thought with a touch of irony. Not even when she was a teenager had she managed to work up such a king-size crush on a man—let alone a man who, when last seen, was bent on suing her.

The plane braked to a stop a few yards from the hangar, and a dispirited Tulley unbuckled her seat belt and stood up to shake out her trench coat from the empty seat beside her. Buttoning herself into the coat, she snugged the belt in tight around her waist and cast a gloomy eye over the half-dozen or so passengers in front of her, all bustling for a fast exit.

A gust of wind shook the plane as she started down the steps to the ground. Turning up the collar of her trench coat, she ducked her head and bent her shoulders against the driving rain and headed doggedly for the hangar where her luggage would be brought on a baggage cart and where she could call a taxi from the miniscule office/waiting room.

As she splashed across the runway behind the small herd of her fellow passengers, she was indifferently aware of a person—another passenger or a crewman, perhaps—keeping pace with her, scarcely an arm's length from her side. She ducked into the shelter of the hangar and headed for the baggage cart that had just been wheeled in from the plane. Spotting her suitcases, she reached up to retrieve one and was startled when an arm thrust past her and seized the bag with a firm hand, pulling it out of her grip. With a cry of protest, she turned and found herself staring into the face of Cass McCready, looking rather pleased with himself.

She sucked in a quick breath of astonishment and struggled to compose herself as she let the breath slowly out.

"I...wasn't expecting to see you here," she managed to say weakly.

"Why not? Isn't this where I dropped you off?"

A tenuous thought tickled her mind, distracting her from the feckless exchange.

"I hadn't counted on round-trip service," she said inanely.

"You didn't think I'd leave you to come back like a piece of unclaimed baggage, did you?" he asked. "My car's over there."

"Wait. That soft-sided bag is mine, too." Cass reached past her to take it off the cart.

"Is this all?" he asked. "It doesn't look like you expect to stay long."

"Oh, but I do. I have some other things coming by freight."

"Come on, then," he said briskly. "Let's go. Give me a moment's lead so I can get the door open for you. Then run for it."

The suitcase in his hand, he slung the many-pocketed garment bag over his shoulder and left the hangar, taking off through the downpour without waiting for Tulley to say more.

And anyway, what was there to say other than to give voice to the one thought that now, obsessively, filled her mind: *Hey, wait! Does all this service mean the lawsuit is off?* If he'd actually filed the suit, she was at this very moment his adversary in an upcoming court case. But would he be giving her such good-buddy treatment if he'd carried out his threat to sue?

She watched the long, rangy figure loping with easy grace across the glistening wetness of the lighted lot and discarded the notion of calling the question after him. She wasn't sure she wanted to hear the answer.

Pulling her coat collar up again around her ears, she plunged forth into the deluge and set off after Mc-Cready as fast as her feet would go.

"For heaven's sake, get in out of the rain," she called out as she approached to find him waiting for her outside the car. But he held his ground until she was directly in front of him, then opened the door enough for her to scoot in and slammed it shut behind her. She saw that if he'd taken shelter and left the door waiting ajar for her, the inside of the car would have been awash.

"I should have brought an umbrella," he grumbled as he flung open the door on the driver's side and jumped in, pulling it closed behind him.

"Not in this wind," Tulley pointed out practically. She scooted around to get on her knees and lean over the headrest to unzip a front pocket in her bag, which Cass had deposited on the back seat. She pulled out a terry cloth robe.

"Here. You're soaking wet," she said, tossing the robe across to him.

When he'd mopped one of the wide sleeves across his head and shoulders and sopped up the worst of the drip, he leaned over and wrapped the body of the robe around her head.

"You're not exactly what we mean when we say brut yourself," he observed as he grasped her head and began to rub her dripping hair vigorously.

"Mmm," Tulley murmured, luxuriating. "I never had taxi service like this before. Thanks."

"Mere thanks will scarcely suffice, lady. This driver expects to get paid."

"Paid?"

"In case you're ignorant of local custom, the coin of this realm is a kiss."

Using the cloth still wrapped around her head as a sling, he pulled her forward—she barely resisting—until their lips met and clung. He let the robe fall away and caught her face between his hands. The first soft, almost tentative contact deepened into a searching kiss. One...two...three.... The moments moved on, and then, as if by some mutual and unspoken decision, the two drew slowly apart.

"Welcome back, Elizabeth Tulley."

Tulley's eyes widened curiously. Was the name Calhoun still too hard for him to say? But to mention it was as risky as hitting a hornet's nest. The last thing in the world she wanted was to disturb this gentle moment with a rerun of the discussion about her name.

"Know something, Tulley? You smell good," he mused in a voice of contentment. "You smell clean...and...beautiful and...oh, well, cuddly, somehow. Like a...like a wet...a wet...puppy."

"Puppy!" A squeak of derisive laughter escaped her lips. "Back to the drawing board with that one, McCready. The last wet puppy I had anything to do with smelled...well...absolutely awful! W-wet p-puppy, indeed!" The last words clattered out through chattering teeth.

"Good Lord, Tulley, you're shivering!"

He draped the robe into a hood over her damp head and paused long enough to give her nose a small, affectionate pat with the tips of his fingers—a movement so infinitely seductive Tulley shivered from something other than the cold.

"We'll get the engine started and have some heat in a jiffy. We'd better get you in front of a roaring fire before you come down with galloping pneumonia."

As if to make up for lost time, he backed away from the concrete abutment in a spin of gravel, and while Tulley was still wondering exactly what roaring fire he had in mind, they were on the main road, traveling fast toward Hilby. The car warmed up and when her teeth had quit chattering sufficiently for her to talk, she felt compelled to ask him where he was thinking of taking her once they reached town.

Cass answered her question with a question. "Why? You have anyplace in particular in mind?"

She hesitated, trying to think of a way to say what she had to that wouldn't disturb the lovely tenuous peace between them.

"Well, if you don't mind, I'd like you to take me two places. First by the Matthewses' house, so I can, uh, pick up the key, and then…" In spite of herself the words were coming out in too much of a rush. She saw the arch of the heavy McCready eyebrows move up a fraction as he darted her a quizzical glance.

"To the house," she finished. "I have the address here."

"House?"

"Yes. Well, you see . . ." She was rushing her words again, as if by saying them quickly she would somehow spare him the offense of the unavoidable reminder they contained. "There's this house I've inherited, and I thought I might as well stay there since it's—"

Her words were interrupted by—of all things—a burst of startled, albeit completely good-humored laughter.

"Oh, *that* house," he said and, to her amazement, chortled again. "I reckon you haven't discussed this with Sam Matthews."

"Well, no. Not really," Tulley admitted. "I just took it for granted it would be all right, since..." She hesitated and changed her mind. "Maybe you'd better just take me to the hotel. I don't want to bother him tonight. I'll talk it over with him in the morning."

The man's inexplicable amusement seemed to have burned itself out, leaving no more than a shadow of a grin.

"As a matter of fact, I have explicit orders to take you to the Matthewses' house now," he said. "They're looking for you to stay with them."

"Oh, no. I couldn't think of imposing on their hospitality again."

"And I wouldn't think of taking you anyplace else. I wouldn't dare. Not if I hope to stay on the good side of Miss Caroline, which I do," Cass assured her. "Be warned, Caroline Matthews is a honey-sweet, strong-minded Southern lady with a will of iron. She's an unregenerate manager. She's decided you are to move into the Matthewses' guest quarters for an indefinite stay. Take it from the voice of experience—it's easier to give in from the start."

Tulley felt genuinely alarmed. "Cass, I can't do that!" she exclaimed. "If I can't move into the house I'm...uh...inheriting, I'll find an apartment somewhere. I certainly can't—"

"I'm sorry. Looks like I went at this all wrong," Cass said dolefully. "It's not that way at all. Sam and Miss Caroline are offering to rent you their carriage house. It's as simple as that."

Tulley eyed him dubiously.

"I'm not fooling you," he said. "It's at the rear of their property a short distance from the main house. It was converted into a newlyweds' cottage for their son and his wife before his work took them to Savannah to live some years ago. Since then it's been used as a guest house, and they've rented it off and on—among others, to the new librarian for a while, and to the new manager of the health center until he bought a house and moved his family here. It happens not to be in use at the moment, so you're in luck."

"That's wonderfully kind of them, but I really would like to find out if it's all right for me to move into the house..."

"...you inherited?" Cass finished on a questioning note. Did she catch a trace of malicious mischief in his voice?

"Look. Would it help if I told you that both Miss Caroline and Sam consider the house you inherited unsuitable for you to move into as it now stands?" He turned to look at her, and she saw again the glint of wry humor in his eyes. "Wait a few days until you get squared away and then go take a look at it. Make up your mind if you want to stay there. In the meantime, you can make yourself comfortable in the carriage house."

"Well, as long as I'm not letting myself become a perennial bird under the Matthewses' benevolent wing."

"Nothing like it," Cass assured her dryly. "Far be it from Sam and Miss Caroline to be a party to any arrangement to compromise your independence, good lady. Same as the librarian and the health-center man—nobody will come trespassing on your territory as long as the rent is paid."

It was immediately evident when Caroline Matthews flung wide the door and hustled them into the house out of the rain that she was not dressed for a quiet evening at home. The midlength mauve chiffon that billowed around her plump figure could only be described as a gown. Diamonds sparkled at her neck, wrist and ears, and her stylishly coiffured hair had been recently "done." She came with outstretched arms to welcome Tulley.

Tulley backed away, laughing. "Keep away from me, Miss Caroline. You'll ruin your beautiful gown. My trench coat is soaked through. Just let me stand here and drip and admire you. You look absolutely divine."

"Oh, Tulley, honey, welcome back. You too, Cass. I'm just sick about it, but Sam and I have to go out the very first night you're here." The warm, gentle drawl that voiced the apology made Tulley feel it really mattered to Caroline. "There's this banquet in honor of one of our judges—a lifelong friend of Sam's who's retiring—so you see, we're obliged to go. We'd rather beg off and have a nice dinner at home with you and Cass."

"Please don't apologize. I understand," Tulley said. "Finding myself with a ready-made home is more than I could have asked for. I do thank you both."

"Oh, Cass told you about the carriage house. It's all ready for you. The lights and the heat are on, and we'll be proud to have you stay there until you find something more to your liking." She paused to turn her head in the direction of footsteps that sounded in a hallway leading to the back of the house.

"Sam, honey," she called out. "Here's Tulley, and I declare the poor girl's soakin' wet. Bring her the key to the carriage house so she can take her things out there and change into some dry clothes."

There was the sound of a drawer being opened somewhere, and Matthews grumbling something about keys.

"I reckon it'll take him a while," Caroline explained. "That key drawer is a mess."

In spite of her prediction it was but a moment before the lawyer came in from the hallway, his rotund figure encased in a tuxedo, a starched, wing-collared shirt and black tie. His face glowed with pleasure.

"Glad to have you back, Tulley," he said heartily. "My stars, you *are* wet." He raised himself slightly on his toes to place a kiss on her cheek, keeping a safe distance away from her drip, and turned to shake hands with McCready.

"Evenin', Cass. Sorry we have to run out on you folks, but I reckon Caroline explained all that," he said. "We're a little late, so if you'll be so kind as to excuse us I'll explain to Tulley about the keys, and we'll be on our way."

In his hand was a chain holding three keys. "This one's to the carriage house, and these two are for Lamarr's car," he explained. "You'll need a car to get around in Hilby, and this'n 'll do for the time. Lamarr didn't do anything but put gas in it since he bought it years ago, but I had it serviced and cleaned up for you, and it runs real good. You'll find it in one of the garage stalls under the carriage house when you're ready to use it in the morning."

"I'm overwhelmed," Tulley said. "I can't begin to thank you enough for all you've done for me, and at the moment I won't try. I know we're holding you up."

"We'll drip on down to the carriage house, if you'll excuse us," Cass finished for her with a grin, taking her arm and turning her toward the door.

"Sorry we don't have time for a visit, Tulley, but come on over about eight tomorrow and have breakfast with us," Sam said. "We have a little business to discuss, and then I'll take you over to the paper and introduce you around."

His wife, who had slipped upstairs for her wrap, arrived in the hallway with a last word for Tulley. "If you haven't eaten yet, just give our cook, Freely, a ring on the house phone when you get dried out. Freely lives at home, but she offered to come and fix dinner for you."

"Oh, no. I appreciate the thought, but I ate on the plane."

Back in the car, heading around the driveway, McCready asked skeptically, "Since when did they start serving in-flight cuisine on the shuttle?"

Tulley wrinkled her nose and grinned at him defensively. "I couldn't enjoy dinner knowing somebody was coming out in this rain to bring it to me. Besides, I had beer nuts and tomato juice on the flight to Raleigh from New York. I'm not all that hungry."

"When was the last time you ate before that?"

"W-well," she paused to think and then confessed, "come to think of it, the last time was about five-thirty this morning, with my mother in Connecticut."

"After you change into dry clothes I'll take you to dinner," he said flatly, bringing the car to a stop in front of the carriage house.

But the uncertainty Tulley felt while in Cass McCready's presence seemed more than she was equal to. It had been a long day. She was too tired to sit through dinner wondering where things stood with him.

"Thanks, Cass, but all I really need right now is a nice hot shower and a good night's sleep," she said. "I don't think a person's supposed to get jet lag flying in a single time zone, but that's what I feel like I have."

A three-car garage took up half the ground space of the carriage house, Tulley saw as she stepped out of the car and dashed for the attractive roofed-over brick entryway that separated the living portion of the building from the rest. A louvered door opened into a single rectangular room divided by a partial wall with a fireplace, on the other side of which a pleasant compact kitchen could be seen.

Tulley gave a murmur of pleasure as she looked around the room. Carpeted in homespun woven wool of a muted heathery blue, it was generously furnished with a sofa, a love seat and several inviting upholstered chairs in appropriately harmonizing hues and complemented by a decorative assortment of tables, lamps, pictures and odds and ends of interesting bric-a-brac.

"There are two bedrooms and baths up here," Cass said, turning to the stairs. "You'll probably prefer to take the one over the living room. The other, which is above the garage, is quite small. A good part of that side has been walled off for storage space."

Following him up the steps, Tulley observed curiously, "You know a lot about this place."

"I should. I was one of those renters I mentioned before," he said back over his shoulder.

"You were? Somehow I thought the McCready family home was in Hilby."

"It is. It's a long story."

Tulley forgot about it as she followed him into the large, pleasantly furnished bedroom, and her eyes took in an open-hearthed Franklin stove, beautifully fashioned of wrought iron and brass, that jutted out from the chimney wall. Logs laid on the grate awaited only a match. At one side of the hearth sat a rocking chair. Facing the open stove across the room was a large walnut four-poster. A dressing room and bath corresponded in location to the kitchen below. McCready hung up her bag before turning to look at her once more.

"And heaven, too!" Tulley murmured.

"Satisfied with your new home?" he asked, his eyes warming at her obvious delight.

"Satisfied?" she echoed. "I'm ecstatic."

"Sure you won't change your mind about dinner?"

"Not tonight, Cass. By the time I get dried out and warmed through..." She left it there.

The man watched her and shrugged. "Well, in that case...I'll let myself out."

He headed out of the bedroom toward the landing, and Tulley felt a pang of regret. Swiftly she crossed the room after him, but by the time she reached the landing he was down the stairway and almost to the door. She leaned over the railing and called after him.

"Cass...Cass McCready! Wait!"

He came to an abrupt stop. When he looked up at her, she realized she was crazy to have called him back.

She simply couldn't deal with all that uncertainty tonight.

"I just want you to know how much I appreciate all the trouble you've gone to for me," she said breathlessly.

He stood with one foot poised on the bottom stair and looked up at her, waiting, his eyes unreadable. After a moment when she had said nothing more, a secret kind of a smile crossed his face, as if unexpectedly a thought that amused him had come to mind.

"Rapunzel," he said with a faint chuckle, a note of recollection in his voice as he let the syllables roll lovingly off his tongue.

Raising his hand back over his shoulder in farewell, he turned away. She watched him go, knowing she had only to call out to bring him back, wanting to, yet constrained to silence by the unanswered question.

CHAPTER SIX

WHY HADN'T SHE just come right out and asked him if he'd filed suit against her? she wondered as the door closed behind him. Still leaning over the railing, she heard his car start and pull away.

The answer was easy. She'd enjoyed the sweet illusion of peace between them too much to risk its degeneration—in case his answer would be yes—into the kind of stubborn squabbling that had marred those last minutes they had together before she took off for New York.

But it couldn't be yes. Without actually spelling it out, he'd made it fairly obvious he'd changed his mind and decided not to sue. Otherwise why would he drive all the way out to the airstrip on a miserable night like tonight to meet the shuttle and bring her back to town?

She straightened, only peripherally aware of her body's deep chill. In her very center there was a new warmth, fueled by a growing certainty that in spite of what he'd said that last day, Cass McCready had never filed suit.

As she stood on the stair landing, a shiver traveled up her spine, reminding her that she was half-numb with the cold. With a grunt of dissatisfaction, she slipped out of her wet shoes and padded into the bedroom, pulling herself out of the soggy trench coat as she went.

If she was so blasted sure he had dropped the suit, what was she so uneasy about?

Touching a match to the kindling in the grate of the Franklin stove, she noticed that the Matthewses had left a stack of *Hilby Herald*s on the small table between the rocking chair and the hearth. The sight of the masthead depressed her. She refused to read it tonight. She would not think any more about... anything. Not till tomorrow. Not the *Herald*. Not Cass. Not the lawsuit...

Oh, my God! The lawsuit!

Tulley hurried to the small table and grabbed the stack of newspapers. The top one bore today's date. Turning the pile over, she saw that the papers had been arranged in chronological order from the day she'd left ten days ago. Starting with that issue, she began to thumb feverishly back through the stack.

If Cass McCready had filed a lawsuit against her, there'd be an item about it in one of these papers. A story with that kind of public interest in a town the size of Hilby should be on the front page.

She combed every front page, column by column, but found not a line about the suit. Still, she wouldn't let herself give in to a growing sense of celebration. She'd read enough copies of the *Herald* to know it would not be inconsistent for Shelby Haynes to have buried the paper's embarrassment on some inside page, hidden between fillers and boilerplate, where even the most dedicated reader would have to look hard to find it.

Not until she'd gone through every paper inch by inch and found no mention of an impending lawsuit did she allow herself a shaky laugh of triumph.

Why, Cass, you scamp! You were bluffing! she said to herself, resentful for a moment at what his bravado had put her through. But somehow she couldn't see McCready bluffing. She had to believe he'd meant exactly what he said when he said it. When he cooled off, wisdom had obviously prevailed. He'd seen that if he took it to court it would take forever to get the public vindication he was after.

She was sorry she hadn't let Cass take her to dinner, realizing that she was ravenous now. Warm as a biscuit fresh from the oven inside and out, she padded down the stairway to the kitchen, entertaining half a hope there might be left-behind comestibles in the freezer or fridge that she could turn into a meal.

She found both appliances immaculately clean. They were also quite empty, as was the pantry cupboard, of anything edible. She remembered an extra packet of beer nuts she'd picked up on the plane from New York and started upstairs to retrieve them from her purse when the door chimes rang.

It was too early for the Matthewses to be home from the dinner party, and who else knew she was here? The Matthewses' cook, she thought. The poor woman had come, after all. Not wanting to delay her on her round of mercy, Tulley hurried across the room in stockinged feet and without even the obligatory "Who is it?" flung open the door.

Under the sheltering roof of the entryway stood Cass McCready, cradling in his arms a large open cardboard carton. In it she could see a bottle of brandy and a covered china tureen. The handle of a ladle extended through a hole in the lid from which rose a delicate thread of saffron-fragrant steam that aroused wellsprings of hunger-juices in her mouth.

"Mind if I come in?"

Tulley greeted him with a sneeze. Sneezing again, she stepped aside to make room for him to enter and followed him into the kitchen where he set his box down on a counter and turned to look down at her sternly. Standing there shoeless, she felt unreasonably short for someone so tall. To equalize the uncomfortable sense of disadvantage it gave her, she managed a questioning smile that was lost in another sneeze.

McCready handed her a box of tissues from the counter.

"Looks like the only progress you've made in the half-hour I've been gone is to start working on a cold," he observed. "You got yourself out of that wet coat, but your hair and your feet are still damp."

"I've been in front of the upstairs fire. I'm warm, and I'm not catching a cold. My nose just went crazy when it caught a whiff of the delectable head of steam coming out from under that lid." She wrinkled the offending nose as if to assure him the siege was over. He continued to frown at her, unconvinced.

"I'm a firm believer in an ounce of prevention, so I brought a bottle of brandy. I'll heat some water for a toddy while you scoot upstairs and poach yourself in a hot shower," he said. "When you're well-done, wrap up in a robe and come down. I'll get the fireplace going here and keep the tureen warm until you get back."

"What's in it?" Tulley asked, bending over to sniff the steam.

"You'll find out when you're ready to eat." He took her by the shoulders and turned her toward the stairs.

Moments later Tulley found herself humming under her breath in a flurry of relief as the hot water splashed down over her head and shoulders, sure at last that Cass had given up the idea of filing a lawsuit.

She didn't dawdle under the shower. Her hands moving swiftly, she soaped and rinsed, toweled her steaming body dry and applied a blow-dryer to her hair long enough to draw out most of the moisture and leave a cloud of loose curls hanging above her shoulders.

She didn't bother to examine the terry bathrobe she had hung nearby. Even if it was quite dry, she wasn't inclined to appear in front of the man below dressed in a garment suggesting the boudoir. She felt far too vulnerable tonight. Instead, she zipped herself into a reasonably genderless corduroy jumpsuit the color of cinnamon, fastened the belt's snap-buckle at the waist and slipped her feet into a pair of soft needlepoint slippers.

He was waiting for her at the foot of the stairway, a steaming mug in each hand.

"Cheers!" he said, handing one of the mugs to her and clicking the one he kept for himself against hers in a salute.

"Cheers," Tulley responded, but she raised the mug to her nose and sniffed doubtfully. "If I drink this, I may just curl up on the carpet and go to sleep. I should never have let you talk me into taking a hot shower. The effect was absolutely...soporific!"

"If you'll forgive my saying it, you were a sorry-looking specimen when I picked you up at the baggage cart. Something akin to a wet mop. You should see what that shower did for you. Just what you needed to rev you up. You look positively—'' he stopped, clearly looking for the right word ''—revved!''

Revved? Tulley took a sip of the toddy and suppressed a chortle. Let the shower have the credit for warming the arctic chill, but if McCready only knew it, the ''rev'' came from realizing he wasn't going to sue.

Two steaming bowls were set on a small drop-leaf table Cass had opened for them before the blazing fire. He pulled out a chair for her and took the other across the table. Tulley breathed in the fragrant steam hungrily before she dipped her spoon into the thick mixture of rice bejeweled with succulent morsels of crabmeat and shrimp and scallops in a rich herb and saffron broth.

''What *is* it?'' she asked in an awed voice when she'd savored the first spoonful. It tasted like nothing she'd ever put in her mouth.

''An old Hilby-McCready family specialty we call jambalaya. That's a Cajun dish made with rice that has shrimp in it, but otherwise is no more like this than hamburger is like a filet mignon.''

''Then how come the same name?''

''My guess is that whatever high-spirited McCready or Hilby cooked up this version the first time liked the cheerful sound of jambalaya, and latched on to it,'' Cass told her. ''How do you like it?''

''Mmm,'' she murmured ecstatically, raising another spoonful to her mouth. ''That goes for both the food and the name.''

"I'm working on a system to store huge vats of it in the city hall tower and pipe it out to resident subscribers for a small fee. It could replace parking meters as a revenue source."

Tulley grinned. "And you'd be the resident chef, assuming you made this, of course."

"Hey, listen! Don't think I can't," Cass declared. "Among McCreadys and Hilbys, making jambalaya is a rite of passage, regardless of sex. No recipe for it has ever been written down. It's passed from generation to generation—sort of a tribal heritage, you might say."

"So you recognized the hungry look in my eyes and dashed home and whipped up a batch so I wouldn't pass out for want of food," she said with amiable sarcasm.

"Well...that sounds good, but you're only half right. I dashed home, sure enough, and when I got there I talked my Aunt Vinnie into filling a tureen with it to bring to you. It so happens she was in the kitchen making a big pot of jambalaya when I left for the airport to pick you up. I saw the look in your eyes when you lied about eating on the plane, and thought of Vinnie. I figured she'd be more than happy to share what she'd made."

Tulley halted her spoon on the way to her mouth to ask curiously, "You live with your aunt?"

"In a way. The two of us rattle around in that big old house on Robert E. Lee Street where I grew up," he said. "It's such a barn of a place neither of us is more than barely aware the other's around, except when Vinnie decides I'm not feeding myself well and insists on cooking my meals."

"Give her my thanks for the jambalaya. It must be what the gods washed down with nectar," Tulley said, while she wondered how the rather unusual living arrangement had come about.

"The house has been in the family for more than a hundred years and was passed down to my father. When the family's tobacco company fell on hard times some years back, my aunt and uncle sold their place and moved into the house with my folks." He said it with a shrug. "It was either that or let the old place go for taxes. Nobody could quite see that."

"It must have been a very hard time for both families," murmured Tulley, remembering that Sam Matthews had told her that because of McCready-Hilby financial reverses, Cass had worked for a Raleigh construction company every summer to pay his way through college.

He seemed to think about it a moment. "I suppose it was, but there never was any question about doing it. The house is as big as a small hotel, my aunt and uncle had no children, and I was away at school."

"Even so—"

"I never heard any complaints. It must have been to my parents' liking because even after things got better and the money wasn't so tight, they all went right on living there together. After my uncle died, Vinnie stayed on."

"And you? Where were you while all this was going on?"

"After I finished college, I went to work for the construction company in Raleigh that I'd been working for during the summers. Three years back I bought into the partnership," Cass told her. "I moved back to Hilby then and opened a company office."

"And returned to the family fold?"

Cass looked at her in surprise. "Moved in with them? A bachelor in his midthirties?" He laughed with genuine amusement and replied in the vernacular, "Not hardly, ma'am. I rented this carriage house, but you know about that."

He stopped short and gave her an apologetic grin. "See, I warned you it was a long story. One I had no intention of boring you with."

"But I want to know, Cass," she insisted. "I must say you're making me work very hard for it. You still haven't told me how you happened to leave the carriage house and move back to your old home."

He was quiet for a moment, and she wondered if he was going to put her off. "Sam may have told you . . . my father was killed in a car accident in Arizona not too long after I moved back to Hilby," he said with a sigh. "Afterward my mother went into hibernation in the old house with my aunt. Vinnie kept telling me it was bad for her. She was living too much in the past. Then some friends invited her to stay with them on the island of Majorca for a while. In spite of Vinnie's coaxing, she wouldn't go until I agreed to move back home to keep Vinnie company. My mother wouldn't leave her alone.

"It's all right," he answered Tulley's questioning look. "We get along fine. Some days we hardly see each other. If there's any burden, it's all on the side of my aunt."

"You'll stay until your mother comes back?"

"Which could be any time now. Her letters are cheerful, and she's beginning to sound eager to—in her own words—'come home and get on with life.'"

"And then you'll want your carriage house back, won't you, and I'm already attached to it."

Cass rolled his eyes in a stunning Groucho Marx leer. "Any objection to sharing it?"

BRANDY, THE HOT JAMBALAYA, the heat of the open fire combined to soothe Tulley into a kind of twilight wakefulness. Talk gradually lapsed into lazy silence. Tulley's eyes focused dreamily from under heavy lids on the strong, bold lines of McCready's face for a while, before she realized that Cass was watching her, too; he seemed to question her in some curious, indefinable way with those clear, cerulean eyes. Impulsively she reached across the small table and laid her hand upon his.

"You're a nice man, Cass McCready," she said muzzily.

Almost as if he'd been waiting for the words, McCready rose to his feet and came around the table to pull her up from her chair. She stood directly before him and very near.

"You mean that, Tulley?" he asked seriously. She was surprised at the intensity in his voice.

"Of course I mean it!" she said, and if there was any last shred of the uncertainty in her that had bedeviled her before, it melted away as he folded her into his arms and pressed her head against his chest as if to fix her there for all time.

"I've been about to go nuts, waiting for you to come back," he said hoarsely, his face buried in her hair.

"Me, too," she murmured against the hollow of his neck where the open shirt collar rolled over the vee of his pullover sweater. Her nose explored the small patch of wiry hair in the hollow and breathed in the dry, woolly scent of cashmere, fresh-laundered cotton and the soapy-clean smell of the man. A slight shift of her head placed her ear against the hard, hungry beat of his heart. She closed her eyes, and her breath caught at the sudden small stab of pleasure deep within her. Even when the arm that held her loosened, she kept her head pressed to his chest until she felt his hands curve under her chin. He lifted her face, and she opened her eyes to look into his.

"Where are we headed, Tulley?" he demanded, his voice as taut as a fiddle string. It surprised her to see the man who seemed always self-confident suddenly unsure of himself.

"If you mean *us*, Cass...I don't know. It's too soon. We'll just have to wait and see," she said honestly. "As for the...well...rest of it, it'll be all right, I promise you. We'll make it come out all right."

"Tell me the truth, Tulley. Aren't you afraid?"

"I was, Cass, but not anymore," she said softly. She slipped her arms around his neck and tried to thank him with her eyes for dropping the suit. The issue still seemed too tender to call attention to it with words.

With a soft growl from deep in his throat, Cass crushed her to him, and as if time was fast running out, assaulted her lips with his tongue—softly, insistently, asking to be let in. She opened her mouth in invitation and welcomed him.

She never knew the exact moment the gently probing venture lost its reality and became a wildly passionate metaphor for the act of love it imitated. She only knew that the heat of arousal burned within her like a flame, and that when her seeking body strained and thrust against the strong hard planes of his, an exquisite shudder swept up from some primal spot within her and escaped in a soundless cry.

"No, Cass," she said, her voice thick with the ache of her yearning.

As he let his hands fall away from her, Tulley saw in the man's movements the same deliberate braking process she had imposed upon herself. He turned away and then turned back to gaze at her bleakly.

"I suppose I know why, but tell me."

She drew in a deep breath and let it out before she spoke. "We've come too far too fast, Cass. We're ... we're just not ready for this. Not yet."

He watched her with shadowed eyes that lighted with questioning hopefulness at her words. "That's it?" he asked urgently. "You're sure that's the only reason you pulled away?"

"Isn't that enough? You'll have to admit we hardly know each other, and most of what we know cuts pretty close to the quick," she said and gave him a rueful smile. "It would be hard to deny that we do get each other's juices janglin', if I may put it that way. But Cass, you must understand. One of those 'slam-bam-thank-you-ma'am' relationships is not for me."

She was surprised at the look of bemused satisfaction she read in his eyes.

"You don't have to tell me that, Tulley," he assured her quietly. "Things just got away from me. To be perfectly honest with you, I'd half expected you to cold-shoulder me when you came back. When you said, 'You're a nice man, Cass,' I knew that you'd decided not to hold the lawsuit against me, and I was so elated I got ... carried away."

Tulley smiled a bit uncertainly. "No apologies necessary. I can't say I did anything to discourage you.

As for the lawsuit, why should I hold something you didn't go through with against you? We all change our minds sometimes.''

"That's where you're mistaken, Tulley Calhoun. I didn't change my mind," he said, his eyes suddenly cloudy, his voice bordering on the contentious. "I filed suit against the *Herald* the day after you left. Didn't I say I would?''

Tulley stared at him sickly. She'd been so sure. Her immediate reaction was new concern for the *Herald*; in the next instant a flame of rage licked through her with a fierceness that rivaled the passion-fire that had burned in her only moments before.

"You are despicable, Cass McCready!" she blurted furiously. "Of all the contemptible tricks!''

Cass studied her with no appearance of understanding. "No tricks. I told you I was going to sue," he said in a level voice.

"You told me you were going to sue, but when I came back you never mentioned it. You let me think nothing had been done.''

"If I'd mentioned it, we'd have gotten in a row. I told you before you left that I was going to do it. You had no reason to believe otherwise.''

"Well, I did believe otherwise!" cried Tulley. From the very core of her anger she struck. "How could you make love to me, knowing all the time you'd filed that damned suit?''

There was a slow smoldering in his eyes. "So that's what this is all about. When it's *my* ox that's been gored, we're not to let it make any difference between us, but it's a different story when the ox is yours.''

"You sound like a politician," Tulley said snidely and at once was sorry as she saw the resentment drain out of his eyes as quickly as it had come, leaving an expression that was somehow wistful.

"I should have known I was reading you wrong. But you were the one who pointed out that these matters are not personal and shouldn't be allowed to interfere with what *is* personal between us. When I thought about it later, it began to make sense. I even thought you meant it," he said, a corner of his mouth slanting in a small, humorless smile. "Damn it, Tulley, that's what I thought was going on here tonight. I swear, I thought you'd come back to Hilby with your mind made up not to let the litigation stand between us. I thought you were practicing what you preached. I even felt a little ashamed I'd been so unreceptive when you first made the suggestion to me."

He rubbed his hand through his thick thatch of hair, sending it into disarray, and eyed her sardonically. "I must say it's a sop to my ego to know thou art no more noble than I, fair Tulley."

"It's not the same," cried Tulley heatedly. "I had nothing to do with the injury my uncle did to you. I didn't even know there *was* a Cass McCready when it happened, which can hardly be said of you. You filed this wretched lawsuit knowing it would directly affect me. Don't tell me that's not *personal*."

"You know I'm not going after you, Tulley. I can't get a retraction, so I have to go after the paper to let Hilby County know I'm fighting back. It's nothing against you. It's not even just for myself. My family name's at stake."

"I have a family name to look out for, too, in case you've forgotten. One that's been in Hilby County almost as long as McCready, I'm told. The fact that I didn't grow up here like you did doesn't make me any less proud of what the name Calhoun has stood for in this county...until my uncle Lamarr. When you come right down to it, Cass, you might say my name's in greater need of being cleared than yours," Tulley said defiantly.

With single-minded determination Cass said, "Let's get back to the point. The lawsuit shouldn't make any more difference between us than your uncle's slander. If I'm willing to keep that from coming between us, then it looks like you—"

"Forget it!" Tulley interrupted grimly. "If I'd thought for a minute you were suing, I wouldn't have let you in the house when you came back tonight."

Again Cass turned as if to leave then turned back to eye her curiously. "What made you think I wouldn't go through with it?"

For a moment she hesitated, debating whether she wanted to go any further with a conversation so fraught with frustration. Finally she said stiffly, "The stack of *Herald*s the Matthewses left for me upstairs." A puzzled frown furrowed her brow. "I can't understand it, I couldn't find a word about the suit in a single issue since I've been away. Naturally I assumed—"

"That's Shelby Haynes!" Cass interrupted irately. "He won't print it. He refuses to tell the public that the *Herald* is being sued."

"He *what*?" Tulley gasped. "You mean this lawsuit that was supposed to serve notice on the people of Hilby County that Cass McCready isn't taking anything lying down has yet to see the light of day?" It was so ridiculous she felt a giggle rise in her throat. In spite of her effort to suppress it, it came out in a sputtering laugh. She clapped her hand over her mouth and turned stricken eyes upon Cass only to find him watching her with a shadow of a grin on his face.

At the sight of the faint evidence that he too saw some humor in the situation, she grinned back at him uncertainly, the animosity that had steamed in her moments before unexpectedly boiled out. She watched the smile widen across his face.

"In view of the fact that it's still under wraps, you have time to print that retraction, if you want to, and I'll drop the suit."

"You never give up, do you, McCready," Tulley said, breaking into a laugh and reaching out to him. And then they were locked in each other's arms, teetering from side to side from the force of their laughter.

At last Tulley said, "Don't think for a moment my sympathies aren't all with this Shelby Haynes, but you are entitled to your front page story telling the world you're suing the *Herald*. My first official act at the paper will be to see you get it."

He burrowed his face in her hair and found an earlobe to nibble at. A shiver traveled up Tulley's spine, and she nestled closer to him, suddenly afraid to let go.

He kissed her then as he'd kissed her earlier: a deep, yearning, hungry kiss that promised more than Tulley was prepared to give...or take. She managed at last to pull herself away.

"Cass, we've got to slow down," she said breathlessly. "We're traveling on a pretty fast track for two people who don't even know where they're going."

She tightened her arms around his neck and clung to him in a fierce bear hug.

"Oh, Cass...Cass McCready," she whispered with a kind of desperation, "what are we going to do?"

"I don't know, Tulley. I really don't know," he said soberly, his words half muffled in the thickness of her hair. "But whatever it is, looks like we'd better do it together."

CHAPTER SEVEN

CASS LEFT HER and walked out into the clearing night to his car. The fresh rainwashed scent of her hair, the petal-soft texture of her skin, the sparkling music of her voice, lingered to tease his senses and fuzzy his mind. He stood for a moment in the driveway and stared up unseeing at the moon's pale sickle, lost in the enchantment of the previous moments, her name a tantalizing refrain in his head.

Tulley... Tulley... Elizabeth Tulley. And then—in chilling disharmony—*Elizabeth Tulley Calhoun!* God! He must be out of his mind.

With a disgusted grunt he came down to earth and stalked to the car. What had he said as they stood locked in each other's arms, body to body, as close as two fully clothed persons could be? What had he said in that last moment, when all he could think of was that he wanted to be upstairs with this woman? In the four-poster.

"We'd better do it together," he'd said. He'd said it in answer to the question she'd put to him—not as a suggestion of what was on his mind. A groan escaped his lips. What had he promised her in his state of bemusement that he couldn't go through with?

Nothing! he assured himself.

Nothing. Except an implied consent that whatever they did they would do together. She expected the two of them to go out and dig up proof to clear him. Short of tearing down the walls of the annex to show it met all contract specifications, where could anyone find proof?

Driving slowly through the darkness to the old family home a few blocks away, he realized with a poignant sense of loss that the barrier separating them was not the libel or the lawsuit so much as who they were. When in the history of Hilby had a Calhoun and a McCready been at peace? It was a bitter truth he'd learned at his grandfather's knee. If it was not the libel or the lawsuit, it would have been something else.

Later, in the ancient four-poster he'd slept in off and on most of his life, he found the slight indentation his body had pressed into the mattress over the years. He settled into it, in his ears the voice of his grandfather trembling with the rage of betrayal. *"Don't ever count on a Calhoun, son. It was Ross Calhoun and his damned newspaper that lost me my seat on the bench."*

It was the only time he'd ever heard his grandfather swear. He'd never forgotten those words. Nor could he forget that, when the tobacco warehouse failed, Lamarr Calhoun had managed to make it sound as if his father had gone bankrupt for the sole purpose of putting townspeople out of work.

And so it had gone between the Calhouns and McCreadys into the third generation. He'd been wrong to let Tulley imagine that the two of them could work together on anything, least of all on a relationship.

And yet... Oh, God! The scent of her hair, the sweet taste of her on his tongue! She had a smile like April and a wit that could keep a man alive. She was everything he had ever dreamed of in a woman—and more.

She was . . . not for him! he finished savagely, fighting his way out of the tangle he'd made of his bedding. No woman had ever disturbed him like this before. Having enjoyed the role of wily bachelor up to now, he found it unnerving, to say the least, to be suffering the pangs of a lovesick kid of seventeen.

It was time to cut his losses. Henceforth Cass McCready would stay on the other side of the street from Tulley Calhoun. On that decisive note, he at last found restless sleep through which ran a recurring refrain: *Tulley . . . Tulley . . . Tulley;* a refrain that inevitably ended with *Calhoun*.

When he came into the kitchen in the morning, his eyes heavy from loss of sleep, his aunt eyed him curiously.

"From the look of you, Cass, your bed must be a mess," she commented. "Don't reckon you were lyin' awake worrying about your Grandmother Candy's Limoges tureen you forgot to bring back last night."

The tureen! That damned tureen! He'd have to go back and get it from Tulley tonight. He enjoyed a moment of anticipation before he pulled himself back in line.

The hell he'd go get it! He'd send a messenger to pick up the confounded dish.

IN THAT OTHER FOUR-POSTER a few blocks away, Tulley had been treated more kindly by the night. She'd fallen into a deep sleep almost as soon as she'd slipped her passion-heated body between the crisp percale sheets. Her sleep was broken only once, early on, by a dream in which she imagined Cass climbing over the windowsill like a hero out of Keats, to arrive at her bedside quite naked and in flagrant arousal.

Deep in her loins a white-hot pulse beat fiercely as she opened her bed, her arms, herself, to him, and they were one. She awakened to find a film of moisture covering her forehead, her breasts, her arms, her thighs. So fresh in her mind was the dream that for a moment it seemed real, and she felt betrayed, frustrated, unfulfilled, until she was wide awake and had accepted that her seducer had been a phantom.

She threw back the down comforter, and as her body cooled and quieted she fell asleep again. All that was left of the nocturnal dalliance in the morning was a warm glow and an instant of reawakened desire when she was met on the stairway by the lingering fragrance of jambalaya, bringing with it a sudden reminder of Cass.

"Go 'way, you," she whispered fondly and pushed the thought of him into a secret pocket of her mind as she raced for the big house where she was to breakfast with Sam and Caroline Matthews. She reached it with a scant two minutes to spare.

STEPPING INTO THE ANACHRONISM that was her late uncle's car to follow Matthews downtown later, Tulley felt an uncomfortable sense of foreboding. This car had rolled off the assembly line before the first gas crisis turned motorists away from gas-guzzling behemoths to lighter models. Its chassis was elephantine and nearly filled one of the three stalls in the garage of the carriage house.

With lagging spirit she slid behind the steering wheel, wondering if the car was a sample of what she might expect in the way of machinery at the newspaper plant. What if they were still setting stories at *The Hilby Herald* on Linotype machines!

Sam Matthews waited for her in his Studebaker to lead the way to the newspaper office via her late uncle's house, which Tulley had asked to see.

There was nothing reassuring about the dwelling where Lamarr Calhoun had lived for as long as he'd been sole owner of the newspaper. Built in the late forties, it was a split-level wood-frame tract house with sprung shingles and peeling paint. Not a tree, not a bush, not a plant had been given rooting place to lend grace to the building's bare, nondescript lines.

There was a depressing, long-abandoned air about the place and a look of emptiness that was soon belied by the interior. The blinds were drawn, and the living room lay in shadows until Matthews fumbled for a switch and an overhead light fixture spread a hostile glare over the lifetime accumulation of a man who, to all appearances, had never thrown anything away.

There was a wooden table on which sat three old manual typewriters long past use, a leather sofa with sagging springs, two worn upholstered chairs and a huge rolltop oak desk with a dozen paper-crammed pigeonholes. A threadbare seat pad on the matching swivel chair spilled foam-rubber crumbs onto the floor. In the midst of this roomful of anachronisms was a top-of-the-line electric typewriter and a large-screen late-model television with a VCR.

In, around, under, on top of and beside everything—everywhere she looked—were back copies of newspapers from every part of the country, stacked according to kind, along with piles upon piles of magazines and periodicals. Wastebaskets overflowed with discarded copy and unopened letters. Among the debris were obsolete cameras, calculators, two archaic adding machines, Swiss army knives, flash-lights, odds and ends of tools and a half-full coffee maker.

The kitchen, and what appeared to be the owner's bedchamber, each contained its own variety of clut-ter. The other bedroom was filled with overflow from the living room.

"Wow!" murmured Tulley at last.

"You know, of course, it's up to the two of us to sort all this out and decide what's to be done with it," Matthews told her.

Tulley groaned. "I can't even think about it now," she said. "If it's all right with you, I'll worry about it later. Let's get out of here, please."

"I reckon the first thing you want is to take a look at the paper," Matthews said as they climbed the steps to his office a short time later. "Our business can wait. I'll drop off my briefcase and walk on over with you. The *Herald* is just up the street a ways."

As they came through the door, Miss Eudith said, "Don't forget, you're due in court on a motion at ten, Mr. Sam."

"Dang it! I forgot. Sorry, Tulley. Looks like I'll have to postpone—"

"You don't have to come," Tulley interrupted, not of a mind to delay. "There's no earthly reason for you to go with me. I'll just walk in and say 'Here I am.'"

Matthews hesitated, clearly uncomfortable with the situation. "I don't much cotton to you going in by yourself, Tulley. You never know about Shelby Haynes. He moved into Lamarr's office the day after your uncle died, and I hear he's acting like he owns the place. I told him yesterday to vacate so's you can move in, but I'm not right sure he's done it. I wouldn't want to let you in for a bad time your first day."

"If I can't handle Shelby Haynes, now's as good a time as any for me to find out," Tulley said, suddenly eager to try her wings alone without Sam Matthews's sheltering presence.

The lawyer shot an anxious glance at the old oak clock on the wall. "Tell you what. I've got just about enough time to walk you to the *Herald* and turn you over to Charlie Kettleman. While you're talking to Charlie, I'll take a look on my way out and make sure Shelby's moved back into his own cubbyhole where he belongs."

THE NEWSPAPER BUILDING was three blocks away at the intersection of Court and Calhoun Streets. It was a functional red brick rectangle with an arched corner entryway and a window beside it, upon which was lettered the legend: The Hilby Herald, Since 1872. The entrance sheltered the main downstairs door to the editorial offices and another door that opened onto a stairway to the second floor.

Matthews ushered Tulley up the steep flight of stairs. "Up here is the business end of the paper," he explained. "Circulation and advertising and photography and all that, and here comes Charlie Kettleman."

Tulley's eyes followed his to a rather scholarly-looking man in his late thirties who was emerging from a room at the far end of the hallway.

He was a tallish, balding, slightly round-shouldered man whose pale gray eyes observed her from behind wire-rimmed glasses with a certain off-putting aloofness. Except for a midriff protuberance that could only be described as a pot, everything about him was thin—his mouth, his hair, his face, his whole body structure. The thick glasses rested on the bridge of his thin and rather beaklike nose, above which two parallel lines like a quote mark were permanently etched on his brow.

He acknowledged their presence with no show of enthusiasm. To Tulley's surprise, he greeted Matthews almost coolly and accepted the introduction to Tulley with an absence of expression. She darted an uneasy glance at the lawyer who appeared to see nothing awry. Leaving, Matthews lingered only to explain his departure to Kettleman.

"I'd hoped to be able to introduce Tulley downstairs, Charlie, but I'll have to leave it to you," he said, taking a look at his pocket watch. "I've got a matter in court. If I don't get a hustle on, the judge'll hold me in contempt."

In constrained silence they watched him go down the stairs and through the door. Kettleman cleared his throat and asked formally, "Would you care to look around up here before we go down, Miss Calhoun?"

"Please, call me Tulley. Among people who are going to be working together daily, last names seem somehow...isolating, don't you think?" she asked, turning on her most ingratiating smile in a conscious effort to thaw the man.

Neither the words nor the smile brought a change to Kettleman's closed face. Tulley's uneasiness grew.

"The business offices are at the far end of the hall to the left," he said, failing to acknowledge her overture. "We may as well start there."

It was as if he'd already made up his mind about her, she thought in dismay.

"If you don't mind, I'd rather go downstairs where I'll be on familiar turf. For the time being I'm quite content to leave this mysterious area to you. I have Mr. Matthews's word that as long as you are in charge of the business and production end of the paper, I have nothing to worry about."

Still unbending, Kettleman said stiffly, "That's very kind of Sam, but he seems to have left unsaid a few rather important things you should know."

Tulley answered with a look of puzzlement, hesitated then plunged ahead, her heart beating faster from the stress of her uneasiness. "I may as well be frank with you. My newspaper background has been all on the editorial side. I don't know the first thing about management and would never have agreed to take over the *Herald* at this juncture if Sam hadn't assured me I could count on you. He says I can learn more about managing a newspaper from you than from the best crash courses available."

"That was exceedingly generous of Sam," said Kettleman acidly. "Did he also advise you to start looking for my replacement? And did he tell you I'm only here because I let him talk me into staying until the property was distributed to the heir?"

He came to a full stop on a note of complete exasperation then with a helpless sigh went on, "What he neglected to tell me, Miss Calhoun, was that the inexperienced editor he'd hired was Lamarr Calhoun's niece and heir to the estate."

Miss Calhoun. Not Tulley, as she'd asked. The emphasis on the name was clear. *Here we go again,* Tulley told herself with a sudden feeling of defeat.

Now she understood Kettleman's wintry visage, his restrained manner with his friend, Sam Matthews, and his coolness, which was just short of hostility, toward her. Somehow she had to convince this man he must not prejudge her or the kind of newspaper she would run because she was her uncle's niece.

"I can see why you're...upset," she said quietly with a slight smile as she went on. "He used some of the same tactics on me, I suppose, but you must know Sam Matthews well enough to realize he did it without malice. In both our cases, it was what he thought would be best for us. He knew you wouldn't stay if he told you he'd hired Lamarr Calhoun's niece. At the same time, the shrewd old rascal knew if he could get you to stay we would work well together. I don't know about you, but I'm inclined to think he's right."

She wondered for a moment if Kettleman even heard her. He seemed to be not so much listening as marking time until she was through. It was as if once he'd turned his tongue loose, things too-long bottled inside had to be said.

"I suppose Sam didn't tell you, either, that I'm no longer employed by the *Herald*," he said on a rising note of outrage. "He didn't get around to informing you, did he, that I quit the day before Lamarr died? Or that I promised myself then that I'd never spend another day working under a Calhoun?"

"No," Tulley admitted. "Would you mind telling me why?"

"Let's say it was a long-standing policy disagreement between your uncle and me. He laid the final straw that last day. Whether I said 'I quit' or he said 'You're fired' is immaterial. Suffice to say, my severance was one of the few things Lamarr Calhoun and I ever wholeheartedly agreed upon."

"I don't care whether you quit or he fired you," she said. "Either way is even a better recommendation than Sam Matthews's glowing testimonial on your behalf, Mr. Kettleman. My goal is to turn this paper around. I'll do it alone if I have to, but it'll go a lot faster if you stay, and I don't have to learn management as I go along by trial and error."

He looked at her curiously for a long moment, and she felt a ray of hope as she saw his truculence begin to melt.

"By the way, that 'last straw' you mentioned. It didn't have anything to do with the *Herald*'s gratuitous attack on Cass McCready, did it?" she asked before he could speak.

"You know about that?"

Tulley gave him a wry grin and said, "From the horse's mouth to my ear, the first day I hit town. I can't blame him for being impatient for a retraction, but I can't print one solely on the basis of his word and my intuition. Even Sam Matthews could offer no more than a character voucher. I've got to have proof my uncle was wrong about what he printed before I stake the paper's reliability on a retraction. If I can persuade you to stay, I'd like to start looking into it very soon."

The cool gray eyes assessed her as she talked. "I'll be honest with you, Miss Calhoun. Under the circumstances, I don't consider my agreement with Sam binding. I should have had the intestinal fortitude to tell Lamarr what he could do with the job years ago. Now I've done it, and I'm disinclined to reverse myself. I'm not sure I have a future here at the *Herald*."

Encouraged by a new tone—businesslike rather than bristling—Tulley said with a smile, "I can hardly offer you lifelong employment on such short acquaintance, Mr. Kettleman, but if all I've been told about you is true, I feel sure your future with this paper will be for as long as you wish to stay."

"Shelby Haynes severed my employment with the *Herald* again last week. I told him I'd already resigned."

"I have a few words to say to Mr. Haynes, myself," Tulley said, making no effort to conceal her annoyance. "I understand Cass McCready filed a libel suit against the *Herald* last week, and our editor pro tem has refused to run a story on it."

"Quite true. That lay at the bottom of our most recent altercation. I said I considered it a deplorable way to run a newspaper, and he said—and I quote—that he didn't want 'any lousy accountant' telling him how to run his paper."

"Who's our top reporter?"

"Any one of the four is dependable, but Ed Dawes is the most experienced and usually handles the courts."

"Then I want Ed Dawes to work up a front page story on that lawsuit, with full background. How soon can we get it out?"

For the first time she saw a look of something like respect—even admiration—on Kettleman's face, a hint of warmth in the hitherto judgmental eyes. She sensed an easing of tension, a tentative move in the direction of trust.

He glanced up at the wall clock, which read nine-thirty. "If Ed gets a hustle on, we might get it in today."

Tulley's eyes lighted. "Good. I'd like that." But even as she said it, she doubted it. "Maybe we'd better aim for tomorrow. I can't very well barge in and start doing things my way without serving some kind of notice on Mr. Haynes, and from what I've heard about the man, I don't think he'll take what I have to say lightly. It may take some time."

"May I have the pleasure of informing you that you have nothing about which to concern yourself in regard to Shelby," Kettleman said in what Tulley had begun to recognize as his own pedantic mode of expression. She detected a faint note of satisfaction in his voice. "Shelby's no longer with us. After Sam notified him that he was to vacate Lamarr's office and leave it for you, he removed all of his impedimenta, collected his paycheck and departed."

Tulley stared at him in disbelief. It was too easy. There was a sudden release of tension she hadn't even been aware of within herself. "Departed?"

Kettleman gave an unscholarly grunt. "Never to return, if we're lucky, though I regret to say I've been around Shelby too long to hope we've seen the last of him."

"Well, then," Tulley said in a sigh of relief, "what are we waiting for? Let's get it in the paper today." There was no mistaking the warmth of approval in the thin face now.

She turned toward the stairway and the editorial offices below, but at the landing she paused and turned back to Kettleman, who had followed her.

"Please . . . just a minute," she said. "You haven't given me an answer. I can't leave anything as important as whether you go or stay dangling until a more convenient time. If I ever needed anyone's help in my life, I need yours now, Mr. K. How about putting me on probation? The first time I start acting like my late uncle, feel free to walk out without bothering to say goodbye. When the paper actually belongs to me, we can renegotiate.''

She saw the first real friendliness behind the austere, rather professorial facade. He hesitated a moment and then surprised her with a smile that was more ironic than playful, but it was unmistakably a smile.

''You can tell Sam Matthews he won his point, Tulley,'' he said almost whimsically.

A soundless sigh of relief escaped her, and she held out her hand to meet that of her business manager.

''Somehow, I feel neither one of us is going to be sorry about this,'' she said simply. Then, though she was half-afraid to venture it, ''Will it be all right now if I call you Charlie?''

This time there was no mistaking the look of genuine amusement in the eyes that gazed back at her.

DOWNSTAIRS, KETTLEMAN took her past the front reception desk, down a corridor lined with partitioned cubicles and finally into a room that accommodated four work stations, leaving just enough space for a reasonable flow of traffic in and around them.

A squarely built man in his early forties with a shock of graying hair looked up with quick, intelligent eyes and raised a hand in salute to Kettleman from across the room. They approached his desk.

''Tulley, this is the dean of our reporting staff, Ed Dawes,'' Kettleman said. ''Tulley Calhoun, our new editor in chief, Ed.'' Already she was learning to brace herself against the reaction to her name. In this case, the amusement that lighted Dawes's eyes at being dubbed ''dean'' flickered into a kind of distant politeness as he acknowledged the introduction. Was she getting paranoid, Tulley wondered uncomfortably, or was she going to have to shake the ghost of her Uncle Lamarr with each and every employee?

Kettleman came to her rescue.

"Tulley wants to break down the front page for a story on the libel suit Cass McCready filed against the *Herald*," he said without preliminaries. "Is there time before the press rolls to make the first run?"

Dawes looked from one to the other in patent disbelief. "You gotta be kidding?" The reporter seemed to really look at Tulley for the first time. "You're *not* kidding!" he answered his own question with an explosive chuckle. "Hell, I wrote that story the day the suit was filed. We got it in type and all the way to the final front page makeup before Haynes saw it. It's still waiting, ready to go."

"Good. I'll go out to the pressroom and tell the foreman there's a change coming up," Kettleman said and took off. From a drawer in his desk Ed Dawes dredged up a typeset sheet and handed it to Tulley.

"Maybe you won't want to play it this strong, Miss Calhoun," he said uneasily. "I can rewrite it. We don't have to run any more than just the complaint."

"No. I want the background, too."

"Oh, it's got background, all right. It also has some pithy quotes from Cass McCready. You'd better read it."

Tulley's eyes dropped to the paper she held in her hand. The quotes were pithy, all right, but there was nothing in it Cass didn't have a right to say... or, for that matter, that the public didn't have a right to know. It was a straightforward account of his futile efforts to get a retraction from the *Herald* for accusations Cass denied and for which the paper had produced no proof.

She finished reading and looked up to find that Kettleman had returned. The two men were watching her intently, waiting, she knew, to see if she would run the story as it stood or throw out the damning quotes. Anxieties whirled in her head like dervishes. How much would it hurt the *Herald* if she ran it as written, and what would it do to the respect she'd just won if she ordered it cut? Then she thought of Cass.

"Run it as is, Ed," she said, handing it back to him. "On the front page. How about starting it above the center fold where people will see it. We want them to know that from now on this paper will not be afraid to put its own dirty laundry on the line."

As the two men headed for the composing room to follow the story's transition into print, she heard Dawes say to Kettleman, "Hey, Charlie, I'll keep my eye on the story. You get the masthead changed. This lady's name should be there as editor. Let the subscribers know, by God, we're playing with a brand-new deck."

Through the windows that walled off the adjoining composing room, she could see Dawes hovering over a young woman who worked at a long glass-topped table through which lights shone from below to illuminate a large sheet of graph paper. Arranged on it were an assortment of type-printed papers, fitted together like a jigsaw puzzle, in what was to be the front page of the day's *Herald*.

Watching them, Tulley suddenly realized that in the stress of the morning's meetings her concern that the *Herald* might still be in the Linotype era was forgotten. She turned away from the well-equipped composing room with its bank of light tables and glanced around the newsroom, its furnishings registering for the first time.

A computer terminal at each reporter's desk told her all she needed to know. Her late uncle's choice of transportation notwithstanding, when it came to the *Herald*'s mechanical needs, he'd kept up with the times. The scene before her was as modern as the newsroom she'd worked in on that first newspaper in upstate New York.

As in most newspapers throughout the country, computer terminals had replaced the typewriter and Linotype. Hooked into a central "brain" somewhere backstage that received, stored and transmitted, they performed an incredible assortment of magic wonders Tulley didn't even try to comprehend. She knew from experience that the video screens were used more than the telephone to transmit messages inside the newspaper's offices to other terminals hooked into the brain.

She turned to meet Dawes and Kettleman as they came through the door from the composing room, satisfaction written on both their faces. As they approached, Dawes held out his hand to her and grinned apologetically.

"We gave you a bum rap, Miss Calhoun," he said. "Thanks for making me feel I'm working for an honest-to-God newspaper again."

"She would prefer we were all on a first-name basis," Charlie informed him. "Isn't that right, Tulley?"

It was an instant before Tulley recovered from her surprise. "Right, Charlie . . . Ed."

She saw her own astonishment mirrored in Ed Dawes's face before it split wide open in a satisfied grin. He dropped into the chair in front of his computer terminal. As his fingers flew across the keyboard, Tulley's eyes turned to the video display. Relief and a kind of jubilation surged through her as she read the message.

"Attention all terminals: catch today's front page. The new editor says call her Tulley."

CHAPTER EIGHT

As THE HUGE WEB PRESS began to roll, Tulley watched from the opening between the pressroom and the loading dock where panel trucks waited to pick up the first bundles of papers to be delivered throughout the county. Later output would be taken to the town's coin-operated dispensing boxes and to the various neighborhoods for hand-delivery to subscribers by newsboys.

Kettleman and Dawes had gone their separate ways. Now she stood alone, reveling in the sound of the press and the fresh, clean smell of the newly inked paper. With a kind of hypnotic fascination she followed the endless pristine sheet with her eyes from the point where it flowed onto the press from a gargantuan roll of paper until it became today's newspaper, pouring out a thousand or so a minute at the end of the line.

During the course of her newspapering, Tulley had never missed a chance to slip out and watch when the presses began to roll. It gave the workday a certain fillip that provided impetus for the day ahead. That she now watched the transformation through the eyes of its future owner added a new dimension to her pleasure.

She turned away from the pageant of movement to find she was not the only observer on the dock. Standing a few feet away, his face registering an absorption to match her own, stood a skinny, gray-eyed boy of about fifteen with a shock of unruly sun-streaked hair. His forefinger played absently with a wart on the side of his thumb. Dressed in uniform jeans, he wore a T-shirt with the *Herald*'s logo across the back, and when he turned slightly she could read a message across the front, Remember, You Read it Here First.

He glanced away from the press to find Tulley watching him. A look of uneasiness crossed his face, and he backed off as if to leave.

"Don't go," she said. "I like a fellow press-watcher. Be my guest."

The boy hesitated then darted her an embarrassed grin and turned his attention back to the press.

"You come here often?" she asked curiously.

"Once in a while," the boy said noncommittally. After a moment he added, somewhat defensively, she thought, "I work here."

"I see," Tulley said, not seeing at all. The boy obviously belonged in school.

He waited as if expecting to be challenged then grinned again and confessed, "Well, I don't actually work *here*, but I work for the *Herald*. I'm . . . a paperboy, but I'm going to be a reporter."

Tulley smiled her encouragement. "More power to you. Stick around, and maybe in a few years you can get a job on the *Herald*."

"No, ma'am. I reckon not on this paper."

From the corner of her eye she saw Charlie Kettleman coming across the pressroom toward them, his eyes fixed sternly upon the boy. Was Charlie thinking of running him off, she wondered, prepared to go to bat for the young press-watcher, if necessary.

"What the devil are you doing here, Scott?" Kettleman asked, raising his voice over the noise of the press to catch the boy's attention. The boy looked up in surprise. His face fell.

"You mean I better get out of here before old Shelby runs me out," he said in a tone of resignation.

"I mean what are you doing here? You're supposed to be in school."

"There's no school today. It was in the paper. Some kind of a teacher's meeting, it said."

"That's right. I forgot." Charlie turned to Tulley. "This is my son, Scott. He's an unregenerate newspaper buff," he said, his sternness lost in a note of affectionate pride. "Scotty, this is Miss Calhoun. She'll be in charge of the paper now."

"Pleased to meet you, ma'am," the boy said stiffly, thereby serving notice he wasn't pleased in the least. "'Scuse me. I gotta go."

"Don't go," said Tulley. "The press run's just begun."

The boy looked around him nervously and then up at his dad. "What about old Shelby?"

"He's no longer with us. I told you Miss Calhoun is running the paper. If she says you can watch the press run, it's all right with me."

"You can sit on the sidelines anytime you like. And my name is Tulley," she said, smiling as she reached out to grasp the boy's grubby hand.

"*Miss* Tulley, Scott," his father amended firmly.

Scott's face broke into a joyous, no more than half-believing grin. "Wow. That's neat. You mean I can come any old time and nobody'll run me off?"

"Sure can, as long as you come alone," Tulley said. "You know to stay in one spot out of the way and not run afoul of the machinery or the pressman."

The boy cast her an injured look. "I've got more sense than that, and none of the guys but me want to watch. I always come alone."

The father's eyes had a look of thanks for Tulley. "Lamarr didn't want the newsboys on the premises. For a boy who made up his mind when other kids were wanting to be firemen that he was going to be the reporter who covered the fire, it's been frustrating," he said. About to go, he turned back. "I almost forgot what I came to tell you. Lamarr's office has been cleaned out and is ready anytime you care to move in. If you'd like, I can show it to you now."

"Never mind. I can find it when I'm ready. You go on. Right now I'd like to see a copy of today's paper."

"I'll get one for you," Kettleman volunteered and hurried away to disappear around the other side of the press.

Without taking his eyes off the moving ribbon of paper that threaded its way over cylinders and funneled down metal bars for printing, folding and cutting, the boy spoke to Tulley over his shoulder.

"I bet you didn't know there are more than five miles of paper on any one of those full rolls of newsprint," he said.

She gave a protesting laugh. "Hey cut it out, will you? What are you trying to do? Test me? Wait until you're a reporter. You won't remember all that stuff, either."

The boy answered her with a pleased grin as his father came over with a handful of papers and gave Tulley one.

"I've got to get back to work," he said, reaching out a hand to tousle his son's hair affectionately as he headed off.

With a bottomless feeling in the pit of her stomach, Tulley looked at the newspaper, still warm from the body of the press. Her eyes stopped upon catching the boldfaced headline on the right-hand side of the front page. "McCready Sues *Herald* for Libel, Slander." It looked big and black and damning, and her first instinct was to tear into the pressroom, yelling "Stop the press!" A voice in her head cried out, *My God, what have I done!*

Feeling sick, she read the story in its entirety then read it again. She must have been crazy to authorize this article. She'd opened the paper's columns to this cool, articulate indictment of itself!

Ed Dawes had given her an out when he had offered to rewrite the story and use only the straight complaint. Why hadn't she listened to him?

But she knew why. It was a heroic play to win over Ed and Charlie. She'd bought the staff's approval with the story. Heroic and stupid, but it hadn't looked as damaging in the form of reporter's copy as it did now on the front page of the newspaper in irretrievable print.

In a kind of paralyzed panic she watched a workman wheel the first bales of the day's edition across the loading dock to a panel truck for distribution throughout the county. It still wasn't too late to stop them, she told herself wildly, and at the same time she knew it was. What kind of credibility would she have with the staff—a staff she hadn't completely won over yet—if her first act as editor was to throw out a whole press run she herself had ordered? From the moment she'd sent Dawes and Kettleman into the composing room to restructure today's front page, it had been too late to back off.

Bundle after bundle of the day's papers, newly baled, were carted past her across the loading dock and into the waiting panel trucks, reminding her that whether it turned out to be a disaster or a stroke of genius, it would be on her head.

At least it would make Cass McCready happy, she thought, and with the suddenness of revelation she knew that however much she'd sought to win the staff's approval with the story, the first person she'd wanted to please was Cass.

But would Cass even see it? If he'd ever subscribed to the *Herald*, he would have boycotted it by now.

Turning to Scotty she said, "How'd you like to run an errand for me...like deliver a paper to Cass McCready? You know him?"

"Sure. Everybody knows Cass."

"How soon do you think you could find him?"

"I don't know exactly. He wouldn't be home this time of day, but he's got a trailer across town he uses as an office. If he's not there, I know where he usually has lunch. I've got basketball practice this afternoon at four, but I reckon I can find him before then."

Tulley folded the paper and handed it to him. "Call me before practice, if you can't. Tell him..." She paused and thought. With a sudden grin she cocked her forefinger like a pistol and aimed it at the boy's shirtfront. "Tell him Tulley says 'Remember, you read it here first.'"

The boy let out a hoot of laughter. "Wow!" he said and with a conspiratorial grin took the paper. In the time-honored fashion of newsboys, he rolled it into a neat cylinder and fastened it with a rubber band from his pocket. Tulley opened her handbag and brought out her wallet.

"Hey, no! Don't give me money. I haven't got anything else to do until practice. I don't want to get paid for doin' it."

She could see he really meant it and didn't demean the gesture by pressing. "Thanks."

"Anytime, Miss Tulley!" he said magnanimously and in a sudden burst of energy charged across the loading dock to his bike. Mounted, he took off in a whir of spokes.

THE OFFICE OCCUPIED by the late Lamarr Calhoun for some thirty years lay at the corner of the building down the street from the front entrance. One side faced Court Street, the other faced the post office. Between the two buildings ran an alley that gave access to the loading and unloading docks of both.

Tulley peered with misgivings through the doorway into the half darkness cloaking the office that was to be hers. It looked more like a cave than a room, and until her eyes adjusted to the gloom, she wondered if it had been built without windows. She saw then that there was a window on the street side and two on the longer wall next to the alley, both completely blacked out by old-fashioned roller shades pulled all the way down to the sill.

Feeling her way to the windows, she discovered that the shades were securely stapled to the frames. Groping along the wall, she found a switch next to the door and flooded the room with light from three overhead rows of fluorescent tubing.

Except for a tall wooden cupboard and a large, well-worn oak desk on which sat the ubiquitous computer terminal, the room's only furnishings were a coat tree, an empty bookcase, the desk's old-fashioned swivel chair and three other straight-back wooden ones. The linoleum cork that covered the floor was worn through in spots along traffic lines, and the walls, stained by time and grime and ancient rain leaks, were a dingy buff. There wasn't a picture, calendar, not a single icon of any kind to bear witness to the nature of the man who had occupied the office for so many years.

Her eyes traveled around the dismal room and back to the computer terminal, where she typed out a message to Ed Dawes in the newsroom across the hall.

"Help! Can somebody find me a screwdriver?"

Ed appeared in the doorway shortly, looking mystified, and Tulley accepted with thanks the tool he brought and attacked one of the nailed-down window shades. When Dawes saw what she was up to, he took a Swiss army knife from his pocket and went to work on another of the shades.

Tulley said, "Why would a newspaperman want to shut himself off from the outside world like this?"

"Lamarr?" Dawes paused in his work to nod his head in the direction of a spot on the far wall. "See that hole up there? Somebody took a potshot at him a few years back. Next morning the blinds were nailed down.

"You mean somebody tried to kill him?"

"It was more likely fired to give him a scare. Lamarr used the paper to run roughshod over a lot of people. Some of them have been pretty mad, but no one was crazy enough to try to kill him."

They freed the windows and shot up the shades to let the noontime light flood in. Tulley turned off the overhead tubes and looked around her with satisfaction. The room was still depressingly ugly but salvageable. At least the light was real.

After accepting Tulley's thanks, Dawes returned to his desk. Tulley looked around the empty office with a feeling of helplessness. She'd called a staff meeting for four o'clock knowing too little about the *Herald*. There was homework to be done.

Still she delayed, sorry the huge bound volumes of each year's newspapers once kept on file had been replaced by microfilm. She could call up all the back issues on a viewer, but the real "feel" of the paper wasn't there. It was a little like trying to capture the essence of Princess Diana by looking at her image in a wax museum.

She'd forgotten to ask where the microfilm files were kept, but as she turned to the computer terminal to type out a query, she paused and eyed the big wooden cupboard at the far end of the room, wondering if it was as empty as the oak desk. Opening it, she hit gold.

It was jam-packed from floor to ceiling with back copies of *The Hilby Herald*, many of them so old they threatened to disintegrate. The papers were stacked in a semblance of order day by day and month by month, but with little regard to chronology in years. It was impossible to tell at once how far back they went. She pulled out a random sampling of papers, piled them in chronological order with recent years on the bottom and settled down to work her way through the stack.

Names and people began to take shape and become familiar to her. She began to understand the nature of the county of Hilby and its people and the town: their accomplishments, problems, desires; their victories and defeats. At the same time she gradually began to get the "feel" of the *Herald*. It was then she started to see that the paper had been the heartbeat of the community for generations before Lamarr had taken over. Following its gradual deterioration in the years since, she felt bereaved and at the same time felt a new sense of commitment.

She lost track of time and might have gone on for the rest of the day, if her door hadn't opened suddenly and a man walked in as if he had every right to be there. Tulley looked up and blinked at him in surprise, trying to remember where she'd seen the handsome face before. At the hospital benefit, of course. His name was . . . What was it? Leo . . .

"Mr. Drummond! This is a surprise."

He'd come to a stop when he saw her and for a moment seemed taken aback. "Miss Calhoun! I was looking for Shelby Haynes, but I'd much rather find you. I didn't know you were back."

"I got here late yesterday. It's my first day at the paper," Tulley said. "I'm sorry I don't know where you can find Mr. Haynes. I understand he's left the paper. Maybe the business office can tell you where you might find him."

"Never mind. I've lost all interest in Haynes." His smile was a winning flash of perfect white teeth. The dark eyes observed her with flattering admiration.

"My only interest at the moment is to persuade you to have dinner with me tonight at my club in Raleigh. They have a fine chef and a very good combo for dancing."

For blatant good looks, he was as handsome as any man she'd ever known. He was a heavenly dancer, she recalled, and had a certain calculated charm that tempted Tulley to say yes.

"I can't. I'm sorry. I really can't. I half promised..." She stopped short of the out-and-out lie, knowing as she did what was holding her back. She'd no more than sent Scotty Kettleman off on her errand than a part of her had started waiting for the phone to ring, waiting to hear Cass McCready's voice in praise of her noble deed, waiting for Cass to say he would see her tonight.

She gave him an apologetic smile. "I'm terribly sorry. The past ten days have frazzled me. I'm afraid you'd find me poor company. Tonight I haven't the energy for even a very slow waltz, but it was nice of you to ask."

"Merely trying to get my bid in early, before the local swains start beating a path to your door. The invitation is still open when you get to feeling 'unfrazzled.' Now I'll be on my way and let you get back to your papers."

She watched the door close behind him without seeing, her mind again on Cass McCready. It was nearly four o'clock, the editorial staff would be drifting in for the scheduled meeting in a few minutes, and still no call from him. She'd be hearing from the boy, Scott, if he hadn't been able to find him, she felt sure.

During the long staff meeting, Tulley sketched briefly her kind of paper then turned the floor over to the employees, subtly encouraging them to define the character of the newspaper they would like to work for and to speak out on where the *Herald* succeeded and where it fell short.

After a timid start the meeting warmed up, and Charlie Kettleman, whom Tulley had invited to sit in, assumed the role of moderator, freeing Tulley to sit back almost unnoticed and draw conclusions to use as yardsticks in the weeks ahead.

Dusk shrouded the windows, and the overhead lights had been turned on when Ed declared the meeting over. The whole crew rose and overwhelmed Tulley with a standing ovation.

"Thank you, friends," she said past the lump in her throat. "I just hope you never find out how much more I need you than you need me."

She knew she'd passed the test, but after the last person had walked out, the moment of exhilaration was lost. By now surely Cass had read the paper. Why hadn't he called?

Blast you, McCready! You might at least acknowledge the gesture. So much for his talk of *togetherness.* The word had sung like a bell in her heart last night when he'd said it. You couldn't play togetherness with someone when only one of you knows the rules.

She retrieved her suit jacket from the coat tree where she'd hung it earlier, and her handbag from a desk drawer. Then, in an almost soundless whisper of dejection, "Oh, McCready...McCready, if you only knew what you're doing to me."

Her spirit sagged to a new low when she walked back to Matthews's office where she'd left her car and saw that the venerable Studebaker was gone and the office was dark. She realized she'd been half expecting the old lawyer to be waiting for her, waiting to invite her to share their company again. Come to think of it, the last meal she'd eaten was a hearty breakfast at the Matthewses' table that morning. For such craven dependency she felt nothing but contempt.

Trouble with you, kiddo, is an empty stomach, she told herself crossly, all too aware she was one of those who could go just so long without food before she began to get cranky or headachy or both; on occasion, to her utter discomfiture, she'd even been known to faint.

She stopped at the first market on her way home and loaded a grocery cart with household staples and breakfast items to get her started the following day. That done, she scanned the freezer case indifferently for a quick something to have as a meal when she got home. She settled on a package advertising itself as a complete dinner under the name Glazed Chicken Oriental.

Whether from lack of food or the rigors of the day, she was limp and dispirited as she piloted the big car into the Matthewses' driveway and around the circle that led to the carriage house, hidden at first by the thick growth of laurel and azalea that bordered the drive. When the car was berthed, she rounded the corner of the building, grateful for the sensor spot that cast a half-circle of light across the entry to the garage. Her own doorway lay in shadows, and she made her way gingerly along the brick walk, her vision further limited by the two large grocery bags she carried.

She had almost reached the door when a thrill of alarm shot through her at the sound of feet crunching along the gravel driveway. In the next instant a pair of hands relieved her of the grocery bags.

From out of the gloom beside her, the voice of Cass McCready asked, "Have you got your key?"

The key was in her hand—a hand grown unsteady as her heart thundered in her breast. His name on her lips was lost in sudden breathlessness. She fumbled for the keyhole and struggled to compose herself, stifling words that cried out to be said.

Why didn't you call me, you clown? Did you have to wait all day? But she knew that to start off on the attack was no way to keep peace with Cass McCready. *Stay cool, Tulley. Give him a chance to speak his piece.*

"I forgot the tureen," he said.

The key had found the lock, but Tulley forgot to turn it.

"You . . . what!"

"I came back to get the tureen. Aunt Vinnie . . ."

The phone was ringing inside. Turning the key, she flung the door open in a sudden fury and headed for the phone, ignoring McCready who went past her, carrying the grocery bags to the kitchen.

Breathing hard, Tulley picked up the receiver.

It was Scotty Kettleman on the other end of the line.

"Hey, I couldn't do exactly what you said, so I thought I'd better call you," said the boy.

"Didn't you deliver it?"

"Yeah. I delivered it all right, but not to Cass. I looked all over and couldn't find him, and it kept getting later and later and . . . you know, with basketball practice and all. Well, I finally went to his house and Miss Vinnie—Miss Vinnie's his aunt, you know—well, she said he had to go to Raleigh, and she didn't know when he'd be back, but she'd give it to him when he came, so I left it and went on to practice, but by then it was so late I didn't have time to call. I hope I did right.'' The words poured out in a kind of breathless rush that begged for approval.

"I can't think of anything better. I'm sorry it turned out to be such a lot of trouble,'' Tulley said.

"Naw. I didn't mind. There wasn't much else to do, but I got to thinking after practice...supposing he stayed over in Raleigh and never got it. You'd want to know, wouldn't you? So I thought I better call and tell you what happened.''

She looked up to see McCready across the room from her, watching her curiously. "I think he got it,'' she said. On the other hand, maybe he'd come over straight from Raleigh. Muffling the phone with her hand, she turned to Cass.

"Have you been home or seen your aunt?'' she asked abruptly, and when she saw by his expression he had, she said into the phone, "He got it. It's all right, Scott. Thank you for everything.''

She put the phone back in its cradle and fixed Cass McCready with an accusing eye. "Now, what's this about a tureen?''

CHAPTER NINE

FROM ACROSS THE ROOM Cass said blandly, "The jambalaya tureen. My aunt thinks highly of it. I forgot to bring it back last night."

Tulley stared at him in disbelief for an instant then rallied and marched past him across the room to the kitchen. Under the disappointment and hurt she was conscious of a shakiness, an "all-gone" feeling inside. It was a clear warning that if she didn't eat soon she was going to say something she'd be sorry for, or faint, or worst of all, burst into tears. Any such performance in the presence of Cass McCready was not to be considered. She must get something to eat fast, but first she must get the man out of her house.

Picking up the flower-sprigged tureen from the counter, she turned back to find him watching her with a curious intensity from where he stood by the fireplace. She thrust the bowl into his hands, acutely conscious of the rattle of the china ladle against the slotted lid—a giveaway of her unsteady hands.

He took the dish but made no move to leave as she peeled out of her coat and hung it in the entry closet.

"Will you please go?" she said from between clenched teeth. "I'd like to fix my dinner." She whirled away from him, slipping her tired feet out of high-heeled pumps as she went, leaving them where they lay. McCready stayed put.

Ignoring him, she rummaged through grocery bags until she came up with the frozen dinner she'd bought. If the tureen was all he'd come for, the man was an insensitive clod. Her tongue burned to tell him so, but to acknowledge he'd let her down was to risk severing the last slender thread of control she held on her ragged emotions.

Without looking at him, she was completely aware of his every move. She knew how long he stood watching her, knew when he walked over and placed the tureen back on the counter. She kept her back turned, removing the wrapper from the chicken dish and opening the door to the microwave oven as if he was already gone. Even before he took hold of her and turned her around to face him, she knew where he was and knew the exact moment he moved in directly behind her.

"Why did you do it?" he asked.

She looked back at him without forgiveness. "So you noticed?" she snapped. "Well, don't think my reasons were personal! It's not my fault the columns of the *Herald* were used to put you down, but today you told your side of the story in the same columns. After all, fair is fair."

Still holding her arms loosely, he said, "I don't understand you, Tulley. You won't print a retraction, yet you'll give half a column of front page space to my personal complaints. It doesn't make sense!"

She was helpless and dismayed by his clear lack of understanding. "I can't run a retraction, Cass—even you can see that. The next best thing was to let you give your own account of what happened in your own words."

"What am I supposed to do? Express gratitude by rushing out and dismissing the libel suit?"

"That's not fair, and it's not true," said Tulley, her words muffled. She turned her head away to hide the tears that rose to her eyes.

"I know it's not." His hands came up to clasp her face and turn it to him. He tipped her head and kissed her, touching her only with his mouth and the curves of his hands—a soft, undemanding kiss that carried with it a kind of sweet sadness.

When it was over, he took his hands gently from her face and stepped back from her. "Forgive me, Tulley. If there's one thing I've learned about you, it's that there's nothing devious in you . . . and that your sense of decency is alive and brave. It took courage to print that story. I didn't mean what I said. It was frustration speaking."

"Frustration?"

He hesitated then plunged ahead. "You could as easily have printed the retraction I asked for in the first place. A retraction wouldn't have cost you more."

"It would cost me my credibility as the *Herald*'s new editor," Tulley said flatly. "When I tell the subscribers the man whose paper I'm about to inherit printed statements now known to be untrue, I'd better be prepared to back it up with proof. I can't very well say 'I ask you to believe this because Cass McCready says it's so.'"

"That was McCready talking in that story today," Cass reminded her stubbornly.

"That's just the point. A retraction comes from the heart of the paper, but that story came from you. If your words aren't true, it's your credibility that's at stake—not mine and not the *Herald*'s."

McCready eyed her a second and gave up. "Sorry. It's hard to argue with that kind of logic. I never looked at it that way."

Unexpectedly a wave of giddiness came over Tulley. She felt herself drifting away from reality, and a bizarre thought crossed her mind. She hung on to it tightly, forming her words with care.

"You better hope what you said in that story is right, McCready, because if it's not, I may sue you for libeling the *Herald* in its own col..."

The last fuzzy syllables were lost under Cass McCready's lips. He gathered her into his arms, his mouth coming down upon hers in a hard, demanding kiss. *And none too soon,* she thought wispily, her legs acting like a pair of airstrip wind socks on a still day. He held her to him savagely, as if protecting her against some unseen marauder. A hoarse sound rose in his throat.

"Oh, God, Tulley, when you're near me, I lose all common sense. I never should have come. I wasn't going to, and then..."

But Tulley was beyond caring. From somewhere near his collarbone her voice murmured in a resigned sigh, "I...I th-think...I'm going to pass out..." and faded to silence as her body went limp in his arms.

It wasn't much of a faint. It lasted less than the time it took Cass to cross the room with her in his arms. He lowered her to the sofa, and her lids opened. His hands fumbled with the buttons at her throat and opened her blouse to feel for the pulse in the main artery of her neck. The soft searching fingers along her collarbone sent a lovely sensuous tremor up her spine and gave her no incentive to wake up. She indulged in a moment of pure subliminal pleasure as she drifted unwillingly back to total consciousness.

Struggling against the hand that pinned her gently to the sofa, she croaked, "Let me up."

"Hey...are you all right?"

"Of course I'm all right. Haven't you seen anyone faint before?"

"Don't know that I have," Cass said after a moment, obviously relieved. "I thought only Victorian ladies fainted."

"Victorian ladies and people like me," she said disgustedly.

"Do you do this often?"

"Not if I can avoid it."

His fingers lingered on her pulse a moment longer. Reassured, he said, "I've been told the Victorians laced their corsets too tight. What's your excuse?"

But Tulley, furious with her body for having betrayed its vincibility to McCready and feeling hardly more stable than she'd felt before she fainted, was not of a mind to be teased.

"It's not all that uncommon," she said, bristling. "In my case, it comes from skipping meals. As a rule, I'm not impelled to stage an archaic performance like this. I usually just get crabby."

"You, Tulley? Crabby?"

In spite of her languor she rose to the bait and said crossly, "Yeah! Like right now for instance." Then, more amiably, she added, "My dad was the same. One of the secrets of my parents' long and happy marriage was that my mother had the good sense to feed my father when he began to get crochety."

From where he crouched beside her, McCready rose abruptly, leaving her stretched out on the sofa. She watched him with mild curiosity. He began to paw through the grocery bags he'd deposited on the counter in the kitchen.

In a moment she would get up and put the frozen meal in the microwave, she told herself. She would send Cass McCready on his way. But the thought of telling him to leave had somehow lost its appeal. Before she could rally energy to move, he was back again with a tall glass of orange juice. He set it on the table by the sofa and raised her to a sitting position, poking pillows behind her back.

"This'll hold you until I get you some real food," he said and put the glass in her hands. He pulled up a chair and sat down near the sofa, leaning forward to observe her from beneath a furrowed brow as she took her first sip.

"Mmm. Just what I needed," she murmured and drank thirstily. The energy-giving juice flowed into her, and the washed-out feeling that had come before she passed out gradually gave way to interest in what was going on around her.

She was aware now of a hovering look in McCready's eyes, a helpless, protective look that told her he was attaching more importance to what had happened just now than the embarrassment deserved. His eyes were clouded with concern, with a troubled yearning that made the strong, vital face seem somehow boyish, and her heart raced for a moment in an erratic beat that would have caused him new alarm had his fingers still been on her pulse. She caught her breath, wanting suddenly to reach out and take the big square hands hanging loosely between his knees in her own. What would he do, she wondered, if she settled her body into the vee formed by his legs and pulled his head to where her lips could reach the two small furrows of worry between his brows.

The potential was intoxicating, but she resisted temptation and handed the empty glass to Cass.

"A shot of this stuff wouldn't hurt *you*," she said instead. "You look like you've seen a ghost."

Maybe he had, thought Cass, only not a ghost. More like an apparition—a premonition, really—the instant her body went limp in his arms. A vision of emptiness at the sudden realization that this woman could abruptly disappear from his life.

If it had been any other woman, he would have taken it for nothing more than it was: a common, ordinary faint. Why had he gone into shock over this one?

It was hard to believe—now that the color was back in her cheeks and her eyes met his with spirit—that in those few steps when he'd carried her to the sofa, the very essence of her seemed to have slipped away. It was as if all the warmth and passion and wit that had brought such zest to his life was gone, leaving him holding a beautiful, meaningless body in his arms.

Looking back he felt a little ridiculous, yet in those first seconds a terrible unreasoning fear had possessed him, a fear that she'd been stricken by some mysterious life-threatening seizure that would take her away from him. He'd known then that Calhoun or no Calhoun, she'd come to mean more to him than he'd ever intended, and he'd hoped desperately for a second chance and even more desperately that he'd have sense enough not to waste it, should it come.

"You gave me a hell of a scare," he said. He stood suddenly and crossed the room to pick up the shoes she'd stepped out of when she stalked off to the kitchen earlier.

Dropping to the floor beside the sofa, he took one of her stockinged feet, thinking only to slip her shoe on it, but then he noticed the soft, slender sculpture of the foot. His fingers moved over the instep and traced caressingly along its outer contours, toe to heel, heel to toe. Feeling the delicate bones of her ankle, his fingers followed the curve of the arch, and he wondered at its perfection.

He could feel the involuntary shiver that raced through her and looked up to find her watching him. A small smile played at one corner of her soft, ripe mouth, the full lips parting slightly as if in welcome. Her eyes seemed luminous with desire. In the unexpected poignancy of the moment he bowed his head and brought her foot up to meet his face, laying his cheek upon the satin-soft curve of the sole. Every part of her seemed infinitely precious. The swell of desire in his loins was driving, but with it he felt something more than he had ever felt before. It was as if in some tenuous mystical way she'd become a part of him; as if somehow she made him whole.

It was only a moment, but even after he came to his senses—feeling suddenly foolish, sitting there holding her foot to his face—the feeling of oneness stayed with him, fixed in his heart to give him pause in the days to come.

"Cass," she said softly as he lowered her foot. Looking up, he braced himself against the sensuous invitation he saw in her eyes. Instinct told him this was not the time, and he grabbed a shoe and went through ineffectual motions of cramming her toes into the toe of the pump.

From the upper end of the sofa she said, "If you really want to put that shoe on, I suggest you try the other foot."

With a grunt Cass got the shoes on the correct feet and stood. He reached to pull her up, but a dreamy-eyed Tulley resisted—trying, instead, to pull him down beside her.

"Why are we doing this?" she asked plaintively.

"Merely bowing to the wisdom of your mother, Tulley. It's time you got some solid food in you. I'm taking you out to eat."

"Oh, come on! Let's stay here. I bought—"

"I saw what you bought. I stuck it in the freezer. Chicken Oriental! Hah! A skimpy snack for one, if I'm any judge."

Still she hung back. "If I could find a way to stretch it, wouldn't you rather stay here?"

She said it with a throatiness in her voice and a Lorelei smile that set his heart thundering and called all his will to resist the subtle seduction. He gave her a quick pull that brought her to her feet in front of him.

"Look, lady," he said, "you and I have some serious talking to do, but you're going to have food in you first. I'm not taking any chances on your going crabby on me, much less on your passing out. We've got all we can handle, without that. What you're going to have is a good steak."

THEY HAD FILET MIGNON and fat baked potatoes dripping butter, and green beans cooked with toma-toes and okra and onions at a small, quiet restaurant where everyone from the owner-cook down to the dishwasher seemed to have gone to school at one time or another with Cass. Tucked away in a shadowy wraparound booth at the back, they went undis-turbed after the first hearty greetings upon their arrival, except for occasional interruptions for service.

Watching Tulley demolish the good food, Cass asked on a note of reproach, "How long has this been going on?"

She glanced up from her plate, questioning. "How long has what been going on?"

"This business of starving yourself."

"Honestly, Cass, I don't usually—"

"Hasn't anyone told you, you can't improve on perfection by going without food."

"Thanks...I think," she said, pausing between bites to give him a quizzical look. Suddenly she laughed. "Oh, I get it. You think I'm on a diet. Not me, McCready. I love to eat, but my metabolism burns it all up. I'd be two-ton Annie if it went to fat."

Cass gazed at her reproachfully. "You hadn't eaten all day yesterday, and you haven't eaten today. If that isn't dieting, I don't know what—"

"Yesterday I didn't have a chance all day, and to-day... Oh, today there was just too much happening. Actually, I forgot."

She said it matter-of-factly and went on to tell him about her first day at the *Herald*, beginning with the unpromising encounter with Charlie Kettleman that had turned out better than she'd expected.

"Don't let it go to your head, but I'm afraid I have you to thank for the winning over of Kettleman and Dawes," she said.

The account lasted well through the meal, inter-rupted by an occasional aside from McCready, par-ticularly on the departure of Shelby Haynes. Inevitably, the discussion turned to the matter that had brought them together and at the same time kept them apart.

"Look, Cass, I simply don't believe a newspaper editor would make up the kind of stuff Lamarr printed about you," Tulley said. She was prepared to elaborate on the subject when their waiter appeared with coffee, and she was obliged to wait while it was served. She'd felt Cass stiffen beside her and waited unhappily, aware she'd gotten off to a bad start. She rummaged for something immediately to the point to repair the damage, but when the waiter moved away Cass spoke before she could.

"So you still think what your uncle wrote in the paper is true! It appears you and I haven't come very far," he said, his voice full of resentment.

"Well, if you think I think..." She wrinkled her nose at him and smiled to make light of it, seeking to erase the defensive look from his eyes. "Of course I don't think that, Cass. I really never have. But there's got to be a better explanation than the one that Lamarr made it up, and I think we'd better get busy and find out what that explanation is before this lawsuit reaches a point of no return."

Though his face told her he didn't agree, the defensiveness was gone, and he reached out and pulled her around the curve of the leather upholstered booth until she was shoulder-to-shoulder with him. Encouraged by the slick surface of the seat, she slid a fraction of an inch closer, and they were thigh-to-thigh. For a moment she was so intensely aware of the lean virile leg touching hers lightly that she lost all sense of what they'd been talking about.

"Tulley, honey, the point of no return was reached when I filed the suit. The only thing that would keep it out of court would be for you to print a retraction.''

In a delayed double take Tulley snapped to attention and moved away from him to break free from the distractions of his body's contact with hers.

Cass continued. ''You won't print a retraction. I understand that. I guess I'd do the same thing in your shoes, but it forces me to play the libel suit through to the finish. The suit's the only way I can see to get the McCready name back in good standing—to have a jury of my peers say Lamarr Calhoun willfully and maliciously lied about me in the columns of the *Herald*.''

''I don't believe he did.''

''You still jump to his defense?''

''No. I've just been around newspapers too long to believe any publisher, even my esteemed uncle, would take a chance on losing his paper in a libel suit, no matter what the extent of his malice. If we don't get busy and run down the truth, people will go on believing the lie.''

''The truth, Tulley—and you may as well face it—is that it was all a figment of Calhoun's imagination.''

''You can prove that, for a fact?''

''I've got more basis than you have for your theory.''

''All right, so I don't have proof...yet. But I will. It wouldn't hurt you to give me some help.''

Cass gave a groan of protest. ''Tulley, it's a waste of time. If you'd grown up in Hilby County you'd know there's always been bad blood between the Calhouns and the McCreadys.''

"Always? That still doesn't prove Lamarr 'willfully and maliciously' lied about you in the paper."

His hand closed reflexively upon hers, and a sound of unhappiness escaped his lips. He lifted her hand and pressed a kiss into her palm. When he looked up, she saw in his eyes the clouds of an inner storm.

"The way I feel about you runs afoul of everything I've heard from my family about yours since I was old enough to understand words," he said at last. There was something in his voice that brought a catch to her throat.

"Meaning you're beginning to believe there are Calhouns and then there are . . . *Calhouns*?" she ventured cautiously.

"Meaning there are Calhouns . . . and then there is you."

With sudden breathlessness she waited for him to say more. The silence spun out between them.

"None of which has anything to do with you and me, Cass—not even this business with Lamarr," she said carefully.

"But it does," he disagreed. She picked up the taint of bitterness in his voice. "You don't know what it is to be part of an old Southern family that's locked horns with the same people generation after generation since they all pioneered the town a hundred years or so ago. Injuries are passed down like heirlooms, Tulley."

"You mean the McCreadys would disapprove if they caught you dining with a Calhoun?"

"Those of them that are left," he said with a bleak smile. "I've no doubt there's a certain restlessness in the old cemetery tonight. One of the last things my grandfather said to me before he died was 'Never trust a Calhoun.' My experience with your uncle hasn't given me any reason to believe he was wrong.''

She felt strangely hollow. The modern-day world she was attuned to—a world where relationships were established or broken almost solely on personal considerations by the two involved—left her unprepared for the feudal ties that troubled Cass. She wasn't even sure about her own feelings for him, except that he excited and delighted her more than any other man she'd ever met, and that she liked him...deeply. If she one day grew sure that this liking was love, the accident that he was a McCready and she a Calhoun would not stand in the way.

She broke the silence that had fallen between them. ''Would you rather we didn't see each—''

He pulled her into his arms in a kind of desperate bear hug, not letting her finish. ''Oh, God, no. Not that. Tulley, I don't know what to say...'' He let her slip from his arms, leaving her feeling terribly let down.

''Let's go, Cass,'' she said. ''We've got to talk this out.''

Cass groaned. ''You're right, but we'd better do our talking here,'' he said. ''If I take you back to the carriage house, out of the public eye, I'll forget everything but the fact that I want to make love to you.''

''Would that be so bad?''

He didn't answer the playful question. ''After I left you last night I made up my mind that the best thing for us both was not to see each other again,'' he said broodingly.

Tulley's eyes were like those of a startled deer. ''Then what are we doing here?''

"I saw the *Herald* when I got back from Raleigh tonight."

"Hail to the power of the press!"

"I read your story and knew I couldn't just walk away without telling you why."

"You're here to tell me you don't intend to see me again?" Her voice was as sharp as a blade of grass and as bitter as dandelion.

"It's why I came, but it's not why I'm here. There...at the carriage house when... Oh, God, Tulley. I realized then how much I care, that's all. That's why—in spite of everything we've got going against us—I'm here." In his voice she heard sounds of bewilderment and despair.

"I feel something I never felt for a woman before," he continued after a moment of silence. "If this is the 'real thing' they keep talking about, I can't just walk away from it. I need time to find out."

For an instant Tulley was furious. *Why, the arrogant ba...beast!*

"And if it is?"

At her scathing tone he drew in a long breath and let it out.

"I don't know, Tulley. I honestly don't. All I know is, I've got to find out."

Angry words rushed to her lips, words left unsaid as she realized that, in essence, this was what she'd been saying to herself, but in reverse. So much against them: the libel, the lawsuit, and now what Cass called "bad blood" between their families. And yet this man stirred her in ways she'd never been stirred before. Maybe it was the real thing. If so, like Cass, she needed time.

She gave him a tentative smile of understanding, and his hand tightened on hers. He released it and gave the slightly upturned end of her nose a gentle pat—a gesture at once so tender and playful that she captured his hand and pressed the palm against her cheek.

"Could we go now?" she murmured. Cass signaled for the check.

Once the car was out of the parking lot and on the street, he reached across the divider between the bucket seats and secured her hand. They rode the short distance home in silence. When he turned his head to smile at her, she saw the ripeness of desire in his eyes. Disturbed that he'd read consent in what she'd intended merely to be a kind of moratorium, she consciously withheld any promise from the smile she gave in return.

At the carriage house she didn't relinquish the keys but unlocked the door herself and opened it narrowly, leaving McCready outside as she stepped in and, in effect, barred his way. Dared she risk even so small a thing as a good-night kiss? Turning back to him, undecided, she was disconcerted to see by his expression that he mistook her act for a flirtatious game.

"Are you telling me I can't come in?"

CHAPTER TEN

SHE HESITATED for a long moment, the magic of his presence playing upon her senses until all she could remember of what he'd said was that he felt something for her he'd never felt for a woman before. But even as she was about to stand aside and let him come in, she knew she couldn't. If she did, he would expect to make love to her, and as long as he held her own people against her, something in her heart would always reject him.

Still, he had a right to know how she felt about it.

"No. I want you to come in," she said simply. She stepped back and was not surprised when he took her in his arms as she closed the door behind her. She held him away, the palms of her hands pushing hard against his chest.

"I'm sorry, Cass, but I'd better tell you right now in case you have more than a good-night kiss in mind, the invitation doesn't extend to the bedroom." She hoped it did not show in her eyes how much she hated to say it.

"As a matter of fact, ma'am, I . . . reckon I do have a little more than a good-night kiss in mind," Cass drawled. "Nothin' specific. I was thinking I'd just wing it." In a deft movement he captured her hands and pulled them up around his shoulders, drawing her close to him.

All Tulley's senses seemed suddenly to conspire against her, urging her to wrap her arms tightly around his neck, to rub her cheek against the sandpapery surface of his face, to breathe in the smell of his clean, male body, unlotioned, uncologned—the scent of Cass. She felt the warmth of his breath at her ear. The nip of his teeth on her earlobe raised gooseflesh up the back of her neck, and with it went her resistance. Her hands slipped down and under his arms to clasp and close the last millimeter of distance between them, locking them body-to-body in an ecstasy of arousal. Their seeking mouths joined, clung and slipped away only to meet and plunge into each other's depths again...and again...and yet again until she was filled with the taste of Cass. She was held by the magnet of his lips while his fingers unbuttoned her coat and blouse then pushed the fabric aside to expose her bare flesh.

She felt the tremble of his fingers as they touched her breast. She felt the air on her skin and the cool of his callused hand when he lifted her breast free from the layers of clothing. His fingers played gently with the tumescent bud where the mound peaked, and he covered it with his lips. A wave of sweet, hot pain swelled deep inside her.

He raised his head, and her breast prickled and cooled from moisture left by his mouth.

With a final kiss to the bare mound, he tucked its fullness back under its coverings and guided her toward the stairs.

She'd ridden the wave too far for a quick return, and for a moment she gave in to the yearning of her body and moved with him. But by the time they reached the bottom of the stairs she was again in touch with reality. She came to a resolute halt. Her lips and her breast still swollen from the fire of his mouth, she reached up, kissed him lightly and stepped away.

"Good night, Cass," she said, fighting for control. "This is as far as we go." Then in answer to the stricken look in his eyes, she added, "Oh, Cass...dear Cass... I'm sorry! I never meant... I should have known if you came in it would get out of hand. I should have stopped it. But, oh, I...wanted it."

"Then why stop?" he demanded hoarsely.

"Somewhere deep in your mind I'm *the enemy*. No matter how much I want to make love with you, Cass, I won't...I can't. If I did I'd feel demeaned."

"You're not the enemy, Tulley. Not you!"

"Yes, me, Cass McCready. Me, Tulley Calhoun, the last loathsome Calhoun. I'll be damned if I'll let you blame me for quarrels among people I never knew who are all long dead. It would put a real chill on my passion if that came to my mind in a moment of lovemaking."

Cass looked at her with a strange dawning comprehension in which she saw an equal measure of resistance.

"You're talking about platonic." It wasn't a question; his tone carried flat refusal.

Tulley shrugged and smiled at him wryly. "I believe we passed platonic back down the road somewhere."

After a long moment of silence he asked, "What do you want us to do about it, Tulley?"

"It's not my problem, Cass," she said gently. "It's you who's hung up on this family stuff. I don't care that your name is McCready or that our families have been acting like the Hatfields and the McCoys for umpteen generations. You're the one all that bothers, not me. It's your ambivalence that bothers me."

"There's nothing ambivalent about the way I feel about you."

"Oh, but there is. If you made love to me, you'd be making love to someone you call Tulley and feel guilty at the same time because the rest of her name is Calhoun." The uncertainty she saw on his face told her she'd hit target.

"You're concerned about bringing dishonor to your family," she said. "Well, I'm concerned about dishonoring myself."

After a while Cass said, "If it's not platonic, and we're not going upstairs...what are we going to do?"

Tulley sighed. "Oh, Cass, I don't know. Somewhere in between, I suppose, if we're going to go on seeing each other. Maybe we'd better think about it a few days. Maybe right now... you'd better go."

They faced each other there at the foot of the stairs, and she could see the bleakness in his eyes and knew it was reflected in her own. She reached out for his hands in a gesture of comforting.

"Oh, Cass...Cass...." she whispered as he took her in his arms in an embrace that spoke more of sorrow than of passion. He held her for a moment before he laid a kiss on her forehead and made blindly for the door.

OUTSIDE, CASS SLIPPED behind the wheel of his car, leaving the door ajar. In a state of despair, he stared down the darkened curve of the driveway, of half a mind to go back, to tell her "You're wrong, Tulley. None of that matters—none of that family stuff. It's water over the dam. I don't care that you're a Cal..."

He turned his eyes from the driveway to look at the carriage house, his foot already out the door on the way to the ground. Then the voice of his grandfather rose unexpectedly out of the past. *"Never trust a Calhoun, boy...."*

Who was it who had said, *"Give me the boy the first years of his life, and he'll be mine forever."* Not that, maybe, but something like it, and in a way it was true. The first things he could remember—the things he remembered best—were the things his grandfather had said to him long before he started school. To the small boy, whose father was locked in a round-the-clock struggle to save the family business and whose mother had spent many of her days shut away in her room with a damp towel across her forehead in the throes of migraines, the old gentleman had seemed the fount of wisdom, the heart of compassion. Many were the hours he'd sat on his grandfather's lap, listening to Brer Rabbit yarns told in that mellifluous, loving Irish voice.

The old judge had talked to him as if they were contemporaries: answered his questions; listened as if what the boy talked about was a matter of as grave importance as anything he heard from the bench.

It was his grandfather who had taught him how to catch fish in the slough west of town and how to throw a baseball and how to catch a pass.

Cass was in his seventh year when—after eighteen years on the Superior Court Bench of Hilby County— his grandfather suffered his first defeat at the polls. Cass saw it destroy him. Almost overnight his grandfather became a cantankerous rambling old man obsessed with bitterness. The steady decline of the most important person in Cass's life until he died two years later was something Cass could never forget.

Nor could he forget that it was Ross Calhoun, the grandfather of Tulley, who had masterminded that defeat through the columns of the *Herald*.

Cass brought his foot back into the car and closed the door. He saw the downstairs light go off in the carriage house and the upstairs light turn on. He felt terribly alone, and for a moment wished Tulley Calhoun had never come to Hilby County to haunt his days and nights. But he knew better. Tulley had brought light and laughter and meaning to his life. Unless he could lay the ghosts of the past, he'd lose her.

BY THE TIME SHE'D LISTENED to fulsome praise of the McCready libel story by five separate voices the next morning, Tulley almost wished she hadn't run it. Not that praise wasn't sweet music to her ears—if callers had been willing to leave it there—but each followed the praise with a heated account of some personal embarrassment suffered in the *Herald*'s columns at the hands of Lamarr.

"Talk about having a tiger by the tail," she said to Ed Dawes. "I get the distinct feeling that every one of those people expects the same treatment I gave Cass in yesterday's paper."

Her news editor grinned his sympathy. "I see your problem. If you turn over the front page to everyone who has a complaint against Lamarr, you won't have space left for the news. Don't worry about it. You'll think of something."

"There's no letters-to-the-editor space in the *Herald*," she said. "How about starting one?"

"Good idea. I've always been a great believer in the public's right to a forum, but do you think it will satisfy them?"

"I told these people to write in their complaints to the paper, and they seemed to go for it. We'll just have to wait and see."

"And brace ourselves for some heavy mail," said Dawes.

"Maybe," she said, "but it's a way of getting the message to the public that the paper is now being published for *them*. We may find ourselves buried in a landslide of letters to start off with, but once the novelty wears off, especially when they realize we can't print anything that's unsigned, they'll dribble down to a few a week."

It was the first day of the first full week of Tulley's tenure as managing editor of the *Herald*, and she threw herself into her new job with a singleness of purpose that excluded everything else.

She took a step toward getting acquainted with the people of Hilby under the aegis of Caroline Matthews, who invited her to a monthly meeting of the Garden Club the following day. The club's membership included the oldest and most prestigious residents of Hilby County, and she was met with a genteel hauteur that gradually melted, thanks to the gentle manipulations of Caroline.

Not without guile, Caroline let it be known that one of Tulley's female ancestors had been a charter member of the club. To Tulley's amusement, that was the open sesame that helped them forget she was also the niece of Lamarr Calhoun.

On Thursday she was the guest of Ed Dawes and Charlie Kettleman at the regular lunch meeting of the all-male Hilby Boosters Club. Like the ladies of the Garden Club, the Boosters, after a few uneasy minutes, forgave her Lamarr and welcomed her in the best tradition of Southern courtesy, profusely gallant and loaded with flirtatious chauvinism.

In her efforts to telescope her self-orientation into the shortest possible time that first week, she started her days early and ended them late, thereby earning the respect of the staff. She was gratified to find that after some initial awkwardness they accepted her with the same casual camaraderie they accorded one another.

The killing pace paid off in a quickly expanding grasp of the nature of the community and of the *Herald* and its staff and rewarded her with much of the background needed to understand and deal with the problems of running a small-town daily.

Though the week was full and left little time for thoughts of Cass, he was there—like the sound of a whisper, caressing her consciousness—scarcely heard, but there. His absence was a growing puzzle. She hadn't asked him to drop off the planet—just that they not make love. She wanted them to be together, to talk about this Calhoun hang-up until he understood that to kiss a Calhoun wasn't a betrayal of all the McCreadys that ever lived.

Still, as she explored her family ties in Hilby County with a growing pride in her own ancestral role in its history, she began to understand better the heroic dilemma that tormented Cass. Could cradle-learned loyalties be unlearned? she wondered. If she were the McCready, could she fly in the face of inherent Southern loyalties to embrace the return of a hated Calhoun?

When Friday came and there was still no word from Cass, she went with Charlie and Emily Kettleman and son, Scott, to a drive-in for fried chicken and on to a high-school football game. The boy left them and headed for the rooting section. Tulley followed Scott's parents up the stairs of the bleachers, looking for a place to sit.

They'd progressed only a step or two when a familiar voice called out behind them, "Hey, Charlie!" They turned to see Ed Dawes motioning them frantically from the ground.

"Guess who's covering tonight's football game," Dawes said when they stepped down to join him.

"You?" asked Kettleman in surprise. "Where's Fletcher?"

"He slipped on his basement stairs about an hour ago and broke his damned arm. I haven't covered one of these things since I was a cub," the news editor said worriedly. "Just let me get the wrong kid carrying the ball in tomorrow's paper, and we lose two subscribers—the parents of the kid that didn't and the parents of the kid that did."

Tulley laughed. "Scotty Kettleman's over in the rooting section. Maybe he'd help you cover the game," she suggested, remembering her conversation with the boy a few days earlier on the loading dock. "I bet he knows whatever you don't."

"Great idea, boss. I'll go hunt him up," Dawes said in a relieved voice. He turned to the Kettlemans. "That is if it's all right with you folks?"

Even before the parents gave consent, Tulley saw by their faces it was all right. With a parting wave of his pad of paper, Dawes took off to look for Scotty among the rooters.

"Thanks," Charlie said. "You may not know it, but you just made our son's night. He'd rather be out there feeding names to Ed Dawes than be the star quarterback on the team."

Emily Kettleman gave Tulley's arm a hug. "Charlie would never have suggested it. He'd feel he might be putting Ed on the spot."

As the two teams lined up for the kickoff, Tulley's eyes left the field to look for her news editor and found him hunkered down near the players' bench scribbling notes on his pad of paper. She saw her skinny press-watching friend squatting beside him and felt a shiver of empathy as she remembered the first time she'd covered a story. The boy was talking back over his shoulder to Ed with his head turned to watch the field, as earnest in his new role as if he was covering a superbowl game.

The game was close and exciting and was won in the last thirty seconds by the home team with a pass caught in the end zone. The crowd began to break up, and as the Kettlemans and Tulley reached the ground, she spotted Scotty making his way toward them through the herd of spectators, an air of self-importance in his stride.

"Hey Mom, Dad...you go on," he called out as he drew near enough to be heard. "Ed wants me to come on back to the paper with him while he writes the story. He says he wants me there to make sure he's got all the names and stuff right. He said to tell you he'd bring me home."

Mother and father exchanged looks, and for a moment Tulley was afraid they were going to say no, but then there was a wavering.

After a moment Kettleman said in his precise way, "Tell Ed you have our permission."

"Tell him not to keep you out any later than he has to," the mother appended fondly and got an "Aw, Mom" look from her son in response.

About to dart away, Scotty stopped and turned back to Tulley, clearly feeling the need to say something but unsure how to say it.

"Ed said it was your idea to get me to help him, Miss Tulley, and...I...uh...thanks!" The glow on the freckled face told her far more than his words.

They walked with the crowd from the bleachers, the Kettlemans stopping often to visit with townspeople and to introduce Tulley to some she hadn't already met. She had a comfortable feeling of homecoming.

Earlier, when she'd found herself cheering for the local team, she was astonished at how partisan she'd become in the short time since she'd inherited a place in the town. She felt as if she belonged.

It had been a fine evening, she thought in a sudden burst of good humor. For the most part it had been a good week.

But the evening was not over. Back in the car, when Charlie turned the key to start the engine, he was met with a tired groan from under the hood. Swearing softly under his breath, he tried again.

"You didn't get that old battery replaced," said his wife. It was a flat, nonaccusing, nonreproving wifely statement to which the beleaguered man did not take exception.

"Sorry," he said absently. "It's been working fine lately. I forgot all about it. If I can't find someone with jumper cables to get us started, we'll have to wait for the Triple A."

The parking lot was clearing rapidly as Charlie stepped out of the car to get help, leaving Emily and Tulley behind to spin out thin strands of small talk until Tulley thought to mention Scott.

"I like your son. You must be very proud," she said directly. "He's a bright engaging teenager. If he really wants to be a newspaperman, he has all the right ingredients."

"Thanks. He's a great kid, but he's got too much locomotion and not enough good judgment when it comes to his extracurricular life," his mother said, looking pleased and anxious at the same time. "Trouble is, he's not very good at sports and gets straight A's without half trying. He's got too much time on his hands. I wish we could find something to keep him busy when he's not in school." Struck by a thought, she turned and looked into the back seat. "I knew it. He left his jacket. That boy! It's too cold for nothing but a sweater. I'd better run back and take it to him."

On the other side of the parking bunker a car nosed in facing them, the beams from its headlights piercing their windshield as Emily got out of the car. In the next moment Charlie appeared and reached inside to release the hood.

"I was lucky," he announced. "I ran into Cass. He's getting his jumper cables out of his car."

Something somersaulted in Tully's breast. She caught her breath. It had never occurred to her to wonder if Cass might be up there in the bleachers somewhere, perhaps no more than a row or two from where she sat.

"We do thank you for comin' to our rescue, Cass, honey." Emily sang out to the large, lean figure of the man looming out of the darkness. "Come say hullo to Tulley while I take Scotty his jacket."

Charlie was bent over the front of the car, connecting the jumper cables to the two batteries. Emily was already on her way. When Cass peered in the open door, they were alone.

"T-Tulley! I wasn't... expecting to see you," he said, stumbling over the words with no vestige of his usual sangfroid. In the distorted light from the dashboard, his face appeared strained and unhappy.

Tulley's own composure was shot. "Obviously not," she managed to say. And then because she couldn't help herself, she asked with deadly sweetness, "You mean you weren't expecting to see me here... or ever again?"

"It won't work, Tulley. I knew when I left you the other night. I should have said so then."

"Should have said what?" she asked stubbornly, determined not to let it be easy for him.

"That I'm just not enough of a Spartan to carry on a hands-off relationship with you."

She was surprised at how much it hurt.

"So you'll take the coward's way out!" She *wanted* the words to cut. It was the way she felt about McCready at the moment: angry, disappointed, let down. He refused to rise to the bait.

His mouth lifted in a crooked smile. "When was the last time you ate?"

She almost let go with a caustic reply, then she saw that his eyes were bleak and there was hurt in his face, too, and all impulse to draw blood was destroyed. Why, he was no happier about the way conditions stood between them than she was.

Charlie came from in front to slide behind the wheel and start the car. Leaving the motor running, he stepped back out. When the jumper cables were disconnected and the hood was in place, he and Cass stood by the open car door and did a post mortem on the game while they waited for Emily.

"Let's all go back to our house, and I'll fix something for us to eat," Emily said when she arrived.

"After all that I ate before the game, Emily, I couldn't think of it," Tulley said quickly. "If you don't mind, I'll have you drop me off at my place, and I'll roll into bed." Did she imagine a shadow of disappointment in McCready's eyes as he started to walk to his car?

Emily called after him, "Come on by, Cass. I'll be fixing something. I know Charlie's going to want something to hold him over until morning, and Scotty's a bottomless pit. When he gets in, he'll be starved."

"Thanks, Emily. I'll take you up on that," Cass said over his shoulder as he climbed into his car.

"I couldn't get you to change your mind and come home with us for a snack, could I, Tulley?" the woman asked when they pulled into the driveway to the carriage house.

"Not tonight. Thank you for a splendid evening, but at this point I need sleep more than I need food."

She might have added that she was simply not up to a purposeless hour in the presence of Cass McCready. The less she saw of him, the quicker she'd get him out of her mind and . . . yes, out of her heart. Biting down on a sore tooth wasn't her idea of fun.

As she turned the key in her lock, the peal of the phone sent her blood racing through her veins. Maybe it was Cass. Maybe seeing her tonight had made him realize they were on the threshold of something too important to let family differences stand in its way. Maybe now they could talk.

In her haste she dropped the key, and by the time it was back in the lock she was so afraid he would hang up that her hands were trembling and she almost dropped it again. By the time she finally got in and snatched the phone off its cradle, she was completely unstrung.

"Hello there, Miss Tulley Calhoun. I trust it's not too late to call. This is Leo Drummond," the male voice at the other end greeted her breezily. Her disappointment was so profound she wondered if it telegraphed itself across the wire. "Now that your first week in the editor's seat is over, I thought you might be ready to consider a bit of R and R for tomorrow night."

A feeling of resignation settled upon Tulley. Why not? she thought dully. Her relationship with Cass was over. That didn't mean she was ready for the cloister.

"What did you have in mind?"

"I thought we might have dinner at my club in Raleigh, for starters," Drummond said. "I may have told you the club has a five-piece orchestra that plays on Saturday nights for dancing, if that suits your fancy. Or we could go to a show, or—"

"Dancing sounds fine," she said, trying to put a ring of enthusiasm into the words. "What time should I be ready?"

She said good-night and hung up, telling herself it was what she wanted...not Drummond, perhaps, but to get to know people in other circles instead of only those people who had known Cass and his family since the beginning of time.

But when she reached the kitchen, she saw the jambalaya tureen, forgotten on the counter and looking reproachful, somehow.

CHAPTER ELEVEN

IF LEO DRUMMOND wasn't the handsomest man she'd ever had anything to do with, he was certainly in the running, admitted Tulley, observing her dinner partner across the small linen-covered table at the Prometheus Club the next night. The lean, aquiline face, the flawless nose, the dark, equivocal eyes added up to a kind of glossy perfection that seemed to echo the sleek art deco lacquer work of Drummond's club, where a scaled-down replica of Rockefeller Center's Prometheus Fountain guarded the entry court.

The man was an elegant dancer, the music was good, the food above reproach, the surroundings chichi. Why wasn't she enjoying herself?

She knew the answer. Part of her was somewhere else. When they danced, she followed Drummond's flawless footwork absently, wishing for the risky abandon of McCready's unconcerned gallop across a floor. The delicate hint of saffron when the waiter lifted the silver cover from her dinner plate triggered a longing for the full, heady aroma of a tureen of jambalaya shared with Cass.

Drummond was adept at small talk well-larded with flattery and a kind of covert sensuality that left little doubt as to his intentions.

Having dined and danced, they sipped after-dinner coffee. Tulley toyed with pleading a headache to forestall any suggestion they dance again. It was a feminine ploy she considered beneath her, and she was a little ashamed at how sorely tempted to use it she was.

"I suppose every man tells you you're beautiful," Drummond was saying. "You may not know this, but I have a special interest in you as a person, too." He said it like an actor pouring out lines in a play.

He covered her hand with his, silk-skinned and well-manicured. For an instant the memory of Mc-Cready's rough palm, exciting to the touch, played upon her senses. The soft hand that enclosed hers felt steamy. She squirmed inwardly against the small entrapment and decided it was not enough to take issue over.

With a cynicism born of experience, she recognized there was more on Drummond's mind than dining and dancing. The best she could hope was to hold him at bay without a confrontation. Few things could be more uncomfortable than riding back to Hilby with a man she'd repulsed for something as silly as holding her hand. Twisting her wrist, she made a conspicuous effort to look at her watch.

"If you don't mind, I should be getting home," she said. "I have a long day at the paper ahead of me."

"But tomorrow's Sunday."

"Yes, and that means I'll have the place to myself with no interruptions. I'll never get any changes made at the *Herald* unless I work Sundays for a while."

Drummond's hand still held hers captive. The tips of his thumb and forefinger moved caressingly around the line of her wrist. It seemed a patent come-on, and Tulley made ready to parry an advance, but she saw by his eyes that the caress was no more than an absent gesture. Whatever Drummond had on his mind at the moment, it was not seduction.

As if suddenly reaching a decision, he let go of her hand. Signaling the waiter for the check, he signed it with a flourish and escorted her to the club entrance. By some kind of magic his car already waited at the curb with a doorman standing by to see her in.

Drummond and the showy black sports car seemed made for each other, thought Tulley, watching him slide in behind the wheel. Out on the highway, with a straight stretch of timber-lined asphalt ahead of them, he reached again for her hand and turned to her fleetingly with a quick, dazzling smile that found no reflection in his eyes.

"Mmm. That's better. Such a lovely hand," he murmured, the actor again, and turned his attention back to the road. Tulley suffered her recapture in guarded silence, waiting curiously to see what would come next.

"You were speaking of changes," he said after a moment. "I hope you won't take it unkindly if a longtime friend and admirer of your uncle suggests you forget about making changes at the *Herald* in the immediate future."

"Friend . . . admirer?" she repeated, hearing only those two words, scarcely believing her ears.

"Your uncle was a maligned man," Drummond said grandiosely. "I can truthfully say that the town of Hilby lost a man of vision when he died. A man of progress. A man who would have done big things for the town, had he lived. That's something for you to remember when his detractors run him down."

"That's a minority opinion in Hilby, I believe," Tulley said coolly.

"He had his detractors." Throughout the evening, there had been a tone of cajolery in all Drummond said. In its place now was an ugly note of toughness. "The town's full of people like your friend, Sam Matthews, who wants to keep Hilby in the horse and buggy days. See that they don't take advantage of your youth and inexperience to use the newspaper to their own ends."

Tulley could feel her hackles rise. Abruptly she freed her hand from his grip. Drummond seemed not to notice, so intent was he on his point.

"I've been newspapering too long to be called 'inexperienced.' And I'm closer to thirty than twenty-five, so you need hardly concern yourself about my 'youth,'" she said flatly. "As for the other, *nobody* is going to use the *Herald* for a power play, and that includes myself."

"To these jaded, fortyish eyes you are young—enchantingly young—and innocent," Drummond said, segueing smoothly for a disarming instant into the stagy purr of flattery under which she could still hear a note of hardness. "What I'm really talking about is maturity, which has more to do with knowing the pitfalls than it has to do with years."

"Pitfalls?"

"This may come as a surprise to you, but I worked closely with your uncle. He understood there were certain pitfalls to our mutual concerns that could be circumvented if we worked together. It's to both our interests that you understand what they are and your part in dealing with them."

"And what are these pitfalls, if I may ask?"

Drummond's voice turned to steel. "That McCready story you ran last week, for instance. That's one mistake you'd never have made if you'd been getting the right advice.''

''Would that all my mistakes could be so successful! The public loved it.''

''Ah, yes, the public. Forget the public! McCready already has quite a following,'' Drummond said with a new edge. ''That story makes a fool of the paper. Lamarr knew what he was talking about when he printed what McCready calls libel. I happen to know he had the facts to back it up.''

''Facts, Leo? Tell me about the facts,'' she said, her voice suddenly tense.

For a moment Drummond said nothing. Half-fearfully Tulley waited, wanting to hear yet dreading what he might tell her. Suppose it was damning to Cass, so damning it couldn't be denied or explained away.

Oh, Cass, I'm sorry, she cried inwardly. As suddenly as it came, her fear passed. Cass was innocent.

Drummond stared out into the funnel of brightness cast by his headlights upon the highway, his face expressionless. With a sense of despair she knew he was not going to tell her what she needed to know.

''All right...to be perfectly frank with you, I don't actually know the facts,'' he said, still not looking at her. ''He told me he had facts to back up what he wrote about McCready. Knowing Lamarr, I've no doubt he did.''

Did Drummond know something and was lying? Or was he embarrassed that she'd called his bluff and forced him to admit he really knew nothing at all? Half-sick with disappointment, Tulley felt as if she'd walked headlong into an unyielding door. In her preoccupation, she hardly heard him as he continued.

"I'm not sure you understand, Tulley, that it's not in our best interests to play cozy with Cass Mc-Cready," he said smoothly.

She did a double take, her attention caught by a single word.

"*Our* best interests?"

"Yours, the paper's...ours. As heir to your uncle's estate, you stand to lose a great deal of money if McCready influences the city council the way he influenced the planning commission on that property we hope to develop."

"Are you using the editorial 'we'? Or are you saying my uncle was in some kind of partnership with you?"

"A silent partner, if you like. Where do you think the money came from for all that computerized machinery at the *Herald*? Not from advertising and circulation, you can be sure."

"Sam Matthews did tell me the paper was on shaky ground," Tulley said hesitantly. "When I walked in and saw all that equipment I couldn't believe—"

"Well, now you know," said Drummond bluntly. "Lamarr kept it afloat with money he made from real estate. He had a knack for it, but let me tell you, sweetheart, the money to be had on this deal will make all Lamarr's other little house-trading look like a penny-ante pot."

"Sam mentioned something about real property in the estate, but we haven't had time to go into it yet."

"The only property that matters is known as the Food Basket block in the west end of town—a bunch of ramshackle houses and run-down garden patches with a vacant supermarket at one end. Lamarr and I bought it for development. The plans call for condominiums built around a shopping center and mall. We've got some big retail companies and fast-food chains signed up for it already. If Cass McCready hadn't thrown a monkey wrench in the works, we'd have the bulldozers in there right now.''

''What's Cass have to do with it?''

''Not a damned thing, but that didn't stop him from going before the planning commission and talking them into denying us a building permit.''

''I'm not sure I understand.''

''The area is zoned for single-family dwellings, which means getting permission from the city planning commission—a variance, it's called—in order to build anything else. No more than a formality if McCready hadn't taken it on himself to interfere.'' There was no mistaking the malice in his voice, the grimness in the saturnine profile.

''Why did he?''

''What difference does it make why? What matters is that we've appealed it to the city council, and if we play it right, the council will override the planning commission and give us the variance.''

''What do you mean 'play it right'?'' Tulley asked, finding his casual assumption that the two of them were in it together suddenly intolerable.

''That's where you come in,'' Drummond said. ''All you have to do is lay low until we get that clearance from the council. The piece you ran the other day was a mistake, but at least it didn't clear up any of the suspicions that hang over McCready. As long as he stays under a cloud, he won't have the clout to freeze us out.''

"I c-can't believe what I'm h-hearing," Tulley stuttered. "What kind of a person do you think—"

"Grow up, Tulley. You're heir to your uncle's estate. It's up to you to carry out his wishes. I'm telling you what he'd do if he'd lived," Drummond said coldly. "There's also another factor that seems to have escaped your lovely head. There's a lot of money in it for you if you do as you're told."

The audacity of what he said restored Tulley's composure. "You have a mistaken idea that I feel some sort of loyalty to my late uncle. I'm surprised you don't know I'm his heir by default."

"Default?"

"He died intestate, and I happen to be his only living descendant," Tulley said. "Ironic, isn't it. He drove my father out of the newspaper only to have it come back to my father through me. I can assure you, I don't owe Lamarr anything—least of all loyalty. I owe loyalty to my father and to those of our family who founded the *Herald*. I owe it to *them* to make up to Hilby for the sleazy journalism my uncle inflicted upon them while he was alive."

"You have a beautiful face and a nasty tongue," Drummond said poisonously. "You'd better think twice about doing your part to get this variance passed by the council. Where do you think the money's going to come from to run the paper without Lamarr around to make it in real estate?"

"From the advertisers and subscribers Lamarr lost during the past twenty years," Tulley said. "An honest newspaper will bring them back. The *Herald*'s failures began and ended with Lamarr. You can count me out of any dealings you may have had with my late uncle."

SHE WAS WAKENED from a restless sleep the following morning by the phone. Across the lot, less than a hundred yards away, the comfortable voice of Caroline Matthews at the other end of the line drawled out a lazy invitation.

"Tulley, honey, you awake? I made a batch of Sally Lunn bread for breakfast, and it turned out right good. Reckon you could come help us eat it?"

Showered and dressed in an oversize crimson sweatshirt and a pair of age-softened jeans, Tulley arrived at the Matthewses' back door fifteen minutes later.

Sated with Sally Lunn bread and fried apples and country sausage, her mind cozy with warm, gossipy talk concerning the small world of Hilby and Hilby County, she sipped her second cup of coffee and queried Sam Matthews head-on about what she'd learned the night before.

"What's this about Lamarr being in partnership with Leo Drummond?"

Matthews glanced at her blankly. "I don't know anything about a partnership between them. What gave you the idea there was one?"

"I had dinner with Drummond last night," Tulley said and followed with a quick report on what had transpired during the remarkable evening, including a nearly verbatim account of their conversation on the way home from Raleigh.

Caroline drawled in disgust, "Sam, honey, didn't I say it the very first time we met him? I remember sayin' that Leo Drummond is not a nice man."

Matthews grunted. "Well, if such a partnership exists, it was indeed a silent one. I haven't run across anything about it among Lamarr's papers. But Lamarr was too canny to have relied upon an oral agreement, so there's got to be something in writing somewhere."

"Maybe Leo Drummond was lying to me," suggested Tulley.

Matthews shook his head. "I doubt it. Somehow it has the ring of truth."

"But why all the secrecy, Sam?"

"That's easy. Because Lamarr was using the newspaper to persuade the public to back the code variance. He wouldn't want it to get around that he had an interest in the development. If the town found out he stood to gain from the variance, it would queer everything."

"If you listen to Drummond, the development's all in the best interests of the community. Honestly now, Sam, is it really so bad?" Tulley asked. "Wouldn't a shopping center and condominiums be good for the economy? They would create jobs. Isn't that progress, as Drummond says?"

"I've got nothing against progress, Tulley, but in the past twenty years Hilby has more than doubled in population," Sam informed her. "Our sewers, our water supply, our waste disposal system are already overextended. Same with the schools and the fire department and the police. When someone like Drummond starts talking in the name of progress about building housing for hundreds of families and turning Hilby into a commuter city for the state capital thirty miles away, it's time somebody hollered 'Whoa!'"

Tulley gazed at the lawyer thoughtfully for a long moment. "And Cass was the someone who hollered whoa."

"Cass just acted as spokesman for a lot of us folks who doubt the wisdom of replacing old, solidly built homes on lots where a poor family can raise most of the food they need to live on for a year, with cheap high-rise housing that in a few years will be slums."

"Then Lamarr discredited Cass to spike his guns when the matter comes up on appeal," Tulley said slowly. "That makes more sense than to think Lamarr did it purely out of malice—what Cass calls bad blood between the Calhouns and the McCreadys."

She saw Sam and Caroline glance at each other questioningly.

"I never heard anything about bad blood, did you, Sam?" asked Caroline. "Oh, sure, I reckon Lamarr was mad at Cass's daddy for marrying the girl he wanted himself, but I hardly think he'd pick on Cass for that. You know something I don't, Sam, honey?"

"Not a thing. We all know Cass's old granddaddy, the judge, was bitter against yours, Tulley, but then the poor old man was senile. It's my understanding that the rest of the McCreadys were all mighty grateful to Ross Calhoun for using the *Herald* to get the judge off the bench before he did something real crazy to disgrace them all."

"I'm sure there's more to it than that," Tulley said. She hesitated for a moment before she went on, uncomfortable with what she was about to say. "Cass as much as admitted to me that all the living McCreadys would look askance on any real...friendliness between us."

The genuine puzzlement she saw on the faces in front of her did nothing but add to her own confusion. She gave them a wry smile and pushed back from the table to leave.

"If you happen to see Cass you might tell him what Drummond said. It's about time he found out who his enemies are. He'd better know there's someone out to get him who's very much alive," she said.

"You better tell him yourself," drawled Matthews.

"I'm not really expecting to see him, Sam. I haven't seen him all week." In spite of herself she could not keep the bleakness out of her voice.

THE PROSPECT OF SPENDING THE DAY alone in the barren room that had been her uncle's office sent her back to the carriage house to forage through the belongings she'd brought from New York, in search of something, anything, to brighten the dismal environment she'd inherited. It was as if she must put her own stamp on the room to erase the taint of her uncle.

A scattering of bright posters, prints and cartoons on the walls in informal arrangements and an assortment of her own books on the shelves relieved the forbidding starkness of the bare room. That done, she settled her body down at her desk to work, but her thoughts wouldn't follow suit. Would Sam tell Cass about her conversation with Drummond?

She reached for a copy of Saturday's *Herald* and spread it out before her, running her eyes expertly down its front page in search of a small boxed item she suddenly remembered she'd seen without grasping its full significance. Halfway down one of the columns she found the piece: "County Calls for Bids." The story announced the opening of bids for the construction of the new county hospital. It meant time was running out for Cass.

She couldn't wait for Sam to tell Cass about her evening with Drummond. He had to know now that the cause of his troubles didn't die with Lamarr.

Her fingers darted through the Hilby County telephone book as she looked for a number for Cass.

"Good mornin'. This is Vinnie speakin'," a woman's voice answered, gentle, Southern, but as dry as ashes. Struck with instant panic, Tulley nearly hung up.

"Good morning. This is Tulley Calhoun at *The Hilby Herald*," she managed to croak, half expecting to hear the click of the receiver at the other end when she identified herself. "I wonder if I could speak to Cass."

"Why, I'm right sorry, Miss Calhoun. He left town Friday night and neglected to mention when he was comin' back."

It was a moment before Tulley could muster the bland voice to hide the magnitude of her disappointment. "Would you mind asking him to get in touch with me as soon as he returns...or with Sam Matthews," she added, hit with the disturbing thought that he might not care to talk to her.

"I'll be glad to, Miss Calhoun."

Tulley thanked her and hung up, thinking distractedly that the Calhoun name hadn't daunted the Southern courtesy of Cass's Aunt Vinnie.

She swiveled herself around in the big desk chair and stared, unseeing, out at the empty tree-lined street. In her mind she could hear time ticking away. How strange for him to leave town after the football game, late at night. Where had he gone and why?

When Charlie Kettleman pulled up to the curb in front of her window ten minutes later, Tulley was still gazing out at the gathering gloom of a rain-threatened day. Not until he was parked and out of the car did she bury her frustration and return his wave with a smile.

By the time Kettleman made his way to her office, she had turned back to her desk and was tidying memos from the spindle into neat little random piles.

"Don't let me interrupt you. You look busy," Kettleman said. "I just came in to say hello. I've got a lot of work waiting upstairs."

"I'm working on some things we might do to give the paper a new image," Tulley informed him, not quite truthfully since she hadn't done anything yet. "I'd like to talk them over with you and Ed Dawes in a few days."

"Anytime," said Kettleman agreeably. "Now, if you'll excuse me . . ."

Tulley was suddenly reluctant to be left alone with her fruitless thoughts. "Stick around a minute. I want to tell you what a good job your son Scott did for us Friday night. Besides helping Ed, he wrote that funny little box item about the mouse in the quarterback's jersey. Ed said the piece was all Scotty's. He has a nice sense for the bizarre."

Charlie's quick look of pride and pleasure ended in a slightly worried frown. "It's been a big weekend for the boy. He got his first story in print, and he discovered girls . . . or rather, I should say, girls discovered him."

Tulley laughed. "Coincidence, I presume."

"That's where you are mistaken! Cause and effect. Girls that age want heroes, and there's nothing particularly heroic about a skinny, freckle-faced adolescent—except, of course, to his mother," Kettleman said ruefully. "At least that's the way it was until Ed

Dawes decorated him with a card that says Press. Ed made him look like an accredited sports reporter in front of a bevy of nubile cheerleaders. The phone's been ringing off the hook ever since.''

"Isn't that what teenaging's all about?"

Kettleman massaged his receding hairline absently. "I suppose so, but it takes getting used to," he said with a resigned sigh. "He went to a party last night and would have accepted an invitation for tonight if we hadn't made him turn it down. The topper is he's suddenly rebellious about an eleven o'clock curfew, and his mother and I are unreasonable to expect him to stay home when there's school the next day."

"Poor Charlie," Tulley said with a sympathetic smile. "This, too, will pass away."

When he had gone upstairs to his own work, Tulley forced herself to return to her stack of memos in earnest. She sorted them first according to related ideas, which she expanded into a number of fully developed proposals for changes at the *Herald*. These she organized into a program for discussion with Kettleman and Dawes and other key members of the staff.

Once she was into it, she turned her mind to meet the challenge of the work by simply not giving in to the inner voice that whimpered for her attention: *what am I going to do about Cass?*

What *could* she do about Cass? Until she found a place to start, she must get on with her own work.

On his way out in the late afternoon, Kettleman again stuck his head in her door to say good-night and suggest she call it a day, but Tulley worked on as if driven. In a way she was—driven by fear of what she'd inevitably think about when she turned her mind from her work.

It was dark outside when the proposal was complete, ready to be presented to her staff the following morning. She could think of nothing to add to it, nothing to take away.

She pushed her chair back from the desk and rose to her feet stiffly, half dazed with weariness. Since the late Sally Lunn breakfast with Sam and Caroline, she'd had nothing to eat. Recent experience and a warning shakiness told her she'd better fortify herself with a bottle of orange juice from the vending machine, before she got behind the wheel of the behemoth for the drive home where food awaited only to be heated.

Reaching for her leather handbag to find money for the machine, she spilled half of its contents when she pulled out her coin purse. Keys and pencils and the like skittered across the bare linoleum in every direction.

"Rats!" she muttered. It was as if the thumb had been pulled out of the dike. Everything she'd managed to keep damned inside her all afternoon came flooding out.

"Cass! Where are you? Dear God, Cass... What are we going to do?" she wailed softly, and started to pick up her lipstick and checkbook. Scooting around on her knees, she garnered her truant belongings, some of which had rolled into the kneehole under the desk. Tulley retrieved what was there and started to back out of the small dark cave when her head came up hard against an obstruction. She turned the beam of her key-chain flashlight on the obstacle, rubbing her head and wondering what it was doing there.

Suddenly she knew. It was a bug! Lamarr had bugged his own desk. Not only was it against the law to record conversations without consent, she couldn't think of any occasion a small-town editor like La-marr would need to do it. She sat there on the bare floor of the kneehole, puzzling over her discovery, and at last shrugged it aside. There was no question about it—this late uncle of hers was bizarre!

She scrambled out from under the desk and was up on her feet. Her head reeled, reminding her to get a coin from her purse—this time very carefully—for a bottle of orange juice and a package of mixed nuts from the machine. She drank the juice and was fin-ishing the last of the nuts when an idea suddenly hit her.

Maybe there was something on tape that would point to where Lamarr got the information he used to defame Cass. At last she had someplace to start!

CHAPTER TWELVE

SOME MILES SOUTH OF NAGS HEAD on one of the long spits of dunes that make up the Outer Banks of North Carolina, Cass's grandfather McCready had built a sturdy three-room cottage he lovingly called "the shack." Set in a hollow of sand made secure by a heavy thatch of oat grass, it faced inland over Pamlico Sound, sheltered from the ravages of the Atlantic on the other side by a fortress of dunes.

From the year Cass gained the freedom of a car, this place had been a retreat where he came to lick his wounds, where, alone, he could weigh problems and come to terms with his adolescence and later with his life. It was where he came to rethink his future when the family business went down. It was where he headed that Friday night when he'd run into Tulley after the football game.

Since those last minutes together at the carriage house, the words they'd said to each other would not go away. *"I don't care that your name's McCready,"* she'd said. Cass was filled with her declaration of trust, and it told him with a growing certainty that Tulley deserved no less from him. Throughout the next days while he pored over blueprints, talked to subcontractors, worked on figures for a construction bid, her voice threaded in and out of his thoughts, and when he asked himself if he cared that her name was Calhoun, he was no longer certain that he did.

With this new ambivalence came the discovery that he'd spoken too glibly of bad blood between their families. He had spoken not from knowledge but from a gut feeling that had been with him for as long as he could remember. In this new light of reason, he knew he didn't give a damn about ancient quarrels. If the rest of the McCreadys did, it was not his problem.

Which wasn't entirely true. There were his mother and Aunt Vinnie, who would not be docile about it, he guessed, but he was reasonably sure they'd put up a good front to Tulley for his sake, and when they got to know her, they'd forget their reservations about Calhouns.

But even after he'd reached this state of understanding, he did not go to Tulley. It wasn't enough that his own problems with the issue were resolved. An unreasonable feeling that his grandfather, were he still alive, would look on their relationship as betrayal held him back.

In bed at night, in internal dialogues with his late grandfather, he argued the folly of one generation passing its hostilities on to the next and extolled the virtues of Tulley, only to hear the enraged voice of his grandfather roar down to him over more than twenty-five years, *"Son, don't ever count on a Calhoun!"*

Friday came, and he had yet to see her. Nor was he any nearer to purging this nagging sense of guilt when he ducked his head in the window of the Kettleman's car and found Tulley, bundled up to her ears in a down coat, so near he could have picked her up in his arms and run off with her. He knew then that he couldn't go through another week like the one just passed.

He had a piece of Emily Kettleman's pecan pie and two cups of coffee before he headed for home, where he bundled a few things into a duffel bag, hauled out rubber boots and oilskin rain gear from a back-porch closet and loaded them into his car. The last thing he did before he locked the door and left the house around midnight was to write a note he left on the drainboard for his aunt to see when she came down in the morning.

"Dear Vinnie," the note said, "I'll be at the shack. If needed, you know how to reach me. Hard to say when I'll be back. Love, Cass."

He stopped in Tarboro for a cup of coffee around two in the morning and for breakfast in Nags Head before he started the last short lap of his night-long trip to the shack. In spite of the cold air from an ocean grown wintry, he rolled down the window and reveled in the smell of the sea that seemed to welcome him back.

The happiest times of his childhood were those fleeting weeks of summer he'd spent here with his grandfather during the judge's yearly vacation from the bench, far away from the pale sighs of his pain-ridden mother and the quick reproach of a father preoccupied with business affairs.

With a sense of homecoming he turned from the road, careful to stay on the wind-washed track that was the only ground a car could travel on to the house without getting buried in sand. Inside he stowed his gear and the groceries he'd bought at an all-night store along the way and built a fire in the old Franklin stove to warm the place and get the dampness out of the air. He was bone tired, but he hadn't driven all the way to the Atlantic Ocean to crawl into bed. He'd come to find his grandfather or say goodbye to him—he wasn't sure which.

Outside he climbed to the highest point of the surrounding dunes, which jutted up from the center of the narrow strip of land like the backbone of a prehistoric beast. Less than a hundred yards on either side, they sloped down in sandy beaches to the water. Over there was the Atlantic where he'd chased incoming tides and hunted shells on warm days and watched through his grandfather's spyglass for ships that came up over the horizon with the suddenness of a jack-in-the-box; and on the other side stretched Pamlico Sound where he'd paddled in the shallows and caught crawdads and with sharp young eyes watched for birds and small furred creatures that were the sole inhabitants of his realm. His grandfather, while always covertly in charge, had let him be monarch of all he surveyed. Cass wasn't sure just what role his grandfather had played. To the boy, something close to God.

Under the porch he found the decaying remains of the aluminum-clad boat they'd fished from, for whatever the waters might yield. Seeing it, he could hear again the slap of the waves against its metal sides. His stomach remembered the feeling of the up-and-down motion and went suddenly queasy.

And then the storm broke, and he ran for it.

Inside he changed into dry clothes and rebuilt the fire and thought about his grandfather with a terrible sense of frustration. Everything spoke of his grandfather: outside in the dunes, in here. Why then couldn't Cass find him?

What had he expected? he wondered disgustedly. Had he imagined if he came to the shack his grandfather would reach down from some celestial throne and give him absolution—a sign or something that would make everything all right?

Sitting in his grandfather's old Boston rocker before the fire, he dozed and wakened and thought of Tulley and remembered the venom in his grandfather's voice when he had said ''Calhoun,'' and, in a kind of escape, went back to sleep.

And so the day went while the storm raged outside. Toward evening, Cass rose and stretched and looked around him with a sense of helplessness. What was he doing here? Why had he thought he might find understanding from a man who'd been dead more than twenty-five years?

But he knew why. From his earliest recollections, his grandfather had been the source of all wisdom. Ultimate understanding could be counted on from him. At the peak of his career, he'd been a judge, respected throughout the state for his even-handed justice.

That's who he'd come up here looking for, Cass thought dully, not the shrill, betrayed old man whose terrible rage the boy had been witness to. How could he make peace with a grandfather whose one remaining passion at the time of his death was hatred for all Calhouns?

He felt a deep sadness as he realized that his trip to the shack was in reality a kind of goodbye. For all the good there was here for him, he could leave tonight were it not for the torrential storm that had blown up and the fact that he hadn't been in a bed for more than twenty-four hours.

Even with the blazing fire he felt unexpectedly chilled by a sudden wintering of spirit. He went into the kitchen and poured Scotch in a glass with a splash of water and was heading back to the fire when a thin rectangular object on the narrow edge of wainscoting caught his eye. Setting his glass back on the counter, he picked the object up and blew into it.

He gave it another tentative blow and made a wry face. They should have had two of them, he thought. He'd never really gotten the hang of it. His grandfather had loved playing it so much himself he never got around to teaching the boy.

Scotch forgotten, he settled back in the Boston rocker and went to work on the rusty harmonica, filling the shack with strange alien sounds that both offended and pleased his ears. God, the old judge could play anything, he marveled. But neither of them could carry a tune.

Yet they sang together on those long-ago summer evenings as if they could—folk ballads, sea chanteys, minstrel tunes—making up the words they didn't know as they went along, more words than the ones they knew.

This was the man he'd come to find, thought Cass suddenly. This was the man he should be listening to, not to words of hatred from the passing stranger his grandfather had turned into that last year or so of his life. Why, for so long, had he mistaken the sick voice of that broken old man for the true voice of the man he had known and loved from the beginning?

He knew then he'd found his grandfather. Storm or no storm, he'd start the long journey back to Tulley in the morning.

AT THE CARRIAGE HOUSE in Hilby, Tulley ate leftovers and brooded. Shelby Haynes had done such a thorough job of stripping the office when he had left

that it had taken her no time to determine there were
no tapes hidden there. Barring the unthinkable possibility that Haynes, himself, had beat her to them, the
next likely place to look was among the rubbish that
filled Lamarr's house, she thought bleakly.

Cass...Cass! His name whispered through her
consciousness like a held-back cry of pain. In a surprise twist that brought a wry smile to her face, her
mind paraphrased an old jazz song. *Won't you come
home, McCready, won't you come home? You've been
away too lo-o-ong!*

In bed later she thought again of the first time she'd
seen Cass, from the annex balcony. Something ineff-
ably lovely had happened between them that day—
something she could never forget, she thought wist-
fully. Then a strange, faint sound wafted up to her
from outside, driving everything else from her mind.

Curiously she raised her head and listened. It was a
moment before she recognized it for what it was—a
sound she hadn't heard in a long time. Of all things,
somebody was playing a harmonica under her window. She slipped out of her bed and walked softly
across the room, pausing on the way to listen again to
the painful caterwauling; she was surprised to recognize, in this trial-and-error rendition, the first few bars
of the breathtaking balcony song from *West Side
Story*. When a certain point was reached, the musi-
cian went back to the beginning to replay the same few
bars. She ran the last steps to look out the window and
drew a shaky, ecstatic breath.

There he stood under her window, spotlighted in the
flood from the garage: Don Quixote in navy blue
parka with the hood up, wrenching horrendous sounds
from the harmonica with the aplomb of a concert star.

A wild, wonderful bubble of laughter welled up in Tulley.

Softly she raised the bottom sash of the window to instant silence.

Then Cass's voice called up to her, "Rapunzel! Rapunzel Calhoun... let down your hair."

Tulley's laughter spilled over the windowsill. "Cass, you idiot!" she cried in a joyous whisper that ended in a slightly hysterical giggle. He touched the harmonica to his forehead in a gallant salute and brought it again to his lips.

"No more, Cass," she called softly on a last gasp of laughter. "No more, please. Not that it isn't lovely. Come. I'll let you in before Sam Matthews calls the police."

Flying now, she reached the stair landing before she remembered she wore only a thin film of a nightgown. Snatching her soft woolen robe from the end of her bed, she tied herself into it, and still in her bare feet, raced for the stairs again. Pulling back the dead bolt, she threw open the door and came to a halt, caught in a sudden wave of unaccustomed shyness. Why was he here?

He stood on the doorstep, a film of mist glistening on his hair and the shoulders of his parka. He reached out and touched her face as if in wonder at finding her there. She knew then that *why* didn't matter. What mattered was that he'd come back to play Romeo under her window.

He stepped across the threshold and caught her to him, drawing her hard against the rain-misted parka that smelled of the sea. An electric thrill raced through her, setting the pace for her break-dancing pulse. She hugged him and curled her fingers into the thick helmet of mist-dampened hair, her throat tight with happiness, her heart singing to dovelike sounds of endearment that needed no words. She shifted in his arms and raised her face to be kissed, brushing her warm cheek in passing across the outdoor coolness of a face overlaid by that provocative reminder of maleness: a day-long stubble of beard.

In that first moment of the kiss their lips tantalized, playing upon each other in quick, hungry samplings. He scattered small random kisses at the corners of her mouth and along the curve of her lower lip, catching its fullness softly between his teeth as her fingers played with the feathery edges of his hairline and stroked the outer shell of his ear. When she rubbed the lobe between her forefinger and thumb, a light shudder of arousal telegraphed up his spine to her fingers, and in her own expanding arousal, she touched her tongue to his lips. It was the end of play. Their mouths joined them in a deep, bottomless kiss. To Tulley it was as if they flowed into each other and were one.

Her arms encircled his neck. His hands molded around the curves of her buttocks, and as he pressed her to him she gave her full weight to him, seeking the reality of the body beneath the bulky parka. Forgotten in the ardor of her sensual arousal was her reason for sending him away. She knew only that she wanted to ignore everything that lay between them and lose herself in this man.

During the kiss they strained to find each other until Cass, with a thwarted groan, put an end to it and gently released her.

"Damned parka," he muttered, pulling away to attack the fastener with more haste than care. One impatient yank, and the zipper was stuck.

As if awakening from an erotic dream, Tulley watched for a moment in a kind of daze.

"Could you do something about this blasted zipper?" Cass asked plaintively. "I can't see what I'm doing. It's stuck too close to the top."

Tulley blinked and shook her head in an effort to restore her senses.

"It is a little like hugging a sleeping bag," she admitted shakily.

By the time she had the zipper back on track, the erotic heat within her had cooled, and so had her head. While Cass peeled out of the offending parka, she moved across the room and leaned against the mantelpiece a safe distance away.

The one thing she really wanted to know as he moved toward her was why he had come back. She was surprised to find herself asking a different question in an accusing voice.

"Where have you been?"

"Not now. Later, my love," he said. "First I want you to know I've found out that you are right. The only thing that matters is how we feel about each other. There's nothing between us but you and me."

She could feel the pounding of her heart in her throat. "Are you telling me the McCreadys are declaring peace with the Calhouns?"

"I mean *this* McCready has declared peace," Cass said, moving closer to lay a hand upon her waist, but Tulley put out her own hand and held him off.

"Wait a minute, Cass. How does your family feel about it?"

"It doesn't matter, Tulley. As you pointed out, it's not my problem. I'll tell Aunt Vinnie, and she'll see that the word gets around, but it doesn't really matter."

Tulley's detaining hand pressed lightly against him. "How can you say that until you know how your family will react?"

Cass gazed down at her thoughtfully. "I know myself, Tulley. It doesn't matter to me. But how about you? Would it make a difference if my family showed...well...a certain amount of...resistance?"

Tulley hesitated. "Maybe," she said at last. "It depends upon whether it makes a difference to you."

"Tulley, darling, I've already told you. Don't you believe me? I won't change."

"I believe that's the way you feel now. What I don't believe is that you can really know for sure until you've told them and heard what they have to say."

Cass gave a surprised snort of laughter. "My God, Tulley, do you think there's some kind of McCready family council I'm obliged to appear before? I have relatives all over the county, and they take a lively interest in one another's affairs, but most of them I barely know, and except for a few, I couldn't care less what they think."

"But the few—your aunt, for instance—you do care very much," insisted Tulley.

"Of course I care what Aunt Vinnie thinks, but the point is, it's completely irrelevant to how I feel about you."

She wanted terribly to believe him, to be sure that an emotional scene with his aunt wouldn't bring in him yet another change of heart.

"I have to be sure." Though it was hardly more than a whisper, her voice was firm.

It brought a dawning look of understanding and an exclamation of disbelief from Cass.

"Tulley...love...it's close to midnight. Be reasonable. You know it will be tomorrow before I can see my aunt."

"I didn't expect you to discuss it with her tonight."

Her palm still lay flat against his chest, distancing him from her. His long arms reached out, and he clasped her shoulders and looked down into her face intently. Through his cotton knit shirt she felt the strong beat of his heart against her palm as she met his eyes unswervingly. After a moment he sighed deeply.

"You really do think my family could cause me to change my mind," he said in the dull voice of reluctant concession. When she didn't deny it, he sighed again and pulled her head into the curve of his neck, burying his face in the soft mist of her hair.

"There's nothing more I can say to you, Tulley," he said dispiritedly then after a long moment added, "except good night."

Her head came up from his shoulder. "You're leaving?" But she'd known, of course, that he would. "We haven't talked."

"You ask too much of my willpower, my lady. I'll be back tomorrow after I've seen Aunt Vinnie. The way I feel now, my control's not up to an evening that offers nothing but talk," he said a bit grimly. He walked away from her to pick up his parka from the newel post of the stairway where he'd hung it. Following him, Tulley was dimly aware of an ephemeral whisper of reason nagging for attention...something she should tell him before he was gone.

At the foot of the stairs he turned back to her suddenly and caught her in his arms, holding her to him so tightly she could scarcely breathe, driving everything from her mind but the play of his body on hers.

"Oh, Cass, please..." But she couldn't think what she was about to ask him as her body quickened to his hard, hungry embrace. As if by an act of will, he let her go, still holding her lightly, his arms encircling her waist.

"I'm going now," he said hoarsely, "but the time's not far off when I'll ask you to let me sleep in my old bed again. Give a lot of thought to your answer, Tulley, because I'm dead serious about this. When we climb these stairs together, it won't be for a one-night stand."

His words filled her with a suffocating joy that left her breathless and unable to speak as he walked away from her. He opened the door and looked out. A driving rain slanted fiercely onto her small stoop. Quickly he shut the door again and thrust himself into the parka. As he unrolled the hood from where it was tucked under the collar and started to pull it over his head, Tulley watched with a feeling of helplessness, wanting desperately for him to stay, yet knowing what she would have to withhold if he did.

What an irony! She was sending him away after a whole day spent wanting... Suddenly she knew what that nagging whisper was telling her to remember.

"Cass, wait a minute. I really have something I've got to tell you." It took effort to hide all hints of the sensual yearning that still burned within. She tried for a crisp practical tone that would imply no unmeant promise.

Cass turned to look at her curiously before he pushed back the hood of the parka and slid the zipper down to let it hang open.

"Sit down and take off the parka. It'll take a minute," she said. "While you were gone, I found out some things you should know."

He seated himself with a kind of caution on the edge of the love seat, as if ready to spring to his feet and away. Tulley sat down beside him, curling her bare feet under her for warmth.

"I was right about the libel," she said triumphantly. "There's more to it than just Lamarr."

Cass eyed her skeptically. "I'm all ears. Tell me what."

Tulley frowned. "I wish I knew. It's all such a scramble. That's why I need your help."

Beginning with her evening with Drummond, she quickly went through the conversation between them on the way home from Raleigh and was gratified to see Cass's face respond with growing interest. When she came to the end, he let out a low whistle.

"So Drummond was in on it! That still doesn't prove Lamarr didn't make up the insinuations."

"I think it does. Drummond's sure Lamarr based what he printed on something he found out and took for fact," Tulley insisted. "I'd swear he was telling the truth, but he may have been lying when he said he didn't actually know what Lamarr knew."

"Which doesn't put us much further ahead than we were before," Cass said with disgust. "We're sure as hell not going to find out from Drummond what Lamarr was going on."

"Maybe that's where the tapes come in," Tulley said smugly, with wicked timing.

"Tapes?"

She told him then about the recording device she'd found secreted beneath her uncle's desk. "If somebody said something incriminating about you in his office, it would be like insurance to have it on tape— particularly if Lamarr didn't really trust his source," she finished.

Cass nodded in stunned agreement. "Right. If the person later backed out and claimed he'd never said it, Lamarr could hold the record of the conversation over his head." He sat for a moment in thought then reached over and grabbed her face between his hands and gave her a resounding kiss.

"I think you're on to something, Miss Marple!" he said exuberantly.

"Miss Marple, indeed. Define your terms! I'm not *that* old," Tulley said with an offended sniff.

"Or that plump. But honey, you're sure that smart," he said, getting to his feet and reaching down to pull her up beside him. "Let's go after the tapes."

Tulley groaned. "My best guess is they're someplace in his house, and it has more trash in it than an open landfill."

"When do we start?"

"I'd planned to ask Sam to go over with me tomorrow afternoon if he has time. How about giving me a call, and you can meet us there?"

Their earlier sexual tension forgotten for the moment in the intrigue of their common cause, they moved together to the door, their arms around each other. He stopped to lay his cheek against her hair and place a kiss on the top of her head. He was out the door when she called to him.

"Cass, wait." He looked back to find she was not in the doorway where he'd expected to see her. A moment later she appeared again, the flowered jambalaya tureen cradled in her arms.

"How about taking this family heirloom back to your aunt? I'd just as soon it wasn't held against me, along with everything else," she said.

She leaned across the fat porcelain bowl between them and kissed him with the sudden fury of passion contained—a hard kiss flat on the mouth.

CHAPTER THIRTEEN

WHEN THE BIG WEB PRESS began to roll out the first edition of the day's *Herald* the next morning, Tulley went back to her office and called Sam Matthews. The lawyer's curiosity about the recording device under Lamarr's desk was evident, and he agreed to go with her to her late uncle's house to look for the tapes at four that afternoon. Stifling her impatience, she went looking for Ed Dawes to discuss the proposed changes she'd worked on throughout the long Sunday.

She returned to her desk with growing restlessness, Cass never far from her mind. Why hadn't he phoned? By now he'd talked to his aunt. Had it gone so badly he couldn't bring himself to call? Like worry beads on a string, she anxiously rolled her doubts over and over in her mind.

Turning to the video terminal, she asked Charlie Kettleman if he could spare a few minutes to see her then climbed the stairs to his office.

"Have you noticed that except for sports the *Herald* isn't paying much attention to the young people in the Hilby schools? I think we should, if for no other reason than that most of them are potential subscribers."

Charlie nodded thoughtfully. "That makes sense. If they form the habit of reading the *Herald* when they're in high school, it's reasonable to presume they will subscribe to it when they become adults. Have you something specific in mind?''

''Yes, but I need your help. Well, what I really want is your permission to ask for your son's help.''

''Scotty? He'd leap at the chance, I have no doubt, but I must confess I'm at a loss to imagine what good he could be to you.''

''We need someone who sees things from a kid's point of view.''

Kettleman shook his head dubiously. ''I don't know, Tulley. He's up to here in adolescence right now, and he's cocky, and he doesn't know a damn thing about newspaper reporting except what he sees on TV.''

''He's also eager and very bright, and he can be taught,'' argued Tulley. ''That little piece he did for Ed on the game the other night shows a lot of originality, and he also knows how to spell and punctuate.''

''What are you thinking of having him do?'' the father asked cautiously.

''Help us with a section of the paper for young people once a week,'' said Tulley. ''School news and pictures, current school-ground fads and foibles, features about people and things kids are interested in. Scotty could be kind of our roving reporter and maybe do a gossipy column every week.''

''Who do you propose to put in charge?''

''Oh, Ed and I'll be in charge,'' she assured him. ''You and Emily both say he doesn't have enough to keep him busy. I guarantee, this will take up the slack.''

Kettleman pushed back his chair and got to his feet. ''I don't want you to think I'm unappreciative, Tulley, but I'm afraid you're letting your heart rule your head. Suppose he doesn't work out?''

"O ye of little faith!" Tulley said. "Why shouldn't he? I'm not going to throw him in the river to teach him to swim, Charlie. I expect to work with him myself until I'm sure he knows what he's doing and what will be expected of him. Then I'll turn him over to Ed Dawes, and he'll be under the keen eye of Ed the same as everyone else on the news staff."

"What's Ed going to say about this added responsibility?"

"I've already talked it over with him, and it's as much his idea as mine. He's all for it."

"I'll talk it over with Emily tonight," he said. "If she's agreeable, I suppose it will be all right."

"Good. Let me know what you decide, but if you don't mind, I'd rather you didn't mention it to Scott. Ed and I still have the format to work out, and besides, it will sound more official if it comes from me rather than Dad."

Downstairs in her office again, Tulley picked up the phone and dialed her mother's number in Connecticut to make up for her failure to make her usual weekend call. Her mother had an uncanny ear for nuances of trouble in her daughter's voice, and Tulley had wanted to spare her the sound of discouragement that had darkened her mood until Cass's visit the night before.

"Tulley, darling! You do sound as chirpy as a chipmunk this morning," her mother greeted her affectionately. "I take it all's well in the land of sorghum and grits."

"Better than just well. All's marvelous," Tulley said, taking pleasure, as always, in the sound of the dry, humorous voice at the other end of the line. How lucky she was to have a mother she liked better than her best friend, she thought as they settled into their customary weekly exchange: a potpourri of fact and foolishness that kept mother and daughter abreast of each other's lives.

As the conversation drew to a close, Tulley said suddenly, "By the way, when you and Dad lived in Hilby, did you happen to know the McCreadys?"

"The name sounds familiar. One of the old families, I think, but honestly, Tul', I never got to know anybody in Hilby during the two and a half years I was there," her mother said. "Your father and I met in college, you know, and then there was the war. Lamarr made a hash of the paper while your father was away, and rather than try to defend the *Herald* to people I might meet, I just lay low while we lived there."

"That doesn't sound like you, Mom," Tulley said curiously.

"I suppose not," her mother admitted, "but you have to understand that I was pregnant with you and sick the whole nine months, and your poor father was going through hell with Lamarr. Neither one of us had any heart for socializing until we moved up here when you were two. What about these McCreadys, hon'?"

"Oh, nothing. Well, yes.... There's this man..."

"...you find interesting, and his name's McCready," her mother finished for her when Tulley came to a stop and showed no sign she was about to go on. "Tell me about it, sweetie, and don't leave out a thing."

Tulley laughed shakily. "I find him *very* interesting..."

"Yes?" prompted her mother.

"Dear, nosy Mother, that's all there is. There isn't any more."

"Elizabeth Tulley Calhoun!"

Tulley sighed. "I promise, if anything comes of it, you'll be the first to know." And she finished with what had become, through the years, their ritual sign-off. "Love you, Mom."

And over the wires from a few hundred miles to the north, the wry, loving voice of her mother replied, "I love you, Tul'."

TULLEY WENT BACK to her work with a growing fear that Cass's meeting with his aunt had gone badly. As noontime approached, she debated whether to skip lunch and stay at her desk to answer the phone if he called or, as had become her practice, lunch uptown in one of several restaurants and cafés, each of which drew a different group of regulars. The lunch crowds had begun to recognize her and to invite her to share a table. In an oblique way she'd been given to understand that printing Cass's remarks about the libel had done much to relieve the burden of being related to Lamarr.

Reluctant to leave her desk, she caught Ed Dawes as he left to pick up a sandwich for himself from a nearby deli and asked him to bring back something for her.

"I don't care what kind of sandwich . . . and a glass of milk, please," she said indifferently.

The tension of waiting that had filled the morning with uncertainty made her heartily sick of her own company, and when Ed came back with two brown bags a short time later, she asked him to pull up a chair and join her.

Her anxieties were lost in the unfailing pleasures of talking shop, and Tulley forgot for a while the call she'd been waiting for all morning. The phone rang twice before she reached for it. By the time she lifted the receiver to her ear, her heart was pounding fiercely in her breast. She was vaguely surprised that her hand was steady, considering the sudden trembling that had arisen within her.

"Tulley Calhoun speaking," she said breathlessly.

"I love you, Tulley Calhoun," said the voice she'd been anxious to hear—the most heart-stopping voice in the world. His words took her by surprise. *Oh, Cass, don't say it. Please, darling, don't say it...unless you are sure.*

She felt paralyzed, totally unprepared for the unexpected declaration. She looked helplessly at the stubby figure of Ed Dawes across from her, munching unconcernedly on a Swiss-on-rye, then back at the phone.

"Tulley? Are you there?" Cass asked across the distance, from wherever he was.

"I...yes, I'm here," Tulley said when she could find the words.

"Did you hear me? I said I love you."

"I heard." Her voice was barely a whisper.

"You *do* believe—"

"I...I do. I'm not sure why. You did talk to...?"

"Aunt Vinnie. Yes."

"Cass! Tell me!" she cried, forgetting Dawes, whose head came up at the sound of the name. Suddenly flustered, she said formally, for the benefit of Ed, "Or perhaps you'd prefer another time."

"Someone's with you?"

"Yes."

"Can you meet me at the carriage house in fifteen minutes?"

She hesitated, suddenly afraid to hear what he had to tell her. But did it matter? He'd said he loved her. She realized then that therein lay much of the cause of her panic. Love with Cass was something she'd never let herself consider. She needed time to think, time to be sure she was ready to say the same to him in return.

"I can't. I'm sorry. There's too much to be done here before four, which is when Sam Matthews and I are going to go through that mess at Lamarr's house."

"It's all right if I come, too?"

"If you still want to. I wasn't sure . . ."

"You mean about my talk with Vinnie. . . . It's a long story that I'll tell you when we have time alone together, but as I said last night, it's irrelevant."

"Irrelevant?"

"Irrelevant to the fact that I love you."

"Oh, Cass . . ."

"See you around four, then? And Tulley . . ."

"Yes?"

"I love you." The line went dead.

AFTER HE LEFT HER the night before, Cass had slept the sleep of emotional and physical exhaustion and had awakened in a sensual explosion, with Tulley's name on his lips. He was filled with the delicious illusion she'd been in his arms the moment before.

Then the reality of the morning intruded. Cass checked the time and saw it was eight o'clock. He lay back on his pillow and campaigned the day ahead. He didn't welcome the upcoming conversation with his aunt and after some consideration decided not to start the day with it. Not because he wanted to postpone it—once he'd made up his mind he wanted only to get it behind him—but because he knew his Aunt Vinnie. Until she'd had two cups of coffee and breakfast, Vinnie was not at her tractable best.

He dressed and slipped quietly out of the house so as not to disturb her and drove across town to the

mobile unit that housed the Hilby office of Mc-
Cready & Co., General Contractors. There he set the
coffee brewing and rolled out the blueprints and specifications for the new Hilby County hospital he was
preparing to bid on.

It was after ten o'clock when he greeted his aunt in
the kitchen, where he found her shuffling through a
handful of letters the mailman had just left.

"Cass, honey, when did you get back?" she asked,
offering her cheek for his peck. "Here's a letter from
your mother. You had your breakfast? Read it. I'm
dyin' to hear when she's coming home."

Oh, God, he'd completely forgotten his fragile
mother. No matter how dead set Vinnie might be
against his relationship with Tulley, she wouldn't get
sick over it—which wasn't necessarily true of his
mother. Matters that affected her emotionally had,
more often than not, sent her to bed with a migraine,
and the accident that killed his father had left her
deeply depressed—a condition her extended stay
abroad had greatly relieved, judging from her letters
and the occasional long-distance call.

Apprehension knotted his stomach. He'd grown up
protecting his mother. Would the development between him and Tulley plunge her into a state of
depression again?

Aunt Vinnie, who hadn't waited for answers to her
questions, was already moving back and forth between the stove and the refrigerator. The first aroma
of frying ham, usually so tantalizing, reached his nostrils and met with indifference. He knew suddenly that
he had to have the whole thing out in the open before
he could face food.

"Put it on the back burner for a while, will you,
Vinnie," he said to his aunt in a tight voice that

sounded strange to his own ears. It brought her head around, and she peered at him with a troubled look. "I've got something to talk to you about. I wouldn't mind a cup of coffee, if you have it."

"Something happen up there at the shack, Cass?" she asked anxiously as she poured coffee for them into fragile Haviland cups that Cass took from her and carried to the breakfast table. He held out a chair for his aunt before he took one across from her.

"There was a little weather going on, that's all." He paused, deciding how to approach the subject, then plunged in headfirst. "How would you take it, Vinnie, if I told you I'm interested in the niece of Lamarr Calhoun?"

"You serious, Cass?"

"I wouldn't go to the trouble of asking if I wasn't serious."

"I don't recall you ever askin' anyone's approval of a lady you happened to take a shine to before," his aunt said.

"I'm not asking for anyone's approval now. All I'm asking for is your opinion, and how it'll set with the rest of the family."

His aunt gazed at him with puzzled eyes. "If you're not lookin' for approval, Cass, why you askin'?"

"She wants to know."

"Why in the world would she care what any of us think, if she likes you?"

It was going to be harder than he expected. Cass groaned inwardly and forged ahead.

"It's complicated, but believe me, she cares. You might say she wants to know how much hostility she's going to have to contend with, getting mixed up with me," he answered grimly.

His aunt looked genuinely confused. "Hostility? I haven't met the young lady myself, I'm sorry to say. I was coming down with a cold and missed the meeting the day Caroline took her to the Garden Club, but I hear nothing but praise."

"There's nothing about her not to praise," said Cass. "But that's not what I'm talking about. It's who she is."

"She's Lamarr's niece, and we all know Lamarr was as mean as a water moccasin. But, Cass, you can't hold Lamarr's meanness against an innocent young woman. It looks like she's doing all she can to straighten out what he did to you in the paper. If she's not holding your libel suit against you, looks like it'd be uncharitable for us to hold the sins of Lamarr against her."

"Forget Lamarr. I'm talking about the rest of the Calhouns."

His aunt gave a disdainful sniff. "If you mean one rotten apple in the barrel spoils the rest, I never did believe that applies to people."

"It's not just Lamarr, Vinnie. He wasn't the first Calhoun to try to destroy a McCready. I don't have to remind you the two families have always been enemies. I'll never forget—"

Aunt Vinnie leaned forward in her chair to lay a hand on Cass's arm, a strange look on her face.

"Cass, honey, where in the world did you get an idea like that?"

"I've grown up *knowing* it. Didn't everybody? If for no other reason, there was Grandfather."

"I'd almost forgot," his aunt said in a shocked voice. "It appears to me, Cass, you spent too much time with poor Daddy when you were too young to understand. He was a sick old man, your grandfather. Until Lamarr came along, any problem between the McCreadys and the Calhouns was what he imagined. I never realized you didn't understand what was going on at that time.''

So from his Aunt Vinnie, nearly thirty years after the fact, Cass learned that his grandfather was brought down from the bench not by a Calhoun, but by the ravages of advanced senility; he learned that his own father had given the McCready family support to Tulley's grandfather in the *Herald*'s campaign to elect the old judge's opponent in that final election.

''Why didn't anyone tell me that what he was saying was all in his head?'' Cass asked in dismay when she was through. ''I had a right to know.''

''You were only a boy, Cass, and you worshiped your granddaddy. I reckon we felt a need to protect you, or that you wouldn't understand, or that it would cause you to shy away from an old man who thought the sun rose and set on you. Or maybe it just never occurred to anyone to explain it to you. I don't remember exactly what. By the time you were older, nobody wanted to remember the awful deterioration of that noble mind. I don't know as I recall hearing any of us bring it up unless we were obliged to, and even then we'd turn away from it as quick as we could. Come to think of it, I don't recall you ever askin', Cass.''

''Asking? Why would I? I took it for granted McCreadys hated Calhouns like Grandpa said, and it wasn't something to be talked about. With Lamarr the only Calhoun in the county, it wasn't hard to believe...until Tulley came along,'' Cass said thoughtfully.

He understood now why, during the last year the judge was on the bench, his parents wouldn't let him go to the Outer Banks with his grandfather alone. He'd fought them about it bitterly. His grandfather had tried to sneak him away once, and the state police had stopped them just outside of town and brought him back.

"You'd think somebody would have stopped him from driving up there to the shack by himself," he said after a minute, remembering his grief when he'd been told the old man's car had crashed through a guard-rail and plunged down an embankment on the way to the Outer Banks, and that his grandfather was dead.

"Did you ever hear of anybody stopping your granddaddy from doin' something he was set to do?" his aunt asked with pride.

ON THE CHANCE that Cass might arrive at Lamarr's ahead of time and they could catch a few minutes alone to talk, Tulley pulled into the driveway of the house early. As she stepped out of the big car that she still couldn't think of as hers, Cass's car rounded the corner at the end of the block. She hurried to the curb to meet him. Her heart pounded the exuberant welcome Cass's appearance always aroused in her, but before she could call out a greeting, the sight of Sam Matthews's car right behind him brought a slowing of her pulse.

While Sam was maneuvering his stout body out of his car, Cass came up beside her. In the early winter gray of the lowering gloom, the blue of his eyes seemed as pure as the sun-drenched sky of summer, and there was a look in his strong irregular face she'd never seen before, as if some secret celebration was going on inside him. At the same time she saw a kind of peace.

What had gone on between him and his aunt to-day? Was this the look of a man who had cut himself loose from family ties for the woman he loved? Was there something of self-discovery in his gaze? Suddenly she felt a heaviness within her; she did not want to tear Cass away from the very roots that had made him what he was.

"Cass, tell me quickly. What did your aunt say?" she asked quietly, urgently.

"There's no way to tell you fast. There's too much to it. It'll have to wait till later when we're alone. Don't worry. Everything's all right. I love you."

There was no time for more. Sam Matthews was within earshot, rattling the house keys as he hurried up the walk with the graceful light-footed steps that sometimes go with weight, calling for them to follow.

In spite of clutter beyond a pawnbroker's wildest nightmare, the search went faster than any of them expected. There was a surprising limit to the number of places where tapes might be concealed. Matthews began with the ancient oak rolltop desk, which he emptied methodically, drawer by drawer, while Cass looked behind all the books in the numerous shelves and foraged through two oak file cabinets. Tulley left the front room to the men and searched through the drawers in the other rooms, including the bathroom and the kitchen.

At the end of three hours there was no place left to search except among the waist-high stacks of news-papers and magazines that took up much of the floor space. Tulley looked around her in disgust.

"I'm about ready to give up. Maybe there aren't any tapes," she said crossly. From where he bent over a bulging file cabinet, Cass glanced at her and reached into a jacket pocket for a large bag of salted peanuts.

"Catch," he said, tossing them to her. "Eat a handful. Things will look better."

Tulley pulled the peanuts out of the air and looked at them then eyed Cass suspiciously.

"Do you always carry peanuts in your pocket?" she asked, breaking open the bag with her teeth and emptying a fistful into her hand.

"Just since I got to know you better," he said with an innocent grin that made her heart do a sudden tango. Handing the bag to Matthews, she said aloud, "Have some peanuts, Sam. Cass thinks if he doesn't feed the animals, we'll pass out on him, and he'll have to finish the job alone."

Cass said, "Cass thinks Sam should go home to his lovely wife, who is no doubt waiting with dinner, and you and I should get a hamburger at the bowling alley and come back here and look for the damn tapes until we find them."

As if on cue, the front door opened and in walked Caroline Matthews, dressed in country-club casuals and not a hair out of place, loaded down with a huge basket. Tulley caught a look of complacence on Sam's face.

"Looks like you're still at it," Caroline said, relinquishing the basket to Cass. "Just find a clear place to set it down, will you, Cass, honey?" And then to Tulley, who was watching, mentally agape, she said, "Sam said if he wasn't back by seven to come and bring y'all something to eat." She turned to Sam again. "I brought along a little bourbon. I reckon what runs out of Lamarr's tap is as good a substitute for branch-water as what runs out of ours."

Warmed by bourbon and "branch," the foursome sat around Lamarr Calhoun's kitchen table and ate fried chicken and biscuits and a variety of other prov-

ender from Caroline's basket, which also gave forth a
blue linen tablecloth, four china plates, four crystal
tumblers and four place settings of antique sterling
marked with an "H" for Hilby—passed down to
Caroline from a great-aunt who married a Hilby and
went to her grave childless.

Dawdling to postpone the unfinished job, they
cleaned up the lemon chess pie and emptied the coffee thermos and worried about the limited areas still
left to search while Caroline wandered off into the
front room to explore.

"You suppose he could have hid them someplace in
the car?" Tulley asked suddenly.

From the other room Caroline called out, "Sam,
honey, this old desk of Lamarr's is just like the one my
granddaddy used to let me play with when I was a little girl."

"Mmm," mumbled Sam in absent reply.

"I bet this is where he hid them," Caroline's voice
rambled on. "If it was me—"

"You would, sweetheart, but unfortunately you're
not Lamarr," said her husband with a kind of doting
patience as he rose to his feet and moved toward the
other room. "I took everything out of that desk, piece
by piece, and there was nary a thing, except the junk
in that box there on the floor."

"You sure, Sam? Granddaddy's desk had a..."
Caroline's voice tapered off.

From the doorway Tulley watched curiously as the
woman thrust a plump, well-manicured, beringed
hand into the shadowy recesses of the desk.

"You're just going to get your arm all dirty, Caroline. I been all through..." Matthews was saying
mildly when a back panel in the desk fell away under

his wife's hand, and he broke off with a gasp of astonishment.

Caroline gave a triumphant crow. "Sure enough. There it is, the secret panel. I bet it's the exact same desk. Granddaddy let it go to some second-hand store, and I bet Lamarr bought it."

From out of the depths of the big oak desk, Caroline withdrew her hand, her fingers folded around a thin plastic oblong object Tulley recognized as a tape.

"This what you been lookin' for, Sam?"

She reached in again and pulled out another and then another and handed them over to her spouse. One by one, in front of three pairs of astonished eyes, Caroline dredged up a total of thirteen tapes before she hit bottom.

"That's the end of them," she announced as she handed the last tape to Sam. Still, as if reluctant to leave her treasure trove, she reached into the secret compartment one more time. "Wait a minute. Here's something else," she said, pulling forth a white envelope and passing it to Matthews.

From it he took a single sheet of paper that he examined for a moment before he gave a grunt of satisfaction and handed it on to Tulley.

"Just what we've been looking for," he said. "The secret agreement that made Lamarr a silent partner in Drummond's development scheme."

CHAPTER FOURTEEN

"I CAN THINK of a lot of things I'd rather be doing than listening to this dismal rubbish. Going to the dentist, for one," Tulley said as Cass slipped another cassette into the tape recorder they'd brought with them from Lamarr's.

They were at the carriage house—Tulley, Cass and Sam—where they'd fled gratefully from the emptiness in that other cluttered house once Caroline had found what they were looking for. Caroline had gone to a meeting of the hospital board, leaving the three to thaw out in front of a cheerful fire while they explored the suspect tapes.

They had listened to six of the tapes and found them to be, for the most part, acrimonious exchanges between voices identified by Sam as Shelby Haynes and Lamarr, punctuated with bits of salacious gossip from Haynes, and scandalous complaints poured into Lamarr's listening ear by assorted malcontents bent on making trouble for someone else.

"He didn't actually use any of this in the paper, did he?" she asked as the seventh of the thirteen tapes began to roll.

"Some of it," Sam said acidly. "It's my guess that whether he did or not, Lamarr enjoyed hearing folks run other folks down about as much as anything that ever reached his ears."

"Shhh," murmured Cass as a voice came on the tape. "Listen! I know that voice."

It had come up suddenly out of a scramble of noises, as if whoever turned the recorder on had accidentally fumbled in trying to do it unobserved.

"...so I told him what he could do with the job." It was a high-pitched male voice caught in midsentence. "If he wanted to make his bundle putting in sleazy wiring in place of what the county was paying him for, 'well, get yourself another man,' I said."

A second voice came on the tape. Sam said tensely, "That's Lamarr."

"And what did Cass McCready say to that?"

"He said, 'Don't think I won't!'"

A muttered expletive escaped from Cass.

"Figured out who it is, Cass?" Sam asked. Cass nodded grimly, but before he could speak, a third voice sounded.

"If you can get people believing McCready propositioned a subcontractor to cheat the county on the annex wiring, Lamarr, he'll lose what clout he has at city hall. When the variance comes before the council on appeal, I'll butter them up, and we'll be in-like-Flynn."

"Leo Drummond!" Tulley said.

The first voice, anxious now, said, "Hey, listen, you guys, I don't want my name dragged into it. Drummond, you promised."

Lamarr: I reckon we can keep you anonymous, Swift. Leo, you see to it that it gets whispered around town for a couple of weeks, and when we see we've got it well spread, we can slip references in the paper to the rumors that are going around. It'll be easy enough then to quote "sources who ask to remain unnamed for fear of reprisals."

Drummond: What about libel? If McCready didn't go through with the scam, he could decide to sue.

Lamarr: I don't want to know if he did or he didn't, Drummond, as long as we've got enough to make it appear he did. To go the whole way would mean dragging in the building inspector and the subcontractor who actually did the electrical work, and that's too risky. We could wind up with a grand jury investigation on our hands, when all I'm after is to get McCready tied up.

Drummond: What makes you think McCready won't sue you for libel?

Lamarr: Don't worry. I'll take care of it so there won't be anything he can get a handle on. If I know McCready, he'll lean on me to print a retraction. I'll hold off until we get the variance from the council. Let him sue. Long before it gets to court, we'll have got what we want. Hell, once we've got that variance, I can be big about it. I'll tell him I'll print the retraction if he'll drop the libel suit.

There the conversation ended and the tape rolled on to the voice of an unrecognizable husband pouring out the details of a neighbor's affair with his wife. Cass switched off the recorder. Tulley let out an explosive sigh.

"Why, they sound like a bunch of coon-dogs bayin' after a treed coon," murmured Sam disbelievingly, his Southern accent thick in the stress of the moment.

Cass gave him a wry grin. "No thanks for the analogy, old friend! This treed coon is about to take off after the dogs. That other voice is Jack Swift, an electrical subcontractor I had on the first big contract I got. Later he put in a bid on the annex wiring and made me the same proposition he just accused me of making to him."

Tulley jumped to her feet and flung her arms around Cass's neck, hugging him ecstatically.

Matthews watched them broodingly. After a minute he said, "You're not thinkin' of printing any of this in the paper, are you, Tulley?"

She withdrew her arms from Cass's neck and stood beside him, one arm linked loosely through his, the glow on her face undimmed by the lawyer's discouraging tone.

She gazed at him thoughtfully. "I don't know, Sam. It would make me feel good to come up with something we could print, but I'm not sure that we've got anything we can use."

"All I see here is Jack Swift saying that Cass did just about what Lamarr had implied in the paper," Matthews said dourly. "You now have a flesh-and-blood accuser. The tape proves the three plotted to malign Cass, but I reckon it'd do Cass more harm than good to break into print with it now."

Tulley nodded after a moment and shrugged regretfully. "Oh, well, I don't mind having to wait awhile to go public with it. The important thing is we've got proof of a conspiracy. We know who's out to get Cass and why. Until now, we haven't known where to start."

"Tulley's right," Cass said. "Between her conversation with Drummond and this tape, her conspiracy theory suddenly makes sense."

"Thank goodness! I suppose if we hadn't discovered the 'smoking gun,' I never would have gotten your attention," Tulley said a bit caustically.

Cass let it pass, plainly too caught up in his own ruminations to comment.

"I'd like to know what Leo Drummond was up to before he came to Hilby," Cass said, "and how he and

Jack Swift got together, and what brought about that meeting between the three of them. Lamarr obviously taped it to make sure Swift couldn't back down and say he never said it."

"It looks like the one who has a grudge against you was not my uncle, Cass, but this fellow Swift," she couldn't resist pointing out to him.

"Could be. I landed on him with both feet on that annex business. I'm not surprised he wants to put me out of commission," Cass said. "Jack grew up in Hilby, but I never knew him until he came back about three years ago. He'd been away from Hilby ten years or so. One of the reasons I hired him for that supermarket job was to give a local fellow who'd come back a new start."

"Some start!" Tulley said with a sniff of disdain.

Smiling now for the first time since he had started listening to the final tape, Sam Matthews heaved himself out of the deep chair where he sat and onto his feet with a gentle grunt.

"It's late, and I expect Caroline's home from her meeting. If you'll excuse me, I'll be gettin' back to my bride," he said on a swallowed yawn. "You folks seem to have things under control. In any case, I don't reckon you need me around for whatever you got in mind from here on out."

"I suppose someone should listen to the rest of the tapes in case there's something more, but I'd hate to sit through any more of Lamarr's ... garbage," Tulley said, following him to the door.

"Give 'em to me. I'll go through them when I have time," Sam said amiably. "I'm used to Lamarr."

Gratefully Tulley loaded the machine and tapes into his arms. "Thank you, Sam."

From the open doorway they watched the bulky figure of the lawyer move quickly across the lawn toward his house, his bald pate reflecting light from the full moon. Yesterday's storm had moved on. The night was cold and crystal clear.

Tulley gave an involuntary shiver. Cass wrapped his arms around her and lifted her back from the threshold. He slipped an arm across her shoulders and turned her toward the stairs, but they went only a step or two together before Tulley stiffened in sudden resistance and came to a stop. He looked down at her quizzically, turned a significant glance up the stairway and looked back at her face again. In a small test of will they gazed into each other's eyes for a long, hypnotic moment.

It would be so easy to give in, thought Tulley. So easy for her to climb the stairs with him and later listen while in bed and in his arms to what he had to tell her—listen to what, she thought uncertainly, she might be sorry to hear. She raised her chin and slowly shook her head. Up to this point they'd carried on a dialogue without words.

"First we talk," she said. "I've got to know if you've been read out of the McCready family because of me, Cass, before—"

"I said everything's all right, and I love you, didn't I? If that's all that's worrying you, we can talk another time."

All at once she felt like the bystander to a joke she wasn't in on. The uncertainties of the past twenty-four hours suddenly overwhelmed her. She was afraid of the tears that sprang suddenly to her eyes.

"Dammit, Cass. Don't do this to me!" she flared. "It's not something I feel like joking about. It . . . it . . . matters to me . . . a lot!" In spite of herself, her voice broke and Cass pulled her to him, scattering kisses on her head, murmuring endearments into her hair.

Tears were an indulgence Tulley seldom succumbed to in her adult life. It was a moment before she was in full control of the ducts and voice that betrayed her. She made an effort to wriggle free, but Cass held her firmly and tipped her head up to look again into her face. The tenderness and distress she saw in his eyes caught at her heart. She felt the tears near the surface again and knew if she didn't hold them back, there would be no stopping them this time. Two work-roughened fingers brushed lightly across her cheek, wiping away the moisture that had spilled over a moment ago.

"I said I love you. Don't you believe me?"

"I . . . Yes, I believe you, Cass."

"Then why—"

"When you say you love me, I believe you. But what am I to believe when you tell me everything's all right?" she said, carefully choosing her words. "I suppose that means in spite of the fact that your family is unhappy with our . . . relationship . . . or whatever it is, you still love me."

"Tulley. . . . Oh, my God! It never occurred to me you didn't understand. Dear love, what have I put you through?"

She put her fingers to his lips and shut off the flow of his words. "No, Cass . . . please. Let me finish while I still have the nerve to say it. It's not that, so much, that bothers me," she said and made no attempt to keep her worry out of her voice. "It's the . . . *headiness* I keep hearing in your voice today, as if you'd just found out that the trunk full of paper in the attic isn't Confederate money, but Treasury Bills. Cass, are you sure you haven't been looking for an excuse to set yourself free from family pressures grown tedious to a man of thirty-four?''

"Oh, my God!" he said again quietly in a voice of disbelief. She had thought he wouldn't accept it, but she hadn't expected him to look so utterly stunned. He stared down at her, speechless. Gradually his expression lightened, and he laughed—a short, quiet, self-deprecating laugh.

"What a thick-headed klutz I am," he declared, his voice regretful and dry. "I might have guessed the most complex woman I've ever known would read something complex into that simple message. When I said 'I love you' and 'Everything's all right,' that was exactly what I meant. The McCreadys don't hate the Calhouns and never have."

Like the sough of a night breeze, Tulley's breath escaped her lips. "Well, for heaven's sake, why didn't you say so this morning?"

"Over the phone? You'd never have let it go at that, and there's no short way to tell you what Vinnie told me today. You have to know background that goes back thirty years."

She waited. He said no more. She knew he was waiting, too; he was waiting for her to say the story could wait, willing it with the impelling blue of his eyes that kindled the latent flame deep within. Yet, instinctively, she knew it was the right time for them to talk it out. If she let it slip by, some of it might be forgotten and left untold at a later time.

Slowly she shook her head. A sigh rose from his throat.

"It's a long story," he said again. "I'd hoped we could . . . No." Turning away from the staircase, he moved with her across the room.

"You are right, I suppose," he said, though a shadow of regret still hung in his voice. "It's better to talk it all out now and then forget it, because, my love, when you and I climb those stairs I don't want any distractions. It won't do to have part of you off, searching for meanings, while the rest of you tries to make love."

Still standing, he watched her settle into the plump down-cushioned lap of the sofa by the fireplace, and his strong face softened with desire. To the woman looking up at him, the irregular features seemed for the first time to have a kind of beauty.

"I may as well throw a log on the fire," he said absently. "We may be here awhile." As the fire flared up, he reached to turn off the light and let himself down beside her on the sofa. Tulley curled up next to him and settled into the curve of his arm.

"I have to tell you about my grandfather first," he said after a minute's silence. "None of the rest of it makes sense unless you understand about him."

In the bright light from the blazing fire a picture began to emerge for Tulley. A picture of the boy Cass had been: a restless only child in a houseful of grown-ups; not unloved or neglected in any sense, simply overlooked by everyone except wise, wonderful Judge McCready. Cass had been merely a spectator in the endless crises of a failing tobacco empire that left his parents with nothing of themselves to give to their child.

Tulley saw the glow of remembered happiness in Cass's eyes as he spoke of the shack and the Outer Banks and fishing with his grandfather on the sound; and the books and songs and the harmonica; and the questions that found answers and laughter that turned self-pride and adversity into a joke.

As she listened, she saw his face as a kaleidoscope of shifting emotions: affection, wonder, awe; above all, profound respect and admiration for the aging judge with whom he'd carried on a continuing dialogue throughout the first seven years of his life. Spellbound, she saw him lose himself in recollection of his grandfather's endlessly captivating talk that became a part of the boy for all time. With a kind of dreamy amusement, as if thinking aloud, he recalled that the subject from one day often spilled over into another, taken up in the morning where it was left off the night before.

Small wonder, Tulley marveled, that the boy had endowed this grandfather with an infallibility otherwise enjoyed only by the pope. To the boy, the grandfather was Truth and Honor and Courage and Duty and Loyalty. Many of the very qualities she loved in Cass, she saw, were his legacy from the judge.

Listening, she shared Cass's love for his grandfather, and when Cass spoke of the terrible decline of the proud old man into senility and the stubborn independence that sent him out in his car that last night to his death, he was someone she cared for, and tears rolled down her cheeks once more, unchecked.

In the shadowy darkness of the dying fire they sat in silence, each in his own thoughts. After a while a burning log split with a loud crackle, and as the middle fell into the embers the two ends shot up flames in a last flare of brilliance that lighted the space around them. They could see each other clearly now. She raised a hand to touch his cheek with her fingers.

"Cass...." It was a whisper of sorrow. "Oh, Cass, dear Cass."

"Don't be sad," he said quietly. "As long as he was able, he gave me the best he had. No kid ever had more."

From one of his pockets he pulled out a clean handkerchief and wiped away the path of tears that glistened on her cheeks in the moment of light. Tulley took the handkerchief from him.

"May I?" she asked with dignity and blew her nose.

"Tulley, wonderful Tulley." The words seemed to catch in his throat. "I love you," he said and gathered her into his arms.

Now for the first time she knew for certain...was as sure as she had ever been of anything in her life.

"And...I...love...you," she said and drew out the words to make them last, only to have the final one silenced on her lips by his mouth in a long, confirming kiss that left Tulley breathless and her body reawakened to the man.

For all its satisfactions, the kiss carried her on to frustration. Nothing more came of it. Cass cradled her more closely to him, but though his hand slipped under her sweatshirt, he let it lie there loosely, palm down on the flat plane of her bare belly as if it had no further place to go.

"Vinnie missed the Garden Club last week the day you were there, but she tells me you made a great hit with the ladies," Cass said in a conversational tone, settling back into the cushions with her. "She asked me to bring you around to the house to get acquainted."

So now he wants to talk! Tulley thought helplessly. She said politely, "I'd like that. Now that I'm sure of her welcome, I want to meet her, too." Not yet sure what the game was, she decided two could play it.

"Have you heard when your mother will be coming home?"

"According to this morning's letter, she hopes to be here by Christmas. Majorca has been good for her. She's beginning to sound like herself."

"She still doesn't know about the . . . problems?"

"The libel?"

Tulley nodded. "There isn't any danger she'll have a relapse when she hears what's being said about you?" she asked anxiously.

"Lord almighty, let's hope not! You never know about my mother. Sometimes, when you expect her to be weakest, she comes out very strong."

"What about your aunt?"

"Aunt Vinnie's a rock, right along. They're poles apart, but you'll like them both. Vinnie's a Mc-Cready and my mother's a Hilby . . . best friends from childhood."

As he talked, his hand under the sweatshirt had come to life, and the softly abrasive surface of his callused palm moved across the flat plane of her stomach. His fingers eased under the waistband of her jeans, exploring cautiously to the limit of their reach before withdrawing to tug at the button.

And all the time, he kept talking. "Vinnie'll talk an arm off of you if you let her . . ." The button popped open, and he slid the zipper down far enough to slip in his hand. And still he rambled on, his mind clearly paying little attention to what rolled out of his mouth as his fingers reached the silken triangle and curled into the soft hair they found. In the hidden spot below, a wrench of sweet, hot pain brought a shiver of pleasure in Tulley, and the wellspring that flowed to his touch filled her with a yearning for something more.

As if from far off she heard him saying, "But my mother is a quiet woman. She'll..." His hand pressed hard upon her, and in a strained voice he pleaded, "Oh, God, Tulley. Must I keep talking all night? Haven't you heard enough?"

Dazed though she was by the driving intensity of the past seconds, she realized then that he waited for her to invite him upstairs. She stayed for a moment, quiet under his hand, and then gently disengaged herself and slipped away to stand looking down into his stunned face.

Her voice was still thick with desire when she spoke, but her words were a complete non sequitur. "Take care of the fire screen, please, and don't go away. I'll be right back," she said. Reaching down, she picked up her jogging shoes from where she'd dropped them and walked away from him, across the room and up the stairs.

Still in the grip of the desire he'd kept banked too long, Cass watched her go. He watched the lithe, lovely body in its shapeless gray sweatshirt with a deep sensual pleasure that would not let him turn away. As her bare feet took her across the floor, she seemed quintessentially female. The slight, swinging motion of the two perfectly rounded buttocks under the revealing fit of her jeans brought him halfway to his feet to go after her; then, with a derisive grunt, he sank back onto the sofa. Too bad he'd never been able to convince himself there wasn't something obscene in the male assumption that women should be subject to the whims of men.

What a sorry lot civilization had made of man, he told himself sardonically. In another time, another culture, he might have gone bounding after the woman and carried her off to his cave. Now, he got up and took care of the fire screen as she'd told him to.

I love her! he thought and realized that though he'd imagined himself in love more than once in the past, there was something different, something almost mystical in his feeling for this woman that spelled out the fragile distinction between "loving" and being "in love" that had eluded him before. *In* implied there was an *out* on the other side of the coin. There was no out for him, he knew, in what he felt for Tulley Calhoun.

"Cass . . . ?"

But for the faint embers of the dying fire, the room was in darkness now except for a sliver of light that spilled onto the upstairs landing from the room above. He turned his head to the sound of her voice. For an instant he could see only darkness. Then the ceiling light on the landing came on.

In the pale circle of light she stood straight and un-ashamed, her bare breasts erect and beautiful, as un-self-conscious in her nakedness as a Tahitian princess. Her flesh seemed almost translucent under the over-head light. He caught his breath.

In a few steps he was below her, looking up, close enough to see the shadowed face that looked down upon him and to see the unaccustomed shyness it wore, a kind of diffidence, as if she was uncertain of his approval.

For a moment he could find no words. Then, without his willing it, the key word came to his lips.

"Rapunzel . . . Rapunzel," he called up to her softly.

Laughing, she held out her hand to him. "Come up," she said. Turning from the stair rail, she skimmed across the landing and down the steps to meet him.

Taking the steps three at a time, Cass met her on the third step from the top and, from where he stood on the step below, brought her to a sudden stop. He encircled her small waist with his big hands and held her away from him, reluctant to sully the exquisite perfection of her body against the rough fabrics of his working clothes. She leaned over and one of her breasts brushed his lips.

With a murmur of delight he caught and held it. His tongue circled the small, resilient stem that lifted and firmed in erection out of the soft, curved areola before he took it into his mouth. When she raised her head as if to pull away, he clung lightly with his lips, unwilling to let go. For a moment she let it be his. Then she let herself slip down the front of his body until the soles of her feet came to rest on top of his, and he breathed the faint, erotic woman-smell of her flesh. Heedless of the roughness of his clothing upon her bare skin, she pressed herself against him in a fierce, unflinching hug.

Wild with desire, he clung there precariously on the single step, his senses telling him to slow down. His body was a river at flood stage. He must hold back.

Half carrying her, he urged her up the last steps to the landing and let her go. His mind cried out to his body to relax. She walked on, but he stopped and drew a deep breath, willing himself to slow down.

If they were to be lovers, they must find their pace together, and if he let his passions outrun them this first time it might never happen. Their love could become no more than a succession of frustrations.

After a moment he moved on, stripping off his clothes as he followed her into the familiar bedroom. He tossed his shirt over a chair near the bed. By the time he reached where she was standing near the four-poster, he'd shed the last of his clothing. Now, less than an arm's length from the woman he loved, he sensed a new shyness in her and recognized something akin in himself.

As his eyes devoured her, he felt a moment of something like fear. She was a tall woman whose perfectly rounded body with its long, beautiful bones had a glow of health about it. Now, unclothed, she seemed suddenly like a delicate vase that his own square, hard-muscled body could crush.

He saw her eyes travel slowly over him, too, pause for an instant to consider his flagrant arousal then move unhurriedly on. The hard, steady pounding of his pulse was suddenly like a jackhammer in his chest. Disconcerted, he reached out and touched her breast, still cool from the moisture of his mouth, and stopped, everything else forgotten as she, too, reached out and touched.

Her hand fingered the hollow at his neck, moved down to play at the mat of hair on his chest, tracing a burning path as it went. In the suddenness of a new anticipation, he sucked in his breath and waited.

Her hand went the full length of his torso to touch the upthrust stalk then pull away and touch again. He held his breath, restraining a massive shudder that threatened to tear him apart as her fingers, light as seafoam, curled around it in a cautious embrace. She looked up at him from limpid eyes.

"You know, you are really quite...splendid," she said.

Half frantic with desire, he pulled her into his arms and onto the familiar bed where he once had slept alone. He got control of himself again and let the urgency of his passion slow, fondling her lightly as they whispered words of love until he was sure that he could wait for the right moment to come.

His body half resting on hers, he buried his face in the soft valley of her breasts, smothering himself between the firm fragrant mounds, raising his head at last to shape his mouth around one of the soft curves. He let his hand move down across her dimpled belly, over the sensuous rise of her hips and the small mound beneath the flowering of soft, wiry curls. Within the folds below, his fingers found the gamic center they sought. He felt the ecstatic shiver that coursed through her as he stroked the small tumescent jewel and brought from her a soft moan of rapture.

Trembling now himself, he gently withdrew to quell the hot throbbing in his loins, his fingers silken with the cream of her desire. She caught his head in her hands to offer him her lips, and in her face he saw that there was no more need to hold back.

He took her mouth in a deep, hungry kiss, and when they pulled apart their lips—glossy and swollen with passion—played upon each other for a last moment, whispering small, wordless endearments as she urged his body to come over hers. In a swell of joyous relief, he knew the moment for them had come.

But even when he moved above her, he braced himself on the flat of his hands on either side of her body and held himself suspended. He drank in the beauty of her face, her slender neck, the rounded cones of her breasts and thought of the secret he was about to explore between the long, beautiful legs, and he wondered again how he could do it without breaking the exquisite body beneath him.

"Oh, Cass...." she cried out softly. "Lover...come to me! Come!"

Slowly he lowered his body to hers. With a small, murmured cry of abandon she clasped his buttocks with her hands, urging him down. He felt the sudden lifting of her thighs to meet him and heard the unbridled cry of ecstasy roll up from deep in her throat as he plunged down the warm, velvet passage to that hidden center. Reaching it, he lifted and plunged again and again, in unison with her now, rising and falling in a rapidly accelerating rhythm, until in a final climactic thrust his whole body seemed to explode inside her, and the broken cry of her pleasure became a rapturous moan drawn out on a rising scale.

In her breathless sighs of satiation as the moment of thunder receded, Cass understood complete fulfillment for the first time . . . and the meaning of joy.

CHAPTER FIFTEEN

IN THE LAST INSTANT of interrupted sleep, the thready, high-pitched note playing upon Tulley's mind was Cass's harmonica, and then it was a signal-tone on an answering machine. Before she was fully awake it stopped, and from somewhere in the darkened room a disembodied voice droned out meaningless words to her sleep-drugged mind. Then, drowning out all other sounds, came the horrendous wail of a siren. She was conscious suddenly of Cass moving quickly and quietly from under the covers. Wide awake now, she scrambled across the bed to catch hold of him, but he was on his feet, already moving away.

"What is it, Cass?" she asked in alarm, raising her voice to be heard over the siren. "It sounds like an all-out alert."

"Go back to sleep. It's only a fire. The town siren alerts the volunteer firemen to pick up instructions from their beepers."

In dawning comprehension, Tulley said tensely, "And you are..."

"...one of them," Cass finished for her and bumped a bare foot on something in the dark. He muttered an expletive. "I can't find the damn beeper in the dark." Tulley reached for the light switch.

"Thanks, love," he said as her hand pressed the button on a bedside lamp.

Blinking sleepily into the sudden brightness, she watched his square, hard-muscled body as he leaned down to pick up the clothes he'd dropped on a chair on his way across the room earlier. From somewhere he brought up a small gray plastic rectangle. In the sudden deafening lull after the siren had screamed to a stop, Tulley realized this was the device from which had come the ghostly voice. Cass gave it his full attention for a moment. Grim faced, he began to throw on his clothes.

"Where is it, Cass?" she asked.

"Across town...that supermarket...my first building. Empty now. Perfect target for arson. The grocery chain pulled out of Hilby...been vacant for several months," he answered in short hurried statements as he pulled on his pants.

Watching him from bed, she asked curiously, "Don't you have regular fire-fighting clothes?"

"I keep them in the trunk of my car." The words were clipped, giving her a sense of the urgency that drove him, and she fell silent. Slipping out of bed and into a bathrobe, she watched him pull on the heavy Irish knit sweater he'd worn and reach for his windbreaker. She felt somehow that a part of him had already left the room and was hurrying on to the fire.

As a reporter, she'd seen firemen hurt in action. She restrained herself from seizing his arm to keep him from going. Instead, she walked down the stairs at his side. When he took her in his arms at the door and kissed her and let her go, she managed a smile that hid the anxiety churning within.

Looking down at her for a long moment, he said soberly, "Darling Tulley, you know how much I hate to put an end to this night."

"But you'll come back when the fire's over, Cass. We can at least have what's left of it together."

Cass laughed. "You wouldn't say that if you'd ever seen me after a fire." He kissed her again and made a fist to deliver a gentle uppercut to her chin. "Look, darling... Oh God, what am I doing here? I should have been on my way five minutes ago." Abruptly he turned from her and pushed open the door. Outside, he dashed down the driveway to his car.

On a sudden impulse, she called after him, "Where's the building located, Cass?" And feeling a need to explain why, she raised her voice again. "I have to call Ed and make sure we've got someone out there covering it for the *Herald*."

"Tenth and Beaumont, but don't bother," he called back from the car as he reached to start the motor. "Ed'll be there himself, right along with the fire trucks. He always is."

She watched him drive away then closed the door and raced back upstairs. In the bedroom she slipped into a bra and underpants and went into the bathroom where she'd hung her jeans and sweatshirt earlier, smiling faintly as she recalled the awful uncertainty she'd felt at the moment she'd left them there.

Putting the same garments back on now, she was no more sure of her judgment in chasing a fire she didn't need to chase than she'd been about appearing nude on the landing for Cass. Something was driving her to do it, but...

Blocking out the sudden knot of fear she'd felt in her stomach as she watched Cass leave, she devised a rationale more to her liking for what she was about to do. It was her duty as managing editor of the *Herald* to go, she told herself stoutly.

She flew down the stairs and headed for the garage. At Ninth Street and Beaumont Avenue, a block from the fire, a uniformed cop pulled her to a stop. The street was lined with cars and alive with people jockeying for a position from which to see the fire.

"Sorry ma'am, this is as far as you can go," the policeman informed her impersonally.

"I'm Tulley Calhoun from the *Herald*," she said pleasantly, reaching across the seat to her bag in which she carried her press card.

"Ed Dawes and the fella with the camera are already in there someplace gettin' the story for tomorrow's paper," said the policeman before he moved on to take care of the gathering crowd. Tulley considered leaving the car and slipping under the ropes while the officer was involved elsewhere.

She felt a twinge of shame. Cass had said Ed Dawes would be there—Ed, who was ten years up on her in experience and had no doubt forgotten more about fires than she cared to know.

Tulley finally acknowledged that it wasn't concern for the paper that brought her here; it wasn't the burning building. It was a heroic picture of Cass that had sprung to her mind in that last moment in the doorway—a picture of Cass going not for glory or derring-do, but because this was his town, founded and passed down by his forefathers, his to look out for in every way he could.

It was a picture that sent her blood racing through her veins with an almost sensual excitement and at the same time knotted her stomach in fear. It was that fear that drew her to the fire. It was as if, simply by being there, watching him work, she could keep Cass McCready from harm.

Down Ninth Street straight ahead of her Tulley could see the dark bodies of the firemen silhouetted against the mounting flames that licked up one side of the building. An extension ladder shot up and one of the swiftly moving figures raced up the rungs with the agility of a spider monkey. Was it Cass? she wondered anxiously. She stepped out of the car to get a better view and was surprised to see the officer coming toward her again, carrying a motorcycle helmet.

"Here, put this on to protect your head, Miss Tulley, and you can go in a little closer," he said, handing her the helmet. "Stay on the far side of the street all the way to the intersection. Don't go beyond that. You can get a fair view from the corner there."

Without waiting for Tulley's thanks, he turned back to the milling watchers. Tulley pulled on the protective headgear and sped down the roped-off street toward the blazing building, which stood back some distance from the intersecting streets and was surrounded by a parking lot. She was still some distance from the actual fire when she reached the corner, but she had a reasonably clear view of the action. A team manning a fire hose that snaked across the lot like a huge python aimed a great steam of water at a point where flames and smoke billowed out of the roof. The firemen worked swiftly, purposefully, with a precision and economy of motion that seemed almost choreographed.

She saw at once that she'd come on a fool's journey. In the shapeless canvas waterproof coats and the pitch-roof helmets, their faces covered with protective shields, one fireman looked like another. There was no way to tell which one was Cass. Unexpectedly, she was relieved. Even if she knew, it wouldn't keep him from harm. To have imagined her presence could make a difference had been a crazy ephemeron.

From where she stood now, she could feel the heat from the flames. The night was filled with the hiss and roar of water and fire. One by one, the huge plate-glass windows across the front of the store shattered from the heat with an explosive snap and the crash of fallen glass. The thick walls of concrete seemed like a fortress, but she could see that inside the building was a roaring inferno.

A shiver coursed down her spine. She should have listened to Cass and stayed home. She turned away from the fire and hurried back up the block to Ninth Street where she'd left the car. She returned the helmet to the officer, who was leaning against her car and taking a coffee break while a colleague relieved him of controlling the crowd.

"I'm Officer Pinkney," he said after she'd thanked him. "You're doin' a mighty good job at the paper, Miss Tulley. It's looking better every day since you took over."

"Thank you, Officer Pinkney. Those are kind words. I'll do my best to see we continue to deserve them."

BACK AT THE CARRIAGE HOUSE in bed again, struggling with the futility of sleep, Tulley found a new worry. Why hadn't she made Cass promise he would call her the minute he got home from the fire so she would know he was safe.

With spells of fitful sleep from which she would emerge fully awake, her heart pounding fiercely in her breast, her face damp with cold sweat, she agonized the night away. Her bed felt like a prison. At 6:00 A.M. she could stand it no longer and made her escape. She showered and dressed for the office and took time for instant coffee and orange juice and a bowl of Raisin Bran cereal that she forced past the lump of fear in her throat.

At 6:45 she unlocked the front door to the *Herald* and let herself in. The early crew was already hard at it. She found Ed Dawes in the composing room. He was leaning over a light table where the fire story was being assembled.

"Holy mackerel, Tulley, you look like you put out the fire single-handed," he said, turning away from the table to squint up at her amiably.

"Ed, there...weren't any...casualties, were there?" she asked tensely with no preliminary greeting.

Dawes looked at her more closely. "There wasn't anyone in the building. It was an empty grocery store."

"What about the firemen?"

"They did a good job. Relax, Tulley. Nobody got hurt."

Relief surged through Tulley. She waited a second for control of her voice. "How bad was the damage?"

"Almost a total loss. Not much left of the building but a concrete shell."

"What was it, Ed? Arson?"

"It doesn't look like it. I talked to the fire chief, and he said it started off slow and had been smoldering for quite a while before it finally took off. It doesn't have the characteristics that spell arson, according to him."

"Ed..." She had to ask it. "What do they think it was?"

"The chief says everything points to an electrical fire."

IT WAS ELEVEN O'CLOCK in the morning, and Cass McCready didn't want to wake up. Shortly after dawn, the fire fighters had left the smoldering ashes of the gutted building to a small crew of replacements and gone their various ways. Cass headed across town to the family home, so tired that he was physically numb and in a state akin to shock. He peeled out of clothing that reeked of smoke and sweat and rolled into a hot tub like an automaton. From there he made blindly for his bed and fell into the dead sleep of exhaustion.

But for the fact that Cass went into this particular fire with an unreasonable feeling that it was violating something that was uniquely his, it had been like any other fire—like walking into the jaws of hell. Like any fire fighter who cares about living to a ripe old age, he thought only of putting the blaze out without getting himself killed doing it. When he'd reached the point where he wondered how much more of the heat and smoke and screaming muscles he could endure, the last tongue of flame hissed itself out in smoking ash like a dying dragon. The fighters' job was done, and the relief crew was on hand.

But the fire did not immediately let go of the men who had fought it. In a dazed, almost zombielike state they stayed on with the smoldering ruins for a while, looking into the wreckage with no special sense of purpose, almost as if, in some ineffable way, they could not let go.

So it was, in that brief aftermath, that Cass had stumbled half blindly onto the evidence of his own betrayal. In what was left of a melted-down junction box where the electrical conduit lay exposed, he saw aluminum where he knew there should be nothing but copper.

His first thought was that he was hallucinating from heat and smoke and exhaustion, but he looked again and saw the bubbles of silvery metal that was like frozen quicksilver. He knew then it was not an illusion. He accepted it dully and without understanding for what he recognized it to be: a fire caused by bad wiring.

Nausea rolled up in his throat. He'd always looked on this first building of his as one any contractor would be proud to take credit for: a good, solid, unpretentious building; a building with integrity. To learn it had been fatally flawed almost from the beginning filled him with rage as hot as the embers around him. He wanted to get his hands on someone...anyone....

Now in his bed at home some six hours later, he fought against returning consciousness. A warning voice reminded him that the moment he was fully awake he'd have to think about what he'd seen this morning in the wet smoke of the dying embers.

What the hell had become of the copper wiring the specifications had called for? Until the moment he'd seen those blobs of aluminum uncovered by the fire, he'd never doubted it was where it was supposed to be, properly installed between the walls. But now he knew better. Someone had substituted bad wiring for good in that building without his knowing it.

Who? How?

He tried to slip back into the still, undemanding darkness of sleep, but the questions flashed across the blank screen of his mind and stayed there. In a moment they were joined by a name.

Jack Swift.

Cass groaned. He gave up all hope of sleep and opened his eyes.

The only way those materials could be switched would be with the connivance of the electrical subcontractor, who had been Jack Swift. But how could the sub make a switch without the knowledge and consent of the general contractor, who happened to be himself?

Neophyte that he'd been, he'd run scared on that first building and had barely let it out of his sight. He'd made it a point to be on the spot when the first workman arrived in the morning and had stayed until the last one left at night. It had been his regimen every working day until the building was done. Every working day, *except* . . .

"Oh . . . my . . . God," he whispered, seeing again, as if in a tableau, his parents in that Arizona hospital after the accident: his father in a coma that ended with his death three weeks later; his severely injured mother, too distraught to be abandoned. He'd taken the first plane out of Raleigh when the call came and stayed until after his father's death then he had brought his mother home.

And in the meantime, construction had gone on. He'd trusted his subcontractors to carry on without him. In his haste to get to his stricken parents, whose needs came first, he hadn't taken time to arrange for any extended absence. He'd expected to be gone, at most, no more than a few days.

The electrical work was started three days after he left Hilby, and by the time he got back on the job the wiring was finished and passed by the building inspector and already hidden between the walls.

Jack Swift had turned a tidy profit by stringing the cheap aluminum wire through that building instead of copper. Furthermore, it looked like he'd cheated on the installation, as well, Cass thought angrily, knowing that if it was properly installed, even aluminum wiring wouldn't cause a fire.

And to add insult to injury, not satisfied with making one killing at Cass's expense, the bastard had his eye on the annex with the same caper in mind; only this time he couldn't count on Cass for another convenient absence, so he'd had to take a chance on trying to cut him in.

Cass vented his anguish in a tormented growl and again closed his eyes, longing to forget everything but that sweet moment when Tulley had given herself to him in the hours before all hell had broken loose. He wanted to bury his face in the honey of her breasts and drown himself in the mystical scent of her body. But there was the fire and the wiring and Jack Swift to go after, and there was no escaping back into the brief paradise of last night.

Tulley... Tulley, how will this look in your eyes? He lay there for a moment then pushed back the covers and pulled out a phone book from the drawer of the bedside table.

God, how he dreaded the day ahead! When the facts about the wiring came out, the town of Hilby could only see it as verification of what Lamarr had hinted at in the *Herald*. And that didn't make him look good. Sure, he might be able to prove that Swift was responsible for the switch, but Cass knew the buck really stopped with him. It was the general contractor's job to make sure nothing of this sort happened. By not being there when the wiring went in, he'd become Jack Swift's accomplice without even knowing it.

Yet how could he have done otherwise? he asked himself with a desperate sense of defeat. Even if it had occurred to him to do it, there was no way he could have stayed away from his dying father and from a mother who had never been known to make a decision on her own. His place had been with them, and he'd had no choice but to rely on subcontractors he'd worked with and known most of his life. He'd signed them on believing they all shared his own code of honor; with one exception, he knew he'd been right.

As for Jack Swift, the only one of them he scarcely knew, he was from a family of Swifts who'd been tobacco farmers in western Hilby County for as long as Cass could remember. Cass had gone to their place once with his grandfather in that last fatal election year and been invited to stay for their midday dinner. They'd had fried okra and black-eyed peas and fried corn and hot cherry dumplings. It had never occurred to him that anyone from that family of Swifts was not to be trusted.

Finding the number of *The Hilby Herald* in the book, he picked up the phone from the bedside table and dialed.

"Tulley, love, it's Cass," he said when she was on the other end. He hesitated and then plunged into it. "I have something I've got to tell you, but I have to be sure first that you know I love you."

At the other end, in a breathless voice he found infinitely exciting, she said, "I do. You know I do, Cass. And I love you. Thank goodness you called. I had to hear your voice to be sure you came through the fire all right."

He laughed—a short laugh, completely devoid of humor. "Of course I'm all right, which is ridiculous because, in a sense, I feel worse right now than I've ever felt in my life."

"I'm not surprised," she said. "You had a hard night. Go back to sleep. I'll see you when you've recovered."

"No...no. I told you, I'm fine, except for the fact I discovered something this morning after the fire that could put me out of business."

"You *what*?"

"Your uncle wasn't that far off when he implied I built a building that had substandard materials hidden inside its walls. He got everything right but the building."

"What do you mean, Cass?"

Swallowing the bile that rose to his throat, he told her, as quickly and as dispassionately as he was able, what he'd seen in the ashes of the fire and his conclusion that Jack Swift had seized on Cass's absence to make the switch in the wiring.

"So Lamarr was right, except that it wasn't the annex. It was the building that burned up last night," he finished grimly. "The libel suit is a shuck. I'll have it dismissed today."

"Don't you dare, Cass McCready!" From across town Tulley's voice steamed into his ear. "Time enough for that when we've got Jack Swift pinned down."

Cass drew a deep sigh and let it out. God bless the darling, she believed him!

"As soon as people hear about that wiring, they're going to decide Lamarr wasn't so far off base, and that Cass McCready's a crook," he was obliged to point out. "Why wait? At least it takes the *Herald* off the hook."

"Cut that out, Cass. If you dismiss the suit now, it's like an admission of guilt," Tulley argued. "Wait until we've got the whole story and can publish it. There's not a person in town who can hold that bad wiring against you once the truth is out."

"We'll see," Cass said slowly after a moment. "I'm on my way to see Sam. He's always been the family lawyer. I want to talk to him about this new development, but I doubt if he'll have anything to say about the libel suit since he's lawyer for Lamarr's estate and couldn't handle it for me. It'd be a conflict of interests."

"You know who owns the building now, don't you?" she asked suddenly.

Cass let out a soft whistle. "Leo Drummond, of course," he said. "I'd forgotten. It's part of the blasted development."

"Jack Swift and Leo Drummond...and the tape...and the fire. There's got to be a connection there."

Cass dismissed it. "If there is, I don't get it. I'd better hang up and let Sam know I'm coming in."

"When will I see you?"

"Darling, I don't... Listen, I'll call you back after I've seen Sam."

ANYONE LOOKING AT THAT FACE would hardly guess that here was a woman who'd spent the most ecstatic hours of her life the night before in the arms of her lover, thought Tulley with a grimace at the mirror in the women's washroom of the *Herald* a few hours later. It was a lackluster face with faint smoky smudges under heavy eyes—the marks of a near sleepless night that had turned into an anxious day. And the second telephone call from Cass hadn't done much to brighten either the face or the day.

Even Scotty Kettleman, who had come to talk to her that afternoon, had turned strange on her. Tulley wondered if she'd guessed wrong about the boy. He'd been full of enthusiasm when she told him she was thinking of starting a new section for young people in the *Herald*. His reactions had been eager and promising...right up to the point when she asked him how he'd like to be junior editor of the feature. Then, to her dismay, the cocky, self-confident kid turned into an uneasy stranger whose eyes no longer met hers. He stammered out a string of excuses, obviously manufactured on the spot—didn't think he could handle it, didn't have time—then in a sudden about-face begged her not to get someone else until he had time to think about it. Maybe he could work it out, he'd said in a final stumbling burst of words and bolted out as if something was after him.

What could you expect of a day that started out with a fire that spelled trouble for Cass? she thought sourly, touching a bit of color to her lips to brighten her face. The boy's behavior was just part of the general pattern of a bad day.

Cass, when he called back after talking to Sam, had gone spooky on her, thanks to Sam who'd advised him to stay away from Tulley until he could prove he had not been in collusion with Jack Swift when the wiring was switched. Reviewing the conversation between them, Tulley found it hard to believe what had been said, much less what she had agreed to.

"Sam says this is no time to let anyone get the idea we're involved with each other," Cass had said.

"But we *are* involved, dammit!" she'd protested. "We love each other, Cass. Sam doesn't know that, of course. After last night, I thought we were supposed to be in things together."

"And we are, darling. As for Sam, he knows I intend to ask you to marry me, once I'm free of this rotten mess, because I told him," Cass had said. And while she was still reeling from *that*, he'd said, "But at the same time, Sam's right. He's speaking not only as a lawyer but as our friend. I think we'd be smart to do as he says."

And she'd started to argue. "But is it necessary? It does seem a little paranoid to me."

And then Cass had told her how the lawyer felt about even the merest suspicion of a personal relationship between them. Not only could it weaken the town's growing confidence in the *Herald*, Sam had warned, but it could cast suspicion on any effort the paper might want to make in support of Cass.

"Sam's right when he says Swift and Drummond are out to make trouble, and he's right when he says they aren't above putting a watch on either one of us," Cass had finished grimly.

Put that way, how could she argue the matter? Sam had even advised they confine their communication to the telephone, but there, thank God, Cass had drawn the line. The compromise arrangement—that for the time being she and Cass would meet only at the carriage house and late at night when it was easiest for Cass to come without being seen—did not set well with Tulley's open nature, but she had agreed.

With a last dissatisfied look in the mirror, Tulley picked up her handbag. Now might be a good time to get out and talk to people. She'd like to hear what the Main Street folks were saying about the fire.

Stopping long enough in her office to grab her coat, she paused in Ed's doorway a moment to report on her frustrating visit with Scotty Kettleman and say goodnight. The front office people had already departed. She stepped outside as the street lights were turning on.

Two late-day stragglers sat at the counter of the Corner Drug Store on Main Street, drinking coffee, and Tulley took a stool beside them. She ordered a cup of coffee and was lifting the scalding brew for a cautious sip when Leo Drummond eased himself onto the empty stool beside her, looking like the proverbial canary-eating cat.

"Mind if I join you?" he asked when he was already seated. Tulley managed a noncommittal shrug.

"Some fireworks we had last night!" he led off on a bantering note. "You're a dedicated news hen, so I suppose you know what caused it by now."

News hen! If there was one thing Tulley loathed as a woman and a journalist, it was to be called a news hen, but her indignation was second to her curiosity. There was something in Drummond's voice that made her feel as though she was being baited.

"As far as I know, the cause hasn't been determined yet," she said crisply.

Drummond raised a superior brow. "Well, I can give you a scoop for your man Dawes. I know what started the fire," he said. The two people sitting next to Tulley were stepping down from their seats to leave. He raised his voice, as if to make sure they didn't leave uninformed. "The contractor substituted cheap aluminum wiring. With slipshod installation, no wonder it caught on fire." Out of the corner of her eye Tulley saw that the two had paused to listen.

Drummond made sure they heard. "You know who the contractor was on that building, don't you? Cass McCready. It looks like your Uncle Lamarr wasn't so far off, after all."

"How did you find all this out about the wiring? If the fire chief made an official statement, I'm sure Ed Dawes would have known about it and told me immediately," she said in a level voice. For a moment Drummond seemed caught off base.

"I have my sources," he said shortly.

"For a man who has just lost a valuable piece of property in a fire, you seem to be taking it rather well," needled Tulley.

There was only a fraction of a moment's hesitation before Drummond said, "Well, of course I hate like hell to lose the building. But it's not as if it'll bankrupt me."

"Let's hope your insurance carrier feels as sanguine about it as you do, Mr. Drummond," Tulley said in a random shot and was surprised to see a sudden hostility flash in his eyes.

"Naturally, the building was insured," he said stiffly. "Though a more apt term would be *under*insured. Nobody expects his own house to burn down."

Tulley felt in some vague way she had scored, but she couldn't stand the sight of the smug, handsome face any longer. She dropped money on the counter, twirled her stool away from him and left. With a hollow feeling in the pit of her stomach, she walked back to the *Herald* building, picked up her car and headed for home. Gone was all desire to listen to the voice of Main Street.

By the time Leo Drummond took refreshment at every coffee shop and bar in the town's center, half the town of Hilby would have heard that Lamarr Calhoun had been right—Cass McCready had put subgrade materials into a building that called for the best. And unless she could think of some way to deflect the gossip, a lot of the townspeople would take it for fact.

CHAPTER SIXTEEN

THE MOMENT she stepped through the door of the carriage house that evening, Tulley began waiting for Cass. She went about the small routine chores of homecoming, first changing into a loose, rough-knit cotton sweater and jeans. She broiled lamb chops she'd bought on her way home, put a serving of frozen peas into the microwave and tossed a salad.

While she ate her dinner, she watched the news on TV and afterward put the kitchen in order and settled down to reruns of *M*A*S*H* and *Lou Grant* and *Taxi*.

She wandered aimlessly upstairs and manicured her nails then brushed on a few coats of enamel—a pale, iridescent pink—knowing it would be chipped and ready for removal before noon the following day.

And all the time, every part of her waited with a kind of breathlessness—listening, almost, for Cass, knowing he was still endless hours away.

He was a fire within her, this man, and a hunger in her breasts, a sweet, throbbing ache at her core.

And he was a long time coming.

How long was this impossible situation to go on? she wondered. She knew she would never grow used to it. Last night she had taken him openly and without shame to be her lover, and tonight he would come back to her like a thief in the dark.

With a brooding sigh she dropped into a lotus position on the carpet and reached for the bottle of enamel. Pulling her foot within reach, she carefully dabbed a bit of enamel on each toe. It amused her. Traditionally, a woman made herself beautiful to meet her lover. She wondered if Cass would appreciate the beauty of her painted toes, and a giggle rolled silently up in her throat.

Cass had taken her as he found her, dressed in the straightforward ensembles indigenous to her career, or in jeans and the shapeless sweatshirt of last night—until she'd hung them on the bathroom door and came to him starkers, she thought with a remembering smile.

She had a sudden, driving desire to dress up for Cass, to appear in something exotic, erotic... *distracting*. Something that would make him forget a day that must have been worse for him than it had been for her.

But was there anything in her wardrobe that consisted of two styles of clothing—borderline Yuppy and grubbies—to top last night's appearance? she asked herself wryly.

And then she remembered the pajamas. The elegant, exquisitely fashioned satin pajamas that had been a gift from a designer of unconscionably expensive lingerie. Tulley had interviewed her and sold the article to a slick women's fashion magazine. The designer adored the piece and had expressed her gratitude with an original design created, the artist swore, for "you, Toolee...a one-of-a-kind."

Its top was a soft, cunningly structured silk satin chemise printed with peacock feathers on a background of peacock blue. It shaped her breasts teasingly and then floated away as she moved, caught into a smooth, fitted band that rested on her hips over slender, flowing pants. Half hidden by the soft folds of the silk was a deep slash reaching almost to the waist from a modest closure at the throat. It was the most beautiful garment Tulley had ever owned, and she'd never worn it. She lifted it out of its tissue-paper wrappings and laid it on the bed.

Normally she preferred a shower, but tonight she ran a warm bath in the tub and sprinkled the water with bath oil. It gave her skin the same satiny texture the pajamas had, and she delighted in the feel of satin-upon-satin when she slipped the top over her head.

The pajamas caressed her body as gently as a lover's hand. She felt her breasts peak in response to the touch of the silk, and a sensual shiver whispered along her neck. It was a garment designed not only to seduce the observer but the wearer, too, she decided and smiled ruefully, knowing that what she really wanted was for the real lover to come and strip it away.

She brushed a drop of perfume in the hollow of her throat and another in the valley between her breasts. She ran a comb through her hair, and when she couldn't think of anything more to do to herself, she went downstairs in her bare feet with their painted toenails and curled up in one of the wing chairs by the fire. Tulley waited, listening for the purr of Cass's car, the crunch of its wheels on the gravel driveway.

The carriage house lay in darkness. She had grudgingly turned off the outside lights because Sam had called and suggested she should, if she was expecting "a visitor."

With the silence of a shadow, he came. The first notice she had that he was there was a gentle rattle on the front-door handle and Cass's voice calling softly "Rapunzel? Are you there?" In the next instant she was in his arms, and the peacock pajamas sent out pricks of static electricity between them as the satin rubbed against the synthetic fabric of his down jacket. Wordlessly they clung together.

When Cass pulled away and started for the kitchen, she called after him accusingly, "Where are you off to? You might at least give me a kiss." She saw then that he'd been hugging her with one hand and was clutching something in a brown paper bag, which he set down on the kitchen counter.

"Choca-moca ice cream, hand packed," he said, turning back to her. "But it can wa..." A soft, wondering sound—between a whistle and a sigh—whispered across his lips. "Tulley... My God, you are beautiful," he said quietly, his voice filled with something close to awe as his fingers, clumsy with haste, tugged at the fasteners on his jacket. With sudden impatience he yanked it off and tossed it on a chair.

He was dressed in old blue jeans and a rough flannel shirt. He walked across the room with measured steps and stopped less than a hand's reach away from where she had seated herself on the couch. His clear blue eyes moved over her caressingly and came back to watch the rise and fall of her breasts beneath the peacock satin. She held her breath, but still the fabric stirred over the beating of her heart. After a moment his forefinger ventured to touch the peak of one breast and brush lightly over the firm bud that thrust unmistakably against the silk.

"You're so... Why didn't you tell me you were... I didn't have to come in my old..." He left the sentence unfinished, his voice choked. "You're... I can't find the word. Exquisite. Unreal. I feel like a clod in the presence of a... a Persian princess. I'm afraid to touch you—" his finger found the hidden opening in the silk "—almost." His hand slipped inside. She could feel it tremble as he lifted her breast and pushed back the silk until the breast was uncovered and rested exposed in the curve of his hand.

The desire that had been building in Tulley from the moment she began to get ready for his visit was like a pinpoint of fire inside her.

"Cass, darling...." she said with a catch in her voice, which had turned suddenly husky. "Adulation is...dandy, but it's no substitute for love."

He let his hand fall to his side. She caught a glint of humor in the blue eyes. "You know what? I'm afraid of you tonight, my beloved. If I took you in my arms, I'd feel like I was crushing a beautiful flower. I'm not dressed for it."

A soft, sensual laugh slipped from Tulley's lips. "Oh, well, if *that's* all," she said and reached for his shirtfront. He caught her hand, pulled her to her feet and steered her purposefully up the stairs.

She shed the peacock pajamas in a small silken pile on the bedroom carpet beside Cass's worn jeans and rough flannel shirt, and they made love—frenetic, hungry love, as if they had been away from each other for a long time. Up...up they soared to the highest peak together and afterward lay panting in each other's arms while the heat and fluids of their passion blended and cooled on their naked bodies.

And when they were back on solid ground they lay together still, in silence, as the traumatic hours they'd suffered since they'd made love the night before in this same bed closed in around them.

After a while Cass kissed her gently—passion spent—and left the bed to get dressed. Disconsolate, Tulley put on her old plaid bathrobe and followed him downstairs.

"Cass..." she began but couldn't think of anything to say. Maybe they should talk about the fire and what to do about Swift and Drummond—about how they could end this awful thing that was happening to their lives—but she didn't know where to start.

"What are we going to do?" she asked softly, miserably. She could see her own unhappiness reflected in his eyes.

"I don't know, Tulley. I honestly don't know."

They clung together for a long, still moment, then Cass stepped outside and disappeared into the darkness. Tulley leaned her head against the door and closed her eyes. It had been beautiful and exhilarating and all wrong. Not like the night before. There had been none of the sweet, playful titillation, no slow, erotic crescendo of their senses to a rapturous climax. Both of them were already halfway there before they even touched each other. And she missed the lovely, languorous aftermath. It had been more like a ride on a roller coaster: incredibly exciting, over too soon.

It was the blasted peacock pajamas, she told herself crossly as she climbed the stairs to her lonely bed. She was no Persian princess! She was a woman in love. She'd never wear the silly things again.

The feeling of dissatisfaction was still with her when she awakened the next morning and was met by the sight of a kitchen drain board awash with choca-moca ice cream leaking out the seams of a cardboard carton, and a sodden brown bag.

Thus things stood with Tulley the following night when Cass slipped out of the darkness to visit her again. She wore jeans and a newly minted T-shirt from a local silk-screen shop. The shirt was a brilliant greenish-blue and lettered with Persian Princess I'm Not. Cass arrived in a tuxedo that looked as if it had been invented with Cass McCready in mind.

"Cass! I'm...stunned. You're magnificent!" Tulley said with a chortle, delighted that he could make a joke of last night's debacle; nonetheless, she really meant what she said. She looked suspiciously at the brown paper bag he carried. "And if that's what I think it is, we're eating it now."

Cass grinned sheepishly. "Sorry about that," he said.

Over bowls of choca-mocha they tackled head-on the problems upsetting their lives. Cass had talked to two electricians who had worked for Jack Swift on the burned-out building. Both said they hadn't known the job called for copper wiring and that Swift had paid scrupulous attention to the installation. The building inspector, whom Cass knew to be honest, confirmed what the electricians had said. There was nothing wrong with the installation. Some other factor had caused the fire.

Later, upstairs in the four-poster, they made love to a quieter refrain than the night before, and when they lay quiescent afterward, she recognized in it a sound of goodbye. He didn't have to tell her that he had slipped like a cat burglar into the carriage house for the last time. She knew and in a way was relieved.

"I hate it, Tulley. I hate sneaking in here in the dark as if it were something to be ashamed of. It demeans you and it demeans me. I won't do it anymore," he said. "I'll talk to you on the phone, but Sam's right. I won't come here again until the town of Hilby understands to what extent I am innocent and to what extent I failed."

"How long, Cass? How long?" she asked unhappily.

And Cass said grimly, "Until I can clear this thing up."

In the sleepless hours after he'd gone, Tulley devised a plan for going public with Lamarr's tape. While it wouldn't clear Cass, it would point out to the town of Hilby the strong probability that he was being framed.

"I THOUGHT I'D BETTER clue you in on what I intend to do, Boss." It was early the following morning, and Tulley was at the Matthewses' breakfast table sipping coffee with Sam and Caroline.

The lawyer looked up quizzically. "Boss?"

"Sure. You're my boss until the probate's closed and the paper's mine, aren't you?"

Caroline pushed back her chair and started to rise. "If y'all are going to talk business, I'll take my coffee into the back parlor and watch the news."

"No, please, Caroline, don't go. I don't have any business to discuss with Sam that I wouldn't discuss freely with you. I feel terrible interrupting your breakfast."

"You're not interrupting. We're all through," Caroline assured her.

"What's on your mind?" asked Sam.

"I thought I'd better tell you I've decided to turn that tape over to Ed Dawes when I get to the office this morning," Tulley began without preliminaries. "I want him to do a story saying it was found among Lamarr's possessions and using direct quotes from the tape, showing how the three men planned to frame Cass. We won't use any names or clues to who the conspirators are. We will say the voices have not yet been officially identified and that the tapes have been turned over to the proper authorities, which we'll do, of course, before the paper is on the streets. It won't clear Cass, but at least we'll be doing something, and it will throw a new light on—"

"Wait, Tulley. Wait," Sam interrupted. She was surprised to see that he was extremely upset. "You can't do it."

"Why not?" she asked stubbornly.

"Because I can't let you. No, wait," he said again, holding up a hand to stop the argument already formed on her lips. "I don't know exactly how to tell you this, Tulley...but the fact of the matter is, there's, uh, some question whether the paper'll *be* yours when the estate is closed."

Tulley stared at him blankly.

"I came across a will written by Lamarr—at least it looks like his handwriting—in Lamarr's desk the other night when we were out there looking for the tapes. I didn't say anything because I didn't want to upset you unless I had to. One of the fellows in the sheriff's office knows a little bit about handwriting, and he says he thinks Lamarr wrote it."

Tulley gazed at him in silence with stricken eyes for a moment. Then she said dully, "I guess I knew all along it was too good to be true."

"Don't give up yet, girl," Sam said gently. "Wait'll I tell you who the beneficiary is."

"I don't much care, Sam. All I can think of is, where do I go from here?" Her voice was dazed.

"No place, for the time being, at least. Nobody knows about this holographic will but you and me, and I'm not about to make it public until I'm sure it's authentic," the lawyer said.

"Why would you think it's not?" Tulley asked, not really listening, still too stunned to assimilate what came after the unexpected discovery that there was a will.

"Because I find it hard to believe Lamarr would leave everything he owns to Shelby Haynes, for one reason."

His words brought a small cry of pain from Tulley.

"Shelby Haynes? Sam, the whole staff will quit. The *Herald* will die. It could have been such a splendid paper," she said in a voice of mourning, shocked out of her self-concern by this further revelation.

"I reckon so," Sam agreed gloomily. "That's why I plan to hold off and look into it a little more. There's something about it I don't like."

Tulley's interest came gradually to life. "Like what?"

"For one thing, I'd swear there wasn't any will in the desk the day I went there looking for one right after Lamarr's death," Sam said. "I don't see how I could have overlooked it, because it was in one of the pigeonholes just askin' to be pulled out."

"But how—"

"Easy enough. Shelby had plenty of opportunity to be in possession of a key to Lamarr's house," Sam said, "but that doesn't explain the handwriting. The fellow over at the sheriff's office tells me it takes a lot of practice to be able to forge a signature, let alone a whole document, even if it's as short as this, and yet I can't swallow it. The real sticker is I don't believe Lamarr would leave so much as a busted chamber pot to Shelby Haynes. It was a well-known fact around Hilby that they hated each other."

Tulley looked at him in amazement. "Why in the world would anyone keep a man who was incompetent and abrasive and a borderline alcoholic on his staff if he hated him?"

"There's been some speculation about that, and the consensus seems to be they couldn't trust each other out of sight. My guess is it had something to do with fixin' an important county election about the time your daddy packed y'all up and moved up nawth. I always figured Prentiss got wind that Lamarr and Shelby were up to something seriously illegal. He couldn't do anything about it so he made Lamarr buy him out.''

"He could have exposed them to the law," Tulley said indignantly.

"Send his own brother to jail and disgrace the name Calhoun? You wouldn't want him to do that," Sam said in a reproachful voice.

The lawyer's words reminded Tulley of Cass, from whom she'd learned the nature of honor and loyalty among families whose roots went down deep, as did the roots of the McCreadys and, yes, the Calhouns, too. And she understood why her father could cut himself off from his brother for the balance of his lifetime but couldn't turn him over to the law.

"What do you want me to do, Sam?" she asked unhappily.

"Just keep on like you've been doing at the paper. Go on as if you never heard of the will, while I dig into it," he said. Then in sudden afterthought he continued, "But you can't run that tape story you were talking about, Tulley. As I said from the first, it'll do Cass more harm than good."

Tulley sighed. "There's an old saying among newspaper people that if you ask your attorney about printing a story, he knows only one answer: don't print it," she said with a weak grin, which turned into a reluctant but forgiving smile. "You're right, of course. It's just that I feel so helpless! Anything seems better than nothing."

She apologized to Caroline for bringing business to their breakfast table and rose to say goodbye. She was almost at the door when she turned back.

"Cass said he was having lunch with you today, Sam," she said hesitantly. "Would you mind telling him about this will?"

Sam looked at her in surprise. "Don't you want to tell him yourself?"

"It's not that. I just don't know when I'll be talking to him again," she said. "We...uh...we decided to take our lawyer's advice. He won't be coming around for a while."

"Good for you," Sam said. Caroline got up from the table and hurried over to wrap her plump arms around Tulley and give her a sympathetic hug.

"I reckon it's no fun for you and Cass, honey, but you're smart to listen to Sam. He's right, most of the time," she said softly. "No tellin' what that mean old Drummond is up to. It's best not to give him a thing to use against you."

A FEW MINUTES before twelve o'clock that day, Miss Eudith ushered Cass into Sam Matthews's inner sanctum, where he found the lawyer in his swivel chair, which was pushed back from the desk, his hands folded across the mound of his stomach and his eyes focused gloomily on the gray sky outside his window.

Swiveling around in his chair, he brought his feet to the floor with a resounding smack and reached for a single sheet of paper on his desk. He got up and handed it to Cass.

"Take a look at this," he said.

Curious, Cass took it from him—plain white paper with a single line of writing on it and a signature, written with a pen in black ink in a sprawling script, dated the year before. He read the words with a feeling of disbelief.

"I, Lamarr Calhoun, leave everything I own to Shelby Haynes," followed by Lamarr's signature.

"Oh...my...God," Cass said, staring down at the document in shock. He looked up to meet Sam's eyes. "Does Tulley know about this?"

Sam nodded.

A sickness rose in Cass as the injustice of it washed over him. Here was Tulley—the woman he loved, the most decent person he'd ever known, who lived life with her chin up, looking the world straight in the eye—deprived of the inheritance she rightly deserved by a worthless, conniving character Lamarr himself had treated with contempt. It gave Cass a strange feeling of hopelessness contrary to his nature.

"Does it mean she's lost the paper?"

"Not if I can help it," Sam said. Briefly, he told Cass what he'd told Tulley that morning and observed in conclusion that there was something about the will that "smelled like a catfish out of water too long."

After a moment of silence Cass asked thoughtfully, "How about that handwriting fellow at the sheriff's office? Does he know what he's doing?"

"I reckon so," said Sam. "He handles forgeries and the like that come in—a couple or so a year."

"How about giving me this piece of paper for a couple of days?" Cass asked.

Matthews looked at him in alarm. "I can't rightly do that, Cass. I've got a responsibility as a—"

"I know, it's against your professional ethics. You have my word of honor I'll have it back to you in the exact condition it is right now, before you're ready to tell the town of Hilby the will even exists."

The lawyer eyed him uneasily for a moment then asked curiously, "What are you thinking about doing with it, Cass? Never mind. I'd rather not know. Take good care of it. If I didn't trust you like my own son, I wouldn't let you do this. Come on. Let's go to lunch."

They went in Cass's car to a small inn they both favored on the outskirts of town where country food was served in a quiet atmosphere. By unspoken agreement they talked of other things. As he was about to drive off after returning the lawyer to his office, Cass said, "I'll be out of town for a few days, Sam. Keep an eye on Tulley, will you?"

Matthews eyed him shrewdly. "If it was anybody but you, Cass, I'd guess you were running away."

Cass bristled. "What the devil do you mean, running away?"

"So you won't be here when the fire chief's report hits the town."

"You know better than that, Sam," Cass said without rancor. "I told the fire chief yesterday about the switch in the wiring. They'd already discovered the aluminum, but he says that's not what caused the fire, and they're still investigating. There may not be an official announcement for several days."

"As your lawyer I advise you to stay on the spot and take care of your own fences."

"As your client I say I can't. I'll be damned if I'll sit by knowing Tulley could lose her paper and not try to do something about it. I know somebody I think might help," Cass said. "If the whole county of Hilby wants to think I'm running away, I can't help it."

"You've got some problems of your own you better be working on, Cass, you know."

"They can wait. My number one priority is Tulley," Cass said stubbornly. "The rest can wait till I get back."

TULLEY LET THE PHONE slide back into its cradle and stared at it. She felt abandoned. It had been Cass, telling her Sam had told him about the Shelby Haynes will.

"I'd come to you, love, but Sam says no," he'd said.

Longing for the comfort of his arms, she'd said crossly, "Sometimes I wish we hadn't invited Sam Matthews into our lives. If the paper's going to belong to Shelby Haynes in a few days, it doesn't matter what people think."

"Sam says it does. After all, the paper's yours until you're told it isn't, and as long as it is, I think we'd better listen to Sam."

She'd grumbled and given in, and then he'd said, "Tulley, honey, I have to be away on some business for a few days. I'm not sure how long it'll take." Suddenly it was as if the room had been plunged into darkness. His promise to call every night was small comfort.

Her hand still resting on the phone, Tulley wondered at her feeling of desolation. They now talked only by phone, so why should it matter whether he was across town or... With a moan of despair, she realized he hadn't said where he was going, and she'd forgotten to ask. Not knowing where he would be made it seem as if he'd taken off for another planet.

Ed Dawes poked his head through the open door of her office. "The fire chief just told me, off-the-record, that they're beginning to think the fire may have been the work of an arsonist. It wasn't the typical arson, and he asked us to lay off for a few days until they finish the investigation. I hope that's okay with you?''

"Why tell you, if he doesn't want it printed?" asked Tulley impatiently. "Besides, Ed, I don't think it's a good idea for a reporter to listen to things off-the-record."

"I agree. I make a practice of avoiding it when I can, but the fire chief and I are friends of long-standing. When he said it, he was thinking of me as his friend, not as a reporter," Ed told her. "I didn't see any reason for us to rush into print with it. He's afraid if we do, it could throw a monkey wrench into the investigation."

She gave him an apologetic smile. "Sorry, Ed. I'm sure you're right, and I'll cooperate any way I can. I wish there was some more concrete way I could help."

When he had left, she went over the events of the past few days in her mind. After a time she called Ed back to her office.

"Since the chief's your friend, maybe he wouldn't mind telling you when they actually discovered the wiring in the building was aluminum," she said.

Ed reached for the phone and put in a call to the chief, Darin Hughes.

"He says they probably all saw it at the time of the fire. It's not unusual, and since it didn't appear to be the cause of the fire, it didn't get any particular notice at the time," Ed told her when he'd finished the call. His face wore a puzzled frown. "A funny thing. The chief says usually they shut off the power in a vacant building when it's not in use, but the power was on. The owner must not mind paying the monthly electric bill."

"The owner's Leo Drummond," Tulley told him.

"Drummond, huh? Well, maybe he figured he needed it on to show to prospective renters. Anything else?"

"Maybe," said Tulley. "He came here from Florida, didn't he? You don't happen to know what part of the state, do you?"

"No, I don't. Wait.... As a matter of fact, I do. I happened to overhear him talking right after the planning commission turned him down on that development plan," Ed said. "He was grumbling that he hadn't expected to get the same flak in Hilby that he got in Fountain Beach."

"Fountain Beach, Florida. Never heard of it," Tulley said, walking across the room to pluck the F-L volume of the encyclopedia from a shelf and flip through it. "Here it is, on the coast south of Daytona Beach. Thanks, Ed."

Tulley put in a call to her colleague, Stanley Rice, on the New York daily she'd recently left.

"Listen, Stan, do you have any contacts in Daytona Beach, Florida?" she asked when the amenities had been observed.

"Yeah. The paper's got a stringer down there. His name's Dick Brown. He covers the routine news for us when there is any, and if it's something big we send a reporter down from here," Rice said.

"Could you get him to find out all he can about a real estate developer named Leo Drummond who's supposed to have built a subdivision south of Fountain Beach?" Tulley asked. "Drummond moved up here to Hilby eight or nine months ago. Tell Mr. Brown I'll make it worth his while."

"Sure thing, Tulley. I'll get back to you as soon as I have something. No. Better I should have Dick call you directly. It'd save time.'' They chatted a minute longer and said goodbye.

She *had* been happy on the paper in New York, she told herself bleakly as she hung up. Her leave of absence lasted until the estate was closed, so she did have a job to go back to.

She wondered why she hadn't told her old friend Stanley, who'd been the first to know she was inheriting the *Herald*, that she'd just been disinherited and quite likely would be coming back. And yet, how could she go back when it would mean leaving Cass with everything still up in the air?

The prospect of losing the paper and leaving Hilby, on top of the ongoing uncertainty about Cass, was immobilizing her, she realized then. There was nothing she could do about Lamarr's holographic will, but if she was to be of any help to Cass, she couldn't let the fact that she'd lost the *Herald* paralyze her, as it threatened to do.

CHAPTER SEVENTEEN

HE CALLED THAT NIGHT shortly after nine. As she bolted downstairs to answer the ring, Tulley stepped on the dangling belt of her robe. Off-balance, she reached for the phone and as she grabbed the receiver, the cradle clattered to the floor.

"Cass?" His name came out in a gasp.

Back came his alarmed voice across the wire. "Tulley, what's going on there? Are you all right?"

"Where are you?"

"Washington. Where did you think I'd be?"

"State or D.C.?" she asked snappishly, rubbing the shin she'd bruised on the newel post.

Cass gave a tired-sounding chuckle that turned her to jelly. "Didn't I tell you? I'm sorry. I was sure I had. Washington, D.C., of course."

She sucked in her breath and let it out. "Oh, Cass, it's been such an awful day. I wish you were here. What in the world are you doing in D.C.?"

"I'm not sure yet that I'm doing anything. I can't get an appointment with the man I need to see until tomorrow," he said. "It's been a *lot* of awful days, love, and before they get better we may be in for some more."

And so the conversation went, nothing said beyond endearments and goodbye. Tulley felt empty again. It was a moment before she realized he hadn't told her what he was doing in Washington and had forgotten to say where he was staying. If she'd known, she would have called him back at once.

SHE WAS AT HER DESK the next day when Scotty Kettleman appeared in the door of her office. It was late morning, and the paper was rolling on the press. She beckoned him in with surprise.

"What's the occasion? School holiday?"

"Nah," he said and stopped. She waited. She could see the marks of strain on the young face.

"Miss Tulley, I want that job more'n anything, but I reckon you're gonna say 'forget it,'" he blurted out suddenly.

"Why would you think that? I already offered you the job."

"But I... know something, and I can't take the job without telling you, and when you hear, you may not want to take a chance on me."

"Why don't you let me decide that, Scott? Pull up that chair over there, and let's talk."

Mechanically he pulled a chair over to her desk and sat down, looking up at her with miserable but candid eyes.

"It's about the fire, Miss Tulley," he said. "I saw something that night, but I wasn't supposed to be where I was when I saw it, and my folks are going... I don't know what they'll—" He broke off with a moan in midsentence.

"If you hadn't asked if I wanted to work on the paper..." he began again after a moment. "But I was scared to tell, and I couldn't take the job without telling you...and then I heard people say the fire was Cass McCready's fault and..." He rolled it out in one long string, like pasta from a spaghetti machine, until he ran out of breath and stopped.

Again Tulley waited, her pulse accelerating. *He knows something about the fire!* The boy looked at her with stricken eyes.

"Miss Tulley, it's got so I don't like myself much anymore. I gotta tell somebody, but I won't blame you if you don't want to hire me, except I'd promise—"

"I'm not sure what we're talking about, Scott, but I must say I'm listening." Tulley tried to keep the sound of excitement out of her voice, afraid she would scare him off. "Please go on."

For a moment panic again swept his face, but he drew a deep breath, and to her relief, began to talk. In labored sentences, the story came out.

For the first time in his life, the night of the fire, Scott Kettleman had sneaked out of the house after his folks were safe in bed. He rode his bicycle across town to join a party thrown by a high-school cheerleader he fancied, whose parents happened to be away.

There was a generous supply of a sweet fruit wine, and he'd never had wine before. It made him feel very good until he began to feel bad. The girl disappeared with another boy. He got on his bike and headed for home.

The empty supermarket building was on his way, and it was there the wine caught up with him. Wheeling into a clump of shrubbery at the rear of the building, he rolled off the bike and threw up. When it was over, he still couldn't make it back on his bike.

"So I just sat there in the bushes in the dark, Miss Tulley, wishing I'd stayed home and waiting for my stomach to settle so I could get there," he said, his eyes clouded with unhappy recollections of the ordeal. "And then all of a sudden this car pulls in where it was dark up the street, and this guy gets out and comes walking toward me. Man, I was scared. I scrunched down in the bushes, but he wasn't looking for me. He went across the parking lot to where there's a door at the back of the building and went in.''

"Yes, Scott. Go on," Tulley urged as the boy paused in thought.

"By then, I guess I could have made it on home, but I was curious about that guy. There was something fishy about it, Miss Tulley. I still didn't feel all that great, so I scrunched back in the bushes and after a while he came out, kind of running. He came close enough I could have touched him, but he was going too fast to see I was there. He ran to his car and took off like a flash.''

She was almost afraid to ask the question. "Do you know who it was, Scott?''

"Yes, but I didn't right away. It sure didn't *look* like him," Scott said, and Tulley's rising hopes fell.

"He had on a parka that made him look bigger and fatter than he usually looks, and he had the hood pulled over his head, so when I first saw him I couldn't see his face. I'd never have known it was him if he hadn't come so close when he ran back to his car. I got a right good look at his face, and I saw his car when he drove off. There's not another car like it in Hilby County. It was that Mr. Drummond, sure enough. The one, you know, that's such a classy dresser.''

Tulley gave a sigh of satisfaction. "What then?" she asked after a moment.

"Well, when I got up to start off on my bike, I . . . well, I felt like I was going to be sick again, so I stayed there in the bushes awhile longer. I guess with all that throwing up and everything I must have been kinda tired, and I guess I must have fell asleep. Anyway, next thing I knew I was awake and there was smoke pouring out the building, and I forgot all about being sick and lit out for home." The flow of words stopped as if at the turn of a spigot.

"And then what?" prompted Tulley.

"Oh, I got home, and I remembered I had to call the fire department."

"You did?"

The boy looked embarrassed again. "Well...yeah, only somebody beat me to it. I was scared to wake my folks, so first I got into my pajamas and messed up my bed and my hair so if they... Anyway, before I got to the phone, I heard the fire sirens. Honest, Miss Tulley, I was going to call them."

There was a stunned silence from Tulley as the implications of what the boy had seen began to take shape in her mind.

After another moment he asked anxiously, "Are you going to tell my folks?"

Recovering, Tulley said, "No. But you may not feel very good about yourself until *you* do." She wasn't sure what her role should be in the situation. He'd just handed her the key she'd been groping for. At the same time, for his own sake, he must understand she didn't take his escapade lightly. Should she thank him or scold him or do both...or neither? While she was still making up her mind, the boy brought her her answer.

He said, his face anxious, "I guess you don't want me to come to work on the paper, do you?"

"I don't know, Scott," she said seriously. "Come back and see me after you and your parents have settled the matter of your sneaking out at night and after you decide what priority you want to give to wine parties."

Scott's grin was almost normal again, though slightly abashed. "I can answer the last one now," he said. "I wouldn't go to another one of those parties if they came and got me in a limousine. Just the thought of that wine makes me feel like throwing up all over again."

Tulley sat for a moment after the boy was gone. She picked up the phone and called the electric company. Her call was routed through three different persons before she found someone willing to answer her question: had the power been on continuously in the burned-out building?

"No, ma'am," a polite voice in the billing department told her. "The power was shut off at that address for most of the year, but the owner had it turned on again four days ago."

In the early afternoon the call she'd been waiting for came through from Dick Brown, the stringer in Daytona Beach.

"About this guy, Leo Drummond, Miss Calhoun," he said. "No friend of yours, I hope. He's not popular in Fountain Beach. Came here from Texas, a land developer—a self-made capitalist. Started in the construction business as an electrician. Surfaced a few years later as a subdivision developer.

"The problem in Fountain Beach was that the houses he built and sold there came apart in our tropical storms, and when the owners got a look at the sleazy construction, they were ready to lynch the guy. By then Drummond and his partner had hit the road."

"Partner? You don't happen to know the name of the partner, do you?"

"I've got it here somewhere. Swift. Jack Swift."

"You've been most helpful, Dick Brown. Tell me your rates and I'll put a check in the mail today. What you've just told me is going to save us a lot of trouble up here," Tulley said gratefully, making a mental note to add a substantial bonus to whatever charges he made.

"Anytime, Miss Calhoun. Glad to be of service."

IT WAS TO BE A DAY of surprising encounters, Tulley thought a short time later when the receptionist buzzed her to say Jack Swift was at the front of the building asking to see her.

Jack Swift? What in the world was he doing here?

A moment later Swift walked through the door—a stocky, red-faced man in windbreaker and jeans.

"They tell me you're Lamarr's niece and are running the paper," he said. Tulley was surprised to hear a yappy little fox terrier voice coming out of what was definitely a bulldog face.

"That's right, Mr. Swift. And you . . . ?"

"I came to make a statement, and I want it in the paper."

"Oh? And just what statement do you want to make, Mr. Swift?" Tulley asked.

"They're blaming me for the aluminum wiring they found in the supermarket that burned down," yapped Swift in his high, strident, essentially whiny voice. "I want to make a statement that I only put in what the general contractor told me to put in, and I did a good, tight job so the wiring didn't cause any fire. If they want to blame somebody, they better blame Cass McCready. He made me substitute aluminum for copper wire."

She fought for composure within while she eyed him coolly across the desk.

"Now, Mr. Swift, we both know that's not true. We both know that in Mr. McCready's absence you substituted cheap wire for the expensive wire the specifications called for and pocketed the difference," she said in a reasonable voice. "We both know you took advantage of a tragedy in Mr. McCready's family to make a small financial killing for yourself, and we both know you and Drummond and my Uncle Lamarr were conspiring to make the town of Hilby think that Mr. McCready had pulled a wiring switch in the annex similar to yours. We both know all that, don't we, Mr. Swift?"

For a moment Swift looked as if he'd been hit in the stomach with a railroad tie. At last he found words. "It's not true. Where did you get that crap?" he shrilled.

"It is true, Mr. Swift, and you and I both know it. But I know something you don't, Mr. Swift," Tulley said, letting him suffer through a long, deliberate pause. "I know my uncle and Leo Drummond intended to use you as their patsy, if they found they needed one."

"What makes you think that?" demanded Swift sullenly.

"Because I have it on tape," Tulley said, stretching a point for a worthy cause; she had no intention of letting him near the tape. "You didn't know, did you, that my uncle had his own office bugged? If Cass McCready took him into court for libel and slander, he intended to use that tape to prove he had some authority for what he printed."

"Lamarr promised my name wouldn't come into it!"

"You believed him? My uncle was not a nice man, Mr. Swift." She could see she was making points. The man's florid face had paled, and with one hand he picked nervously at the cuticle on a finger of his other hand.

"You don't travel in nice company, Mr. Swift," she said. "Leo Drummond isn't a particularly nice man, either. If it's a case of you or him, Drummond, too, intends to make you take the fall."

"What's that supposed to mean?" He was close to panic. Tulley pressed her advantage.

"I understand you did a good job of installing the substitute wiring in the supermarket, so you aren't likely to be blamed for causing the fire, unless..."

"Unless what? For God's sake, unless what?"

"Unless the investigators have reason to believe you've been tampering with the wiring there lately. That seems to be what they've found caused the fire."

Never had Tulley seen such rage in a person's face.

"Why, that son of a bitch! He burned down his building for the insurance, and he's going to try to pin it on me," yelled Swift in a voice Tulley had no doubt could be heard out on the street. "I got a right to hear those tapes."

"You'll have to talk to Sam Matthews, the *Herald*'s attorney, about that," she said. "The tapes are all in his hands."

It was a highly agitated Swift who stormed out of the newspaper building a minute later.

It had turned out to be a pretty good day, Tulley told herself a few hours later at the carriage house as she waited for the promised call from Cass and reviewed the hour she'd spent earlier with Sam Matthews, filling him in on the extraordinary disclosures of the day. A good day, *except that she was going to lose her paper*.

And what the hell was Cass doing up there in Washington when she needed him here? It was his war! She hadn't enlisted to fight it alone. Whatever happened to "together"?

It was in this frame of mind she answered the phone when Cass called. It was a short conversation, even less satisfactory than the one the previous night.

"I hope whatever you're doing up there in Washington has something to do with the fire, Cass, because if it hasn't, you'd better get back here fast," she said.

Cass answered, "Not that, Tulley, but it's important, and I can't leave until I get a report from the man I came to see."

"About what, Cass?"

"Trust me, Tulley. I'd rather not talk about it until I'm with you, darling."

Two could play the waiting game, she thought, hurt and a little piqued. Though it was burning a hole in her tongue, she'd be darned if she'd tell him what she'd learned from Scott Kettleman and Dick Brown and Jack Swift.

"I love you," he said.

And she responded with "I love you." And both of them said good-night.

THE BIG NEWS in Hilby County the next morning was the first snowfall in fifteen years that left a light frosting on the ground and continued to come and go in flurries. It captured the top headline in the *Herald* that day. The paper had just gone to press when a call came through to Tulley from Sam Matthews.

"You reckon you could get Charlie Kettleman to take his boy out of school for an hour this afternoon and get him to my office around two? I want him to tell his story," the lawyer said in his mellow drawl. There was an underlying note in it that sounded suspiciously smug.

"What's up, Sam?" she asked curiously.

''Wait and see. You be here, too, y'hear.''

It wasn't like Sam to be high-handed, Tulley thought, her curiosity mounting as the time drew near. Well before two she bundled herself into her down coat and headed for his office, hoping he would break down and let her in on his secret.

To her surprise, Matthews ushered her past his office and through the library to a room in back furnished with a handsome oak conference table and eight leather-padded oak armchairs. On a small side table had been placed a heavy sterling coffee service and a number of cups and saucers.

''Looks like you're expecting company,'' she said, but Sam had moved away from her to speak to a sullen, nervous Jack Swift, whom Miss Eudith had ushered through the door.

''What's going on, Matthews?'' Swift demanded without greeting. ''You told me I could hear that tape.''

''Some other folks want to hear it, too,'' Sam said laconically. ''We'll wait till everybody's here.''

Sam designated the seat next to his at the head of the table as Tulley's, and from that vantage point she could see out the window where Charlie Kettleman and son, Scott, were climbing the steps together.

Jack Swift's bulldog face grew progressively grimmer as Miss Eudith next ushered in a tall, big-muscled man with a pleasant face whom Sam introduced to Tulley as Darin Hughes, the fire chief, and a few minutes later another tall man with graying hair who paused in the doorway and looked over the assembly with shrewd eyes before he stepped inside.

''May I introduce our chief of police to you, Tulley,'' Sam said in his impeccable drawing-room manner. ''Chief Jimmy Ballou. This is Tulley Calhoun,

Chief. I don't have to tell you who Tulley is. I believe you know the rest."

There was a strained silence around the table, broken only by some small talk between Sam and the chiefs. Swift was beginning to look trapped. Tulley saw with relief that there was an air of we're-in-this-together between Charlie Kettleman and his son that told her the boy had worked out his problems with his parents.

There were seven now at the table. Then, to her surprise, Ed Dawes peered around the door. For a moment it looked as if Swift was about to bolt, but Miss Eudith appeared at the door once more, escorting Leo Drummond, and Swift settled back in his chair.

Drummond stopped cold just inside the door when he saw the assembly. He made an involuntary move to retreat and ran smack into Miss Eudith, who blocked his way. The handsome face flushed with color, but in an instant he recovered and came into the room with a toothy smile that did not reach his eyes—eyes that were like the police chief's, moving around the table, sizing everyone up.

"Come in, Leo. Sorry there are no more chairs, but you can pull up this yellow one here in the corner. There's room for it next to the chief," said Sam.

"You didn't tell me it was a party, Matthews," Drummond said sourly. "You got me here under false pretenses."

"Now, Leo," Sam said reproachfully. "As I recall, I said that something relating to your land development proposal was being discussed in my office around two today, if you wanted to hear it."

For a moment Drummond didn't move. His face still marked with the flush of anger and a patronizing smile, he said, "All right, Sam. I'll go along with your little game for the moment, but don't . . ." He didn't finish the sentence but walked around the table and pulled up the yellow leather chair.

"I reckon y'all either know or can make a pretty good guess why I asked you to come here," Sam began.

Tulley, next to him, barely suppressed a grin. Sam Matthews had read too much about Nero Wolfe. He was playing the role of Stout's detective to the hilt and loving it.

"We're going to talk about the fire that burned Leo's building the other night," Sam continued benignly in his easy Southern drawl. "Tulley says you know what caused it, Leo. I reckon the fire chief would be grateful to you for any light you might throw on the subject."

"I'll tell him what I told her," Drummond said truculently. "It was that damned aluminum wiring Swift and McCready put in instead of the copper called for."

"Wait a minute, Drummond." Swift was on his feet. He was mad, but he was also scared. "You're not going to pin the fire on me. That wiring was put in right."

Darin Hughes, the fire chief, nodded. "As far as we can see, there was nothing wrong with the installation."

"Mind telling them what you've come up with, Darin?" Sam asked.

"We've found clear evidence somebody tampered with the junction box and deliberately caused the wires to short. We're putting the fire down to arson."

"Well, you won't have to look far to find your arsonist," Drummond said smugly. "Swift and Mc-

Cready were the only ones who knew the building was wired with aluminum."

"You knew, Mr. Drummond," Tulley broke in. "You told me about it the day of the fire."

"You're lying. You're lying to save Cass McCready," Drummond accused coldly.

"You keep bringing up Cass McCready, Drummond. Maybe it's time we got his name out of it," Matthews said. "I'm going to play a tape that changes the picture some."

As the tape began, Drummond was obviously shaken, but when the three-way conversation between Lamarr, Drummond and Swift came to an end and Sam switched off the recorder, Drummond's face had lost its look of apprehension. Tulley, on the other hand, was feeling sick. It was Sam himself who'd pointed out what a terrible mistake it would be to let them hear the tape. She'd meant it only to scare Swift when she'd mentioned it. It had never occurred to her that Sam would play it for them. Swift jumped to his feet, and he and Drummond started to speak at once.

"That doesn't prove anything but that McCready tried to get Swift to—" Drummond began, overriding Swift, but Matthews took the floor.

"That's the first tape we found at Lamarr's house," he said. "Now let's hear the other one I ran across last night."

Why, the old rascal, thought Tulley with a sudden feeling of relief. She might have known he had something up his sleeve.

There were only two voices on this second tape: Drummond's and Lamarr's. The editor expressed his doubts about Swift. Could he be trusted to stick with his story?

Drummond: You've got nothing to worry about, Lamarr. Swift and I worked together down in Florida. He made good money substituting aluminum wiring for copper on the supermarket building, and I know the guy that supplied it. I've got too much on Swift for him to back out on us.

Lamarr: How come McCready let him get away with it?

Drummond: He didn't know. Swift got the wiring done while McCready was in Arizona taking care of his folks.

Lamarr: About that supermarket, Leo. It'll cost us a pretty penny to have it torn down and the land cleared when we get ready to start building out there.

Drummond: I got something in mind. It won't cost us a cent. We might even make some money on it.''

The tape ended, and both Swift and Drummond were on their feet.

"Wait, boys," Sam said. "You haven't heard what Scott Kettleman has to say yet."

"Sit down." It was Police Chief Ballou speaking now, in a cold, authoritative voice. "You don't have to say anything until you've talked to your lawyers, but I'm advising you to hear what this boy has to say."

Scott's face was crimson as he turned to Sam Matthews to ask unhappily, "Do I have to tell it all, right from the first?"

"I reckon you do, Scott. Just tell us what you told Miss Calhoun."

When it was finished, Tulley leaned over and whispered in Scott Kettleman's ear, "Congratulations! The job's yours." The boy's face broke into a broad grin.

Chief Ballou rose to his feet and turned to Leo Drummond, who for once appeared speechless. "You two better come with me. I'm arresting you on suspicion of arson, Drummond, and I have a few questions to ask Swift. You can call your attorneys at the police station.''

"You might like to ask Mr. Drummond why he had the power turned back on in that vacant building a few days before the fire, Chief,'' Tulley suggested as they moved out of the room. Drummond gave her a venomous look.

"I'll do that, Miss Calhoun,'' said the Chief.

"Excuse me,'' Ed Dawes said, looking enormously pleased with it all. "I've got work to do at the paper.'' He departed, and the Kettleman father and son followed close behind.

Tulley was alone with Matthews, and she looked at him admiringly. "Nero Wolfe couldn't have handled it better. I think I'm going to give you a hug.''

"Hey! What's going on here?'' It was Cass, standing in the doorway, with a bemused grin on his face. The hug intended for Sam was lost in McCready's arms.

"You missed the show. Sit down and I'll tell you about it,'' Sam said.

Cass stopped him. "Not until I tell Tulley she doesn't have to worry about that holographic will of Lamarr's. It's a forgery.''

Tulley pushed herself out of his arms to stare up at him in awe. "Darling...*that's* what you were doing up there. You left your own problems to take care of mine! And I was annoyed because you weren't here helping us sort out yours!''

"You sure about this, Cass? Who says?'' asked Sam.

"Three of the top handwriting experts in Washington, D.C. I was in college with one of them. He called in the two other experts, just to be on the safe side.

They're all in absolute agreement it's a fake, and if it ever becomes necessary, they'll be glad to testify.''

Miss Eudith appeared at the door. "This came from Raleigh by special messenger while y'all were closed in the meeting, Mr. Sam." She held out a letter.

Matthews eyed the envelope curiously for a moment before he opened it. His eyes darted over the enclosed letter, then he passed it on to Tulley and Cass while he looked at the sheet of paper that came with it.

The letter was from a small copy shop in Raleigh.

"Dear Mr. Matthews," it said. "Someone apparently copied this and forgot to take the original out of the machine. I'm sorry it has taken so long to get it to you, but it took a while to decide what to do with it. I discovered that you are the administrator for the Lamarr Calhoun estate in Hilby. I'm sure this will be of interest to you. R.L. Thorpe, Thorpe Copy Shop."

"Now look at this." Sam held out the rest of the envelope's contents.

It was a sheet of paper with single words written in Lamarr Calhoun's handwriting, cut from several different kinds of paper and pasted in order to make up the wording of the will found in Lamarr's desk.

"Looks like Shelby put this together and made a copy he could practice on until it looked like the real thing," Matthews said and began to laugh. "I'll bet he'd been nipping the bottle when he went to the copy shop and never once thought about pickin' up the original."

"What do we do about it?" asked Tulley.

"Nothing," said Sam, grinning broadly. "We'll just let Shelby go crazy wondering if it's been found. If he ever comes looking, we've got plenty to shut him up. But you're not the only one who's been busy, Cass.

Tulley's got a thing or two to tell you, too. Come on back in my office. I've got a bottle of sippin' whiskey that I keep there for celebratin' victories, and I must say, this has been a right victorious day."

In the ensuing convivial hour, Matthews and Tulley brought Cass up to date on the events leading to his own vindication.

"If there's anything we've missed you can read about it in the *Herald*," Tulley told him at last with a benevolent smile. "Ed probably has the story already written."

"Just one thing I'm curious about," Cass said. "What about Jack Swift?"

"Nothing much, I reckon. The company you built the building for paid for copper wiring and got aluminum, but they're not likely to go after him at this late date," said Matthews. "The police'll get Drummond for burning his own building to collect the insurance. Swift may even give evidence against him to clear his own slate."

"Now Sam, if you'll excuse us," Tulley said, "I think that retraction is about ready for Cass to see."

CHAPTER EIGHTEEN

DURING THE HOUR OR MORE since the others had left Sam Matthews's office, a light frosting of snow had fallen and covered the marks of their passing. Tulley, stepping outside, hesitated, loathe to be the first to mar the immaculate whiteness with her foot. Cass, coming from behind with no such scruples, stepped around her and then he stopped, too, and turned to look back up at her.

Blue eyes spoke to her of love...desire...promise, and for a moment Tulley felt as if he had taken her in his arms. Then he reached up and wrapped his long, strong fingers around her hand, and she came down to the step behind him. Emotion caught at her throat, and her voice came out in a ridiculously croaky squeak when she tried to say lightly, "Sam has given us permission to go public?"

"High time, too," Cass said gruffly, smiling down at her. "And if you don't cut that out—that blatant seduction in your eyes—I swear I'm going to kiss you like you've never been kissed before. Right here on Sam Matthews's doorstep, in front of the world."

Tulley made a show of considering it and putting it aside. "I'd love it," she said, "but we wouldn't want to embarrass Mr. Sam, would we?" With a tug at his hand, she started down the steps. "Let's go see what Ed is doing with my retraction."

"Forget the retraction. It'll all be there in the exposé."

"You wouldn't deprive me of doing what I've wanted so much to do, would you?"

Hand in hand, they started down the sidewalk to the *Herald* building, leaving behind them the big tracks of his man-size shoes beside the slender ones of her boots in the newly fallen snow. It was a winter world they walked in, but with spring in her heart Tulley felt that the snowflakes on her cheeks were like the kiss of peach petals.

Tenderly, teasingly, Cass said, "Looks like you've managed to keep busy while I was away."

Tulley, matching his tone, replied, "Well, *somebody* had to mind the store."

"You tied it up like a pro, and right in the nick of time," Cass said seriously. "Mother is arriving home from Majorca next Thursday."

"When did you hear?"

"She called the morning I left for Washington. I guess I forgot to tell you," he said in an apologetic tone. "With everything else, it slipped my mind."

"That isn't the only thing that slipped your mind, it seems, dear man. Why didn't you tell me what you were going there for?"

"I didn't want you to get your hopes up. If those fellows I saw had said Lamarr wrote that will, I knew you were through, love." They walked in silence for a few steps, and then he added, "You weren't exactly forthcoming, yourself, you know."

"Oh, darling, I'm ashamed. It was childish to be so out of sorts with you. But just when it looked like we were getting on top of the bloody mess, you took off for Washington without even telling me why."

AT THE PAPER they found Ed Dawes bending over a light table in the composing room and watching a compositor assemble the makeup for tomorrow's front page. He glanced up absently. Seeing Tulley and Cass, he shifted position to let them nearer where they could see what was being done.

"We're just playing around with the makeup right now, so it won't be exactly like this when it comes out tomorrow," he explained to Cass. "This'll give you the general idea of how we plan to run it."

On the surface of the illuminated glass lay a sheet of squared paper the size of a newspaper page, with the *Herald* masthead across the top. A single line of large black type marched across the width of the sheet. "Leo Drummond Arrested as Arson Suspect." Beneath it in smaller type, next to before-and-after pictures of the burned-out market, and over the two outside columns to the right, a two-line heading read "Wire Tampering Cause of Fire, Says Chief."

A well-marked box tied into the rest of the display was topped with a conspicuous headline that said "Public Apology by the *Herald* to Cass McCready."

Dawes handed them a first draft of the main story and the box he'd printed for them to see, apparently assuming they would be there to look it over before the afternoon was done. Tulley let out a small whistle of satisfaction when she'd finished reading and turned an appreciative smile on the writer.

"Looks like you've about covered everything, Ed," Cass said, "except that I'm dismissing the libel suit, of course. You're safe in saying it has been done. As soon as I can get in touch with my attorney in Raleigh, it will be. Things have been happening too fast!"

THE SNOW HAD STOPPED when they left the *Herald*. The afternoon was on the wane. The street had turned slushy under the tires, and foot traffic had worn away the pristine cleanness of the sidewalk snow. Still, the rest of their world was coated in white.

As Tulley and Cass approached the courthouse annex, Tulley thought of her first view of the town of Hilby from the third floor balcony that day she'd had the building to herself. It bustled with activity now. In a ceremonial opening while she'd been in New York the county offices had been installed, leaving the original courthouse building to the business of the court.

She turned to Cass eagerly. "Oh, Cass, let's go in," she said.

He gave her a quizzical look. "Funny you should say that. I was thinking the same thing."

Once they were inside, it was immediately clear that Cass's goal and Tulley's were not the same. He started away from the stairs. She had to pull at his arm to direct his attention that way.

"The balcony, Cass. It's been years since Hilby's had a blanket of snow like this. It may not happen again for twenty years," she said, urging him toward the stairs. "Don't you want to see it before it melts?"

Cass glanced down the broad hallway where people moved around and then back at Tulley. "What I had in mind certainly won't melt," he said with a wicked grin and tucked his arm under hers. Together they climbed the two broad flights of stairs to the third floor.

They stepped out onto the balcony and as the door closed behind them, Tulley let out a small cry of alarm and stuck out her foot to catch it.

Cass watched with amusement. "Don't panic, my sweet. I released the lock." He added fondly, "Nobody can accuse you of making the same mistake twice."

Surprisingly they had the snow-covered balcony to themselves. Tulley let the door close and reached up to wrap her arms around his neck. She lifted her face to rub her nose against his.

"That was no mistake," she said solemnly. "That was the most fortuitous accident any woman ever had. I just wish I could take credit for being smart enough to have planned it."

And then she was in his arms, and he was murmuring endearments.

"Oh, Rapunzel...my Rapunzel. Elizabeth Tulley Rapunzel Calhoun."

And Tulley pushed away from him just far enough to lean her head back and look into his face.

"Would you care to try for *McCready*?" she asked.

He kissed her then, a kiss of love and commitment and joy and desire. After a long time he said, "Rapunzel McCready. I like it." He kissed her again and looked down into her eyes. "Tulley...my unsinkable Tulley Calhoun. Come to think of it, I like the sound of Tulley Calhoun McCready even better." He burrowed his face in her hair. After a moment the sound of his muffled voice reached her ears.

"Oh, God, Tulley Calhoun, how I do love you."

Alone together on the balcony they clung to each other, murmuring soft foolishness between kisses as if, now that the imbroglio was behind them, they must seize the moment for play. The wet snow turned to slush around their feet and dripped noisily off the eaves, but they paid it no heed.

Finally Cass moved his wrist to look at his watch.

"We've got twenty minutes left," he said, taking her arm and pulling her toward the door.

"Twenty minutes?" she asked lazily, inclined to stay on for a while.

"Before the county clerk's office closes. To get a marriage license," he said. "I was about to suggest it when we came in, but you got me all the way up here on the balcony before I could think of a way to say it."

"Cass, darling, if this is a marriage proposal, you must have learned how at the same school that taught you to dance," Tulley said, but her voice cracked again in that ridiculous squeak, and suddenly she couldn't tease him about it.

Nor could Cass, it seemed. "Does this sound better? Will you marry me, Tulley Calhoun?" he asked earnestly.

"Oh Cass, I love you so! I don't care how you ask me," she said. "The answer would always be yes."

"Shall we go then?"

"I guess there's no reason we can't get a license before we have any wedding plans, but I think it's usually the other way around," said Tulley.

"Wedding plans? Did you have something elaborate in mind?" he asked cautiously.

Tulley laughed with delight. "Don't look so alarmed, dearest. How could I have *anything* in mind? You'll want to wait until your mother gets here from Majorca. My mother can come from Connecticut."

They had reached the door, and Cass took his hand from the latch to turn her so he'd be looking into her face.

"Unless you feel strongly about it, that's a lot longer than I want to wait," he said quietly.

For a moment her heart was too full of happiness for her to speak, and she raised her lips to give him a quick kiss.

"Me, too," she said when she could. "I thought maybe you'd want the wedding that joins the Calhouns and the McCreadys to be a family affair."

Cass hesitated. Then, enfolding her in his arms, he said, "If it's just the same to you, my love, I'd like our wedding to be *ours*. Would your mother be hurt if we had that family affair later, after my mother gets back to the States?"

Tulley slipped her arms around his waist, and together they rocked gently on the balls of their feet, caressing each other with their eyes.

"Whatever we do will be fine with her. She's a very independent and understanding lady," Tulley assured him fondly. "Now, about the wedding. I have an open mind. When do you suggest?"

"As soon as the law allows, love. As soon as the law allows," Cass said softly. "We could get the license now and drive out to Nags Head tonight."

"Nags Head . . . the Outer Banks?"

"There's a retired judge out there I go fishing with who could marry us. How does that sound to you? We could stay at the shack."

A warm swell of contentment filled Tulley's heart. In his grandfather's day, he had told her, the shack had been off limits to the female of the species. Cass wanted her there!

"Sounds heavenly," she said.

Cass's brow furrowed anxiously. "Can you get away from the paper for a few days on such short notice?"

"Give me an hour, and we'll be on our way," Tulley said.

Together they left the balcony and descended the stairs. Halfway down Tulley remembered in a bemused sort of way that they had forgotten to look at the snow.

Harlequin Superromance

COMING NEXT MONTH

Harlequin Intrigue

WHAT READERS SAY ABOUT HARLEQUIN INTRIGUE . . .

Fantastic! I am looking forward to reading other Intrigue books.

*P.W.O., Anderson, SC

This is the first Harlequin Intrigue I have read . . . I'm hooked.

*C.M., Toledo, OH

I really like the suspense . . . the twists and turns of the plot.

*L.E.L., Minneapolis, MN

I'm really enjoying your Harlequin Intrigue line . . . mystery and suspense mixed with a good love story.

*B.M., Denton, TX

*Names available on request.

IQ-A-1

Harlequin Intrigue

Because romance can be quite an adventure.

Available wherever paperbacks are sold or through

Harlequin Reader Service

In the U.S.
901 Fuhrmann Blvd.
P.O. Box 1325
Buffalo, N.Y. 14269

In Canada
P.O. Box 2800, Station "A"
5170 Yonge Street
Willowdale, Ontario M2N 6J3

INT-6R

Take 4 books & a surprise gift FREE

SPECIAL LIMITED-TIME OFFER

Mail to   **Harlequin Reader Service**®

In the U.S.   In Canada
901 Fuhrmann Blvd.   P.O. Box 2800, Station "A"
P.O. Box 1394   5170 Yonge Street
Buffalo, N.Y. 14240-1394   Willowdale, Ontario M2N 6J3

YES! Please send me 4 free Harlequin Superromance® novels and my free surprise gift. Then send me 4 brand-new novels every month as they come off the presses. Bill me at the low price of $2.50 each—a 10% saving off the retail price. There are no shipping, handling or other hidden costs. There is no minimum number of books I must purchase. I can always return a shipment and cancel at any time. Even if I never buy another book from Harlequin, the 4 free novels and the surprise gift are mine to keep forever.

Name   (PLEASE PRINT)

Address   Apt. No.

City   State/Prov.   Zip/Postal Code

This offer is limited to one order per household and not valid to present subscribers. Price is subject to change.   DOSR-SUB-1R